The Borough

by

George Crabbe

The Echo Library 2007

Published by

The Echo Library

Echo Library
131 High St.
Teddington
Middlesex TW11 8HH

www.echo-library.com

Please report serious faults in the text to complaints@echo-library.com

ISBN 978-1-40684-897-7

The Borough by George Crabbe (1754-1832) [1]

LETTER I.

These did the ruler of the deep ordain,
To build proud navies and to rule the main.
POPE, Homer's Iliad.

Such scenes has Deptford, navy-building town,
Woolwich and Wapping, smelling strong of pitch;
Such Lambeth, envy of each band and gown,
And Twickenham such, which fairer scenes enrich.
POPE, Imitation of Spencer.

.... Et cum coelestibus undis
Aequoreae miscentur aquae: caret ignibus aether,
Caecaque nox premitur tenebris hiemisque suisque;
Discutient tamen has, praebentque micantia lumen
Fulmina: fulmineis ardescunt ignibus undae.
OVID, Metamorphoses.

GENERAL DESCRIPTION.

The Difficulty of describing Town Scenery—A Comparison with certain Views in the Country—The River and Quay—The Shipping and Business—-Shipbuilding—Sea-Boys and Port-Views—Village and Town Scenery again compared—Walks from Town—Cottage and adjoining Heath, &c.—House of Sunday Entertainment—The Sea: a Summer and Winter View—A Shipwreck at Night, and its Effects on Shore—Evening Amusements in the Borough—An Apology for the imperfect View which can be given of these Subjects.

"DESCRIBE the Borough"—though our idle tribe
May love description, can we so describe,
That you shall fairly streets and buildings trace,
And all that gives distinction to a place?
This cannot be; yet moved by your request
A part I paint—let Fancy form the rest.
Cities and towns, the various haunts of men,
Require the pencil; they defy the pen:
Could he who sang so well the Grecian fleet,
So well have sung of alley, lane, or street?
Can measured lines these various buildings show,

The Town-Hall Turning, or the Prospect Row?
Can I the seats of wealth and want explore,
And lengthen out my lays from door to door?
    Then let thy Fancy aid me—I repair
From this tall mansion of our last year's Mayor,
Till we the outskirts of the Borough reach,
And these half-buried buildings next the beach,
Where hang at open doors the net and cork,
While squalid sea-dames mend the meshy work;
Till comes the hour when fishing through the tide
The weary husband throws his freight aside;
A living mass which now demands the wife,
Th' alternate labours of their humble life.
    Can scenes like these withdraw thee from thy wood,
Thy upland forest, or thy valley's flood?
Seek then thy garden's shrubby bound, and look,
As it steals by, upon the bordering brook;
That winding streamlet, limpid, lingering slow,
Where the reeds whisper when the zephyrs blow;
Where in the midst, upon a throne of green,
Sits the large Lily as the water's queen;
And makes the current, forced awhile to stay,
Murmur and bubble as it shoots away;
Draw then the strongest contrast to that stream,
And our broad river will before thee seem.
    With ceaseless motion comes and goes the tide,
Flowing, it fills the channel vast and wide;
Then back to sea, with strong majestic sweep
It rolls, in ebb yet terrible and deep;
Here Samphire-banks and Saltwort bound the flood,
There stakes and sea-weeds withering on the mud;
And higher up, a ridge of all things base,
Which some strong tide has roll'd upon the place.
    Thy gentle river boasts its pigmy boat,
Urged on by pains, half-grounded, half afloat:
While at her stern an angler takes his stand,
And marks the fish he purposes to land;
From that clear space, where, in the cheerful ray
Of the warm sun, the scaly people play.
Far other craft our prouder river shows,
Hoys, pinks, and sloops: brigs, brigantines, and snows:
Nor angler we on our wide stream descry,
But one poor dredger where his oysters lie:
He, cold and wet, and driving with the tide,
Beats his weak arms against his tarry side,

Then drains the remnant of diluted gin,
To aid the warmth that languishes within;
Renewing oft his poor attempts to beat
His tingling fingers into gathering heat.

    He shall again be seen when evening comes,
And social parties crowd their favourite rooms:
Where on the table pipes and papers lie,
The steaming bowl or foaming tankard by;
'Tis then, with all these comforts spread around,
They hear the painful dredger's welcome sound;
And few themselves the savoury boon deny,
The food that feeds, the living luxury.

    Yon is our Quay! those smaller hoys from town,
Its various ware, for country use, bring down;
Those laden waggons, in return, impart
The country-produce to the city mart;
Hark! to the clamour in that miry road,
Bounded and narrow'd by yon vessel's load;
The lumbering wealth she empties round the place,
Package, and parcel, hogshead, chest, and case:
While the loud seaman and the angry hind,
Mingling in business, bellow to the wind.

    Near these a crew amphibious, in the docks,
Rear, for the sea, those castles on the stocks:
See! the long keel, which soon the waves must hide;
See! the strong ribs which form the roomy side;
Bolts yielding slowly to the sturdiest stroke,
And planks which curve and crackle in the smoke.
Around the whole rise cloudy wreaths, and far
Bear the warm pungence of o'er-boiling tar.
Dabbling on shore half-naked sea-boys crowd,
Swim round a ship, or swing upon the shroud;
Or in a boat purloin'd, with paddles play,
And grow familiar with the watery way:
Young though they be, they feel whose sons they are,
They know what British seamen do and dare;
Proud of that fame, they raise and they enjoy
The rustic wonder of the village-boy.

    Before you bid these busy scenes adieu,
Behold the wealth that lies in public view,
Those far extended heaps of coal and coke,
Where fresh-fill'd lime-kilns breathe their stifling smoke.
This shall pass off, and you behold, instead,
The night-fire gleaming on its chalky bed;
When from the Lighthouse brighter beams will rise,

To show the shipman where the shallow lies.
    Thy walks are ever pleasant; every scene
Is rich in beauty, lively, or serene—
Rich is that varied view with woods around,
Seen from the seat within the shrubb'ry bound;
Where shines the distant lake, and where appear
From ruins bolting, unmolested deer;
Lively the village-green, the inn, the place,
Where the good widow schools her infant-race.
Shops, whence are heard the hammer and the saw,
And village-pleasures unreproved by law:
Then how serene! when in your favourite room,
Gales from your jasmines soothe the evening gloom;
When from your upland paddock you look down,
And just perceive the smoke which hides the town;
When weary peasants at the close of day
Walk to their cots, and part upon the way;
When cattle slowly cross the shallow brook,
And shepherds pen their folds, and rest upon their crook.
    We prune our hedges, prime our slender trees,
And nothing looks untutor'd and at ease,
On the wide heath, or in the flowery vale,
We scent the vapours of the sea-born gale;
Broad-beaten paths lead on from stile to stile,
And sewers from streets the road-side banks defile;
Our guarded fields a sense of danger show,
Where garden-crops with corn and clover grow;
Fences are form'd of wreck, and placed around,
(With tenters tipp'd) a strong repulsive bound;
Wide and deep ditches by the gardens run,
And there in ambush lie the trap and gun;
Or yon broad board, which guards each tempting prize,
"Like a tall bully, lifts its head and lies."
    There stands a cottage with an open door,
Its garden undefended blooms before:
Her wheel is still, and overturn'd her stool,
While the lone Widow seeks the neighb'ring pool:
This gives us hope, all views of town to shun—
No! here are tokens of the Sailor-son;
That old blue jacket, and that shirt of check,
And silken kerchief for the seaman's neck;
Sea-spoils and shells from many a distant shore,
And furry robe from frozen Labrador.
    Our busy streets and sylvan-walks between,
Fen, marshes, bog, and heath all intervene;

Here pits of crag, with spongy, plashy base,
To some enrich th' uncultivated space:
For there are blossoms rare, and curious rush,
The gale's rich balm, and sun-dew's crimson blush,
Whose velvet leaf with radiant beauty dress'd,
Forms a gay pillow for the plover's breast.

　　Not distant far, a house commodious made,
(Lonely yet public stands) for Sunday-trade;
Thither, for this day free, gay parties go,
Their tea-house walk, their tippling rendezvous;
There humble couples sit in corner-bowers,
Or gaily ramble for th' allotted hours;
Sailors and lasses from the town attend,
The servant-lover, the apprentice-friend;
With all the idle social tribes who seek
And find their humble pleasures once a week.

　　Turn to the watery world!—but who to thee
(A wonder yet unview'd) shall paint—the Sea?
Various and vast, sublime in all its forms,
When lull'd by zephyrs, or when roused by storms,
Its colours changing, when from clouds and sun
Shades after shades upon the surface run;
Embrown'd and horrid now, and now serene,
In limpid blue, and evanescent green;
And oft the foggy banks on ocean lie,
Lift the fair sail, and cheat th' experienced eye.

　　Be it the summer—noon: a sandy space
The ebbing tide has left upon its place;
Then just the hot and stony beach above,
Light twinkling streams in bright confusion move;
(For heated thus, the warmer air ascends,
And with the cooler in its fall contends)
Then the broad bosom of the ocean keeps
An equal motion; swelling as it sleeps,
Then slowly sinking; curling to the strand,
Faint, lazy waves o'ercreep the rigid sand,
Or tap the tarry boat with gentle blow,
And back return in silence, smooth and slow.
Ships in the calm seem anchor'd; for they glide
On the still sea, urged solely by the tide:
Art thou not present, this calm scene before,
Where all beside is pebbly length of shore,
And far as eye can reach, it can discern no more?

　　Yet sometimes comes a ruffing cloud to make
The quiet surface of the ocean shake;

As an awaken'd giant with a frown
Might show his wrath, and then to sleep sink down.
    View now the Winter-storm! above, one cloud,
Black and unbroken, all the skies o'ershroud:
Th' unwieldy porpoise through the day before
Had roll'd in view of boding men on shore;
And sometimes hid and sometimes show'd his form,
Dark as the cloud, and furious as the storm.
    All where the eye delights, yet dreads to roam,
The breaking billows cast the flying foam
Upon the billows rising—all the deep
Is restless change; the waves so swell'd and steep,
Breaking and sinking, and the sunken swells,
Nor one, one moment, in its station dwells:
But nearer land you may the billows trace,
As if contending in their watery chase;
May watch the mightiest till the shoal they reach,
Then break and hurry to their utmost stretch;
Curl'd as they come, they strike with furious force,
And then re-flowing, take their grating course,
Raking the rounded flints, which ages past
Roll'd by their rage, and shall to ages last.
    Far off the Petrel in the troubled way
Swims with her brood, or flutters in the spray;
She rises often, often drops again,
And sports at ease on the tempestuous main.
    High o'er the restless deep, above the reach
Of gunner's hope, vast flights of Wild-ducks stretch;
Far as the eye can glance on either side,
In a broad space and level line they glide;
All in their wedge-like figures from the north,
Day after day, flight after flight, go forth.
    In-shore their passage tribes of Sea-gulls urge,
And drop for prey within the sweeping surge;
Oft in the rough opposing blast they fly
Far back, then turn, and all their force apply,
While to the storm they give their weak complaining cry;
Or clap the sleek white pinion to the breast,
And in the restless ocean dip for rest.
    Darkness begins to reign; the louder wind
Appals the weak and awes the firmer mind;
But frights not him whom evening and the spray
In part conceal—yon Prowler on his way:
Lo! he has something seen; he runs apace,
As if he fear'd companion in the chase;

He sees his prize, and now he turns again,
Slowly and sorrowing—"Was your search in vain?"
Gruffly he answers, "'Tis a sorry sight!
A seaman's body: there'll be more to-night!"

    Hark! to those sounds! they're from distress at sea;
How quick they come! What terrors may there be!
Yes, 'tis a driven vessel: I discern
Lights, signs of terror, gleaming from the stern;
Others behold them too, and from the town
In various parties seamen hurry down;
Their wives pursue, and damsels urged by dread,
Lest men so dear be into danger led;
Their head the gown has hooded, and their call
In this sad night is piercing like the squall;
They feel their kinds of power, and when they meet,
Chide, fondle, weep, dare, threaten, or entreat.

    See one poor girl, all terror and alarm,
Has fondly seized upon her lover's arm;
"Thou shalt not venture;" and he answers "No!
I will not:"—still she cries, "Thou shalt not go."

    No need of this; not here the stoutest boat
Can through such breakers, o'er such billows float,
Yet may they view these lights upon the beach,
Which yield them hope whom help can never reach.

    From parted clouds the moon her radiance throws
On the wild waves, and all the danger shows;
But shows them beaming in her shining vest,
Terrific splendour! gloom in glory dress'd!
This for a moment, and then clouds again
Hide every beam, and fear and darkness reign.

    But hear we not those sounds? Do lights appear?
I see them not! the storm alone I hear:
And lo! the sailors homeward take their way;
Man must endure—let us submit and pray.

    Such are our Winter-views: but night comes on—
Now business sleeps, and daily cares are gone;
Now parties form, and some their friends assist
To waste the idle hours at sober whist;
The tavern's pleasure or the concert's charm
Unnumber'd moments of their sting disarm:
Play-bills and open doors a crowd invite,
To pass off one dread portion of the night;
And show and song and luxury combined,
Lift off from man this burthen of mankind.

    Others advent'rous walk abroad and meet

Returning parties pacing through the street,
When various voices, in the dying day,
Hum in our walks, and greet us in our way;
When tavern-lights flit on from room to room,
And guide the tippling sailor staggering home:
There as we pass, the jingling bells betray
How business rises with the closing day:
Now walking silent, by the river's side,
The ear perceives the rippling of the tide;
Or measured cadence of the lads who tow
Some entered hoy, to fix her in her row;
Or hollow sound, which from the parish-bell
To some departed spirit bids farewell!
    Thus shall you something of our BOROUGH know,
Far as a verse, with Fancy's aid, can show.
Of Sea or River, of a Quay or Street,
The best description must be incomplete;
But when a happier theme succeeds, and when
Men are our subjects and the deeds of men,
Then may we find the Muse in happier style,
And we may sometimes sigh and sometimes smile.

LETTER II.

.........Festinat enim decurrere velox
Flosculus angustae miseraeque brevissima vitae
Portio! dum bibimus, dum serta, unguenta, puellas
Poscimus, obrepit non intellecta senectus.
                              JUVENAL, Satires

And when at last thy Love shall die,
Wilt thou receive his parting breath?
Wilt thou repress each struggling sigh,
And cheer with smiles the bed of death?
                              PERCY.

THE CHURCH.

Several Meanings of the word Church—The Building so called, here intended—Its Antiquity and Grandeur—Columns and Aisles—The Tower: the Stains made by Time compared with the mock antiquity of the Artist—Progress of Vegetation on such Buildings—Bells—Tombs: one in decay—Mural Monuments, and the Nature of their Inscriptions—An Instance in a departed Burgess—Churchyard Graves—Mourners for the Dead—A Story of a betrothed Pair in humble Life, and Effects of Grief in the Survivor.

"WHAT is a Church?"—Let Truth and Reason speak,
They would reply, "The faithful, pure, and meek;
From Christian folds, the one selected race,
Of all professions, and in every place."
"What is a Church?"—"A flock," our Vicar cries,
"Whom bishops govern and whom priests advise;
Wherein are various states and due degrees,
The Bench for honour, and the Stall for ease;
That ease be mine, which, after all his cares,
The pious, peaceful prebendary shares."
"What is a Church?"—Our honest Sexton tells,
"'Tis a tall building, with a tower and bells;
Where priest and clerk with joint exertion strive
To keep the ardour af their flock alive;
That, by its periods eloquent and grave;
This, by responses, and a well-set stave:
These for the living; but when life be fled,
I toll myself the requiem for the dead."
    'Tis to this Church I call thee, and that place

Where slept our fathers when they'd run their race:
We too shall rest, and then our children keep
Their road in life, and then, forgotten, sleep;
Meanwhile the building slowly falls away,
And, like the builders, will in time decay.

    The old Foundation—but it is not clear
When it was laid—you care not for the year;
On this, as parts decayed by time and storms,
Arose these various disproportion'd forms;
Yet Gothic all—the learn'd who visit us
(And our small wonders) have decided thus:-
"Yon noble Gothic arch," "That Gothic door;"
So have they said; of proof you'll need no more.

    Here large plain columns rise in solemn style,
You'd love the gloom they make in either aisle;
When the sun's rays, enfeebled as they pass
(And shorn of splendour) through the storied glass,
Faintly display the figures on the floor,
Which pleased distinctly in their place before.

    But ere you enter, yon bold tower survey,
Tall and entire, and venerably gray,
For time has soften'd what was harsh when new,
And now the stains are all of sober hue;
The living stains which Nature's hand alone,
Profuse of life, pours forth upon the stone:
For ever growing; where the common eye
Can but the bare and rocky bed descry;
There Science loves to trace her tribes minute,
The juiceless foliage, and the tasteless fruit;
There she perceives them round the surface creep,
And while they meet their due distinction keep;
Mix'd but not blended; each its name retains,
And these are Nature's ever-during stains.

    And wouldst thou, Artist! with thy tints and brush,
Form shades like these? Pretender, where thy blush?
In three short hours shall thy presuming hand
Th' effect of three slow centuries command?
Thou may'st thy various greens and grays contrive;
They are not Lichens, nor like ought alive;-
But yet proceed, and when thy tints are lost,
Fled in the shower, or crumbled by the frost;
When all thy work is done away as clean
As if thou never spread'st thy gray and green;
Then may'st thou see how Nature's work is done,
How slowly true she lays her colours on;

When her least speck upon the hardest flint
Has mark and form, and is a living tint;
And so embodied with the rock, that few
Can the small germ upon the substance view.
    Seeds, to our eyes invisible, will find
On the rude rock the bed that fits their kind;
There, in the rugged soil, they safely dwell,
Till showers and snows the subtle atoms swell,
And spread th' enduring foliage;—then we trace
The freckled flower upon the flinty base;
These all increase, till in unnoticed years
The stony tower as gray with age appears;
With coats of vegetation, thinly spread,
Coat above coat, the living on the dead;
These then dissolve to dust, and make a way
For bolder foliage, nursed by their decay:
The long-enduring Ferns in time will all
Die and depose their dust upon the wall;
Where the wing'd seed may rest, till many a flower
Show Flora's triumph o'er the falling tower.
    But ours yet stands, and has its Bells renown'd
For size magnificent and solemn sound;
Each has its motto: some contrived to tell,
In monkish rhyme, the uses of a bell;
Such wond'rous good, as few conceive could spring
From ten loud coppers when their clampers swing.
    Enter'd the Church—we to a tomb proceed,
Whose names and titles few attempt to read;
Old English letters, and those half pick'd out,
Leave us, unskilful readers, much in doubt;
Our sons shall see its more degraded state;
The tomb of grandeur hastens to its fate;
That marble arch, our sexton's favourite show,
With all those ruff'd and painted pairs below;
The noble Lady and the Lord who rest
Supine, as courtly dame and warrior drest;
All are departed from their state sublime,
Mangled and wounded in their war with Time,
Colleagued with mischief: here a leg is fled,
And lo! the Baron with but half a head:
Midway is cleft the arch; the very base
Is batter'd round and shifted from its place.
    Wonder not, Mortal, at thy quick decay—
See! men of marble piecemeal melt away;
When whose the image we no longer read,

But monuments themselves memorials need.

With few such stately proofs of grief or pride,
By wealth erected, is our Church supplied;
But we have mural tablets, every size,
That woe could wish, or vanity devise.

Death levels man—the wicked and the just,
The wise, the weak, lie blended in the dust;
And by the honours dealt to every name,
The King of Terrors seems to level fame.
—See! here lamented wives, and every wife
The pride and comfort of her husband's life;
Here, to her spouse, with every virtue graced,
His mournful widow has a trophy placed;
And here 'tis doubtful if the duteous son,
Or the good father, be in praise outdone.

This may be Nature: when our friends we lose,
Our alter'd feelings alter too our views;
What in their tempers teased us or distress'd,
Is, with our anger and the dead, at rest;
And much we grieve, no longer trial made,
For that impatience which we then display'd;
Now to their love and worth of every kind
A soft compunction turns th' afflicted mind;
Virtues neglected then, adored become,
And graces slighted, blossom on the tomb.

'Tis well; but let not love nor grief believe
That we assent (who neither loved nor grieve)
To all that praise which on the tomb is read,
To all that passion dictates for the dead;
But more indignant, we the tomb deride,
Whose bold inscription flattery sells to pride.

Read of this Burgess—on the stone appear
How worthy he! how virtuous! and how dear!
What wailing was there when his spirit fled,
How mourned his lady for her lord when dead,
And tears abundant through the town were shed;
See! he was liberal, kind, religious, wise,
And free from all disgrace and all disguise;
His sterling worth, which words cannot express,
Lives with his friends, their pride and their distress.

All this of Jacob Holmes? for his the name:
He thus kind, liberal, just, religious?—Shame!
What is the truth? Old Jacob married thrice;
He dealt in coals, and av'rice was his vice;
He ruled the Borough when his year came on,

And some forget, and some are glad he's gone;
For never yet with shilling could he part,
But when it left his hand it struck his heart.

    Yet, here will Love its last attentions pay,
And place memorials on these beds of clay;
Large level stones lie flat upon the grave,
And half a century's sun and tempest brave;
But many an honest tear and heartfelt sigh
Have follow'd those who now unnoticed lie;
Of these what numbers rest on every side!
Without one token left by grief or pride;
Their graves soon levell'd to the earth, and then
Will other hillocks rise o'er other men;
Daily the dead on the decay'd are thrust,
And generations follow, "dust to dust."

    Yes! there are real Mourners—I have seen
A fair, sad Girl, mild, suffering, and serene;
Attention (through the day) her duties claim'd,
And to be useful as resign'd she aim'd:
Neatly she dress'd, nor vainly seem'd t'expect
Pity for grief, or pardon for neglect;
But when her wearied parents sunk to sleep,
She sought her place to meditate and weep:
Then to her mind was all the past display'd,
That faithful Memory brings to Sorrow's aid;
For then she thought on one regretted Youth,
Her tender trust, and his unquestioned truth;
In ev'ry place she wander'd, where they'd been,
And sadly sacred held the parting scene;
Where last for sea he took his leave—that place
With double interest would she nightly trace;
For long the courtship was, and he would say,
Each time he sail'd,—"This once, and then the day:
Yet prudence tarried, but when last he went,
He drew from pitying love a full consent.

    Happy he sail'd, and great the care she took
That he should softly sleep and smartly look;
White was his better linen, and his check
Was made more trim than any on the deck;
And every comfort men at sea can know
Was hers to buy, to make, and to bestow?
For he to Greenland sail'd, and much she told
How he should guard against the climate's cold;
Yet saw not danger; dangers he'd withstood,
Nor could she trace the fever in his blood:

His messmates smiled at flushings in his cheek,
And he too smiled, but seldom would he speak;
For now he found the danger, felt the pain,
With grievous symptoms he could not explain;
Hope was awaken'd, as for home he sail'd,
But quickly sank, and never more prevail'd.

    He call'd his friend, and prefaced with a sigh
A lover's message—"Thomas, I must die:
Would I could see my Sally, and could rest
My throbbing temples on her faithful breast,
And gazing go!—if not, this trifle take,
And say, till death I wore it for her sake:
Yes! I must die—blow on, sweet breeze, blow on!
Give me one look before my life be gone,
Oh! give me that, and let me not despair,
One last fond look—and now repeat the prayer."

    He had his wish, had more: I will not paint
The Lovers' meeting: she beheld him faint,—
With tender fears, she took a nearer view,
Her terrors doubling as her hopes withdrew;
He tried to smile, and, half succeeding, said,
"Yes! I must die;" and hope for ever fled.

    Still long she nursed him: tender thoughts meantime
Were interchanged, and hopes and views sublime:
To her he came to die, and every day
She took some portion of the dread away;
With him she pray'd, to him his Bible read,
Soothed the faint heart, and held the aching head:
She came with smiles the hour of pain to cheer:
Apart she sigh'd; alone, she shed the tear:
Then as if breaking from a cloud, she gave
Fresh light, and gilt the prospect of the grave.

    One day he lighter seemed, and they forgot
The care, the dread, the anguish of their lot;
They spoke with cheerfulness, and seem'd to think,
Yet said not so—"Perhaps he will not sink:"
A sudden brightness in his look appear'd,
A sudden vigour in his voice was heard,—
She had been reading in the Book of Prayer,
And led him forth, and placed him in his chair;
Lively he seem'd, and spoke of all he knew,
The friendly many, and the favourite few;
Nor one that day did he to mind recall
But she has treasured, and she loves them all:
When in her way she meets them, they appear

Peculiar people—death has made them dear.
He named his Friend, but then his hand she press'd,
And fondly whisper'd, "Thou must go to rest;"
"I go," he said: but as he spoke, she found
His hand more cold, and fluttering was the sound!
Then gazed affrighten'd; but she caught a last,
A dying look of love,—and all was past!

  She placed a decent stone his grave above,
Neatly engraved—an offering of her love;
For that she wrought, for that forsook her bed,
Awake alike to duty and the dead;
She would have grieved, had friends presum'd to spare
The least assistance—'twas her proper care.

  Here will she come, and on the grave will sit,
Folding her arms, in long abstracted fit;
But if observer pass, will take her round,
And careless seem, for she would not be found;
Then go again, and thus her hour employ,
While visions please her, and while woes destroy.

  Forbear, sweet Maid! nor be by Fancy led,
To hold mysterious converse with the dead;
For sure at length thy thoughts, thy spirit's pain,
In this sad conflict will disturb thy brain;
All have their tasks and trials; thine are hard,
But short the time, and glorious the reward;
Thy patient spirit to thy duties give,
Regard the dead, but to the living live.

LETTER III.

And telling me the sov'reign'st thing on earth
Was parmacity for an inward bruise.
SHAKSPEARE, Henry IV, Part I

So gentle, yet so brisk, so wond'rous sweet,
So fit to prattle at a lady's feet.
CHURCHILL

Much are the precious hours of youth misspent
In climbing learning's rugged, steep ascent;
When to the top the bold adventurer's got,
He reigns vain monarch of a barren spot;
While in the vale of ignorance below,
Folly and vice to rank luxuriance grow;
Honours and wealth pour in on every side,
And proud preferment rolls her golden tide.
CHURCHILL

THE VICAR—THE CURATE.

The lately departed Minister of the Borough—His soothing and supplicatory Manners—His cool and timid Affections—No praise due to such negative Virtue—Address to Characters of this kind—The Vicar's employments—His Talents and moderate Ambition—His dislike of Innovation—His mild but ineffectual Benevolence—A Summary of his Character. Mode of paying the Borough-Minister—The Curate has no such Resources—His Learning and Poverty—Erroneous Idea of his Parent—His Feelings as a Husband and Father—the Dutiful Regard of his numerous Family—His Pleasure as a Writer, how interrupted—No Resource in the Press—Vulgar Insult—His Account of a Literary Society, and a Fund for the Relief of indigent Authors, &c.

THE VICAR.

WHERE ends our chancel in a vaulted space,
Sleep the departed Vicars of the place;
Of most, all mention, memory, thought are past—
But take a slight memorial of the last.
    To what famed college we our Yicar owe,
To what fair county, let historians show:
Few now remember when the mild young man,
Ruddy and fair, his Sunday-task began;
Few live to speak of that soft soothing look

He cast around, as he prepared his book;
It was a kind of supplicating smile,
But nothing hopeless of applause the while;
And when he finished, his corrected pride
Felt the desert, and yet the praise denied.
Thus he his race began, and to the end
His constant care was, no man to offend;
No haughty virtues stirr'd his peaceful mind;
Nor urged the Priest to leave the Flock behind;
He was his Master's Soldier, but not one
To lead an army of his Martyrs on:
Fear was his ruling passion; yet was Love,
Of timid kind, once known his heart to move;
It led his patient spirit where it paid
Its languid offerings to a listening Maid:
She, with her widow'd Mother, heard him speak,
And sought awhile to find what he would seek:
Smiling he came, he smiled when he withdrew,
And paid the same attention to the two;
Meeting and parting without joy or pain,
He seem'd to come that he might go again.

     The wondering girl, no prude, but something nice,
At length was chill'd by his unmelting ice;
She found her tortoise held such sluggish pace,
That she must turn and meet him in the chase:
This not approving, she withdrew, till one
Came who appear'd with livelier hope to run;
Who sought a readier way the heart to move,
Than by faint dalliance of unfixing love.

     Accuse me not that I approving paint
Impatient Hope or Love without restraint;
Or think the Passions, a tumultuous throng,
Strong as they are, ungovernably strong:
But is the laurel to the soldier due,
Who, cautious, comes not into danger's view?
What worth has Virtue by Desire untried,
When Nature's self enlists on Duty's side?

     The married dame in vain assail'd the truth
And guarded bosom of the Hebrew youth;
But with the daughter of the Priest of On
The love was lawful, and the guard was gone;
But Joseph's fame had lessened in our view,
Had he, refusing, fled the maiden too.

     Yet our good priest to Joseph's praise aspired,
As once rejecting what his heart desired;

"I am escaped," he said, when none pursued;
When none attack'd him, "I am unsubdued;"
"Oh pleasing pangs of love!" he sang again,
Cold to the joy, and stranger to the pain.
E'en in his age would he address the young,
"I too have felt these fires, and they are strong;"
But from the time he left his favourite maid,
To ancient females his devoirs were paid:
And still they miss him after Morning-prayer;
Nor yet successor fills the Vicar's chair,
Where kindred spirits in his praise agree,
A happy few, as mild and cool as he;
The easy followers in the female train,
Led without love, and captives without chain.

     Ye Lilies male! think (as your tea you sip,
While the town small-talk flows from lip to lip;
Intrigues half-gather'd, conversation-scraps,
Kitchen cabals, and nursery-mishaps),
If the vast world may not some scene produce,
Some state where your small talents might have use;
Within seraglios you might harmless move,
'Mid ranks of beauty, and in haunts of love;
There from too daring man the treasures guard,
An easy duty, and its own reward;
Nature's soft substitutes, you there might save
From crime the tyrant, and from wrong the slave.

     But let applause be dealt in all we may,
Our Priest was cheerful, and in season gay;
His frequent visits seldom fail'd to please;
Easy himself, he sought his neighbour's ease:
To a small garden with delight he came,
And gave successive flowers a summer's fame;
These he presented, with a grace his own,
To his fair friends, and made their beauties known,
Not without moral compliment; how they
"Like flowers were sweet, and must like flowers decay.'

     Simple he was, and loved the simple truth,
Yet had some useful cunning from his youth;
A cunning never to dishonour lent,
And rather for defence than conquest meant;
'Twas fear of power, with some desire to rise,
But not enough to make him enemies;
He ever aim'd to please; and to offend
Was ever cautious; for he sought a friend;
Yet for the friendship never much would pay,

Content to bow, be silent, and obey,
And by a soothing suff'rance find his way.

 Fiddling and fishing were his arts: at times
He alter'd sermons, and he aim'd at rhymes;
And his fair friends, not yet intent on cards,
Oft he amused with riddles and charades.
Mild were his doctrines, and not one discourse
But gain'd in softness what it lost in force:
Kind his opinions; he would not receive
An ill report, nor evil act believe;
"If true, 'twas wrong; but blemish great or small
Have all mankind; yea, sinners are we all."

 If ever fretful thought disturb'd his breast,
If aught of gloom that cheerful mind oppress'd,
It sprang from innovation; it was then
He spake of mischief made by restless men:
Not by new doctrines: never in his life
Would he attend to controversial strife;
For sects he cared not; " They are not of us,
Nor need we, brethren, their concerns discuss;
But 'tis the change, the schism at home I feel;
Ills few perceive, and none have skill to heal:
Not at the altar our young brethren read
(Facing their flock) the decalogue and creed;
But at their duty, in their desks they stand,
With naked surplice, lacking hood and band:
Churches are now of holy song bereft,
And half our ancient customs changed or left;
Few sprigs of ivy are at Christmas seen,
Nor crimson berry tips the holly's green;
Mistaken choirs refuse the solemn strain
Of ancient Sternhold, which from ours amain
Comes flying forth from aisle to aisle about,
Sweet links of harmony and long drawn out."

 These were to him essentials; all things new
He deemed superfluous, useless, or untrue:
To all beside indifferent, easy, cold,
Here the fire kindled, and the woe was told.

 Habit with him was all the test of truth:
"It must be right: I've done it from my youth."
Questions he answer'd in as brief a way:
"It must be wrong—it was of yesterday."

 Though mild benevolence our Priest possess'd,
'Twas but by wishes or by words expressed.
Circles in water, as they wider flow,

The less conspicuous in their progress grow,
And when at last they touch upon the shore,
Distinction ceases, and they're view'd no more.
His love, like that last circle, all embraced,
But with effect that never could be traced.

     Now rests our Vicar. They who knew him best,
Proclaim his life t'have been entirely rest;
Free from all evils which disturb his mind
Whom studies vex and controversies blind.

     The rich approved,—of them in awe he stood;
The poor admired,—they all believed him good;
The old and serious of his habits spoke;
The frank and youthful loved his pleasant joke;
Mothers approved a safe contented guest,
And daughters one who back'd each small request;
In him his flock found nothing to condemn;
Him sectaries liked,—he never troubled them:
No trifles fail'd his yielding mind to please,
And all his passions sunk in early ease;
Nor one so old has left this world of sin,
More like the being that he entered in.

THE CURATE.

ASK you what lands our Pastor tithes?—Alas!
But few our acres, and but short our grass:
In some fat pastures of the rich, indeed,
May roll the single cow or favourite steed;
Who, stable-fed, is here for pleasure seen,
His sleek sides bathing in the dewy green;
But these, our hilly heath and common wide
Yield a slight portion for the parish-guide;
No crops luxuriant in our borders stand,
For here we plough the ocean, not the land;
Still reason wills that we our Pastor pay,
And custom does it on a certain day:
Much is the duty, small the legal due,
And this with grateful minds we keep in view;
Each makes his off'ring, some by habit led,
Some by the thought that all men must be fed;
Duty and love, and piety and pride,
Have each their force, and for the Priest provide.

     Not thus our Curate, one whom all believe
Pious and just, and for whose fate they grieve;
All see him poor, but e'en the vulgar know
He merits love, and their respect bestow.

A man so learn'd you shall but seldom see,
Nor one so honour'd, so aggrieved as he;—
Not grieved by years alone; though his appear
Dark and more dark; severer on severe:
Not in his need,—and yet we all must grant
How painful 'tis for feeling Age to want:
Nor in his body's sufferings; yet we know
Where Time has ploughed, there Misery loves to sow;
But in the wearied mind, that all in vain
Wars with distress, and struggles with its pain.

    His father saw his powers—"I give," quoth he,
"My first-born learning; 'twill a portion be:"
Unhappy gift! a portion for a son!
But all he had:—he learn'd, and was undone!

    Better, apprenticed to an humble trade,
Had he the cassock for the priesthood made,
Or thrown the shuttle, or the saddle shaped,
And all these pangs of feeling souls escaped.
He once had hope—Hope, ardent, lively, light;
His feelings pleasant, and his prospects bright:
Eager of fame, he read, he thought, he wrote,
Weigh'd the Greek page, and added note on note.
At morn, at evening, at his work was he,
And dream'd what his Euripides would be.

    Then care began:—he loved, he woo'd, he wed;
Hope cheer'd him still, and Hymen bless'd his bed—
A curate's bed ! then came the woeful years;
The husband's terrors, and the father's tears;
A wife grown feeble, mourning, pining, vex'd
With wants and woes—by daily cares perplex'd;
No more a help, a smiling, soothing aid,
But boding, drooping, sickly, and afraid.

    A kind physician, and without a fee,
Gave his opinion—"Send her to the sea."
"Alas!" the good man answer'd, "can I send
A friendless woman? Can I find a friend?
No; I must with her, in her need, repair
To that new place; the poor lie everywhere;—
Some priest will pay me for my pious pains:"—
He said, he came, and here he yet remains.

    Behold his dwelling! this poor hut he hires,
Where he from view, though not from want, retires;
Where four fair daughters, and five sorrowing sons,
Partake his sufferings, and dismiss his duns;
All join their efforts, and in patience learn

To want the comforts they aspire to earn;
For the sick mother something they'd obtain,
To soothe her grief and mitigate her pain;
For the sad father something they'd procure
To ease the burden they themselves endure.
    Virtues like these at once delight and press
On the fond father with a proud distress;
On all around he looks with care and love,
Grieved to behold, but happy to approve.
    Then from his care, his love, his grief, he steals,
And by himself an Author's pleasure feels:
Each line detains him; he omits not one,
And all the sorrows of his state are gone.—
Alas! even then, in that delicious hour,
He feels his fortune, and laments its power.
    Some Tradesman's bill his wandering eyes engage,
Some scrawl for payment thrust 'twixt page and page;
Some bold, loud rapping at his humble door,
Some surly message he has heard before,
Awake, alarm, and tell him he is poor.
    An angry Dealer, vulgar, rich, and proud,
Thinks of his bill, and, passing, raps aloud;
The elder daughter meekly makes him way—
"I want my money, and I cannot stay:
My mill is stopp'd; what, Miss! I cannot grind;
Go tell your father he must raise the wind:"
Still trembling, troubled, the dejected maid
Says, "Sir! my father!"—and then stops afraid:
E'en his hard heart is soften'd, and he hears
Her voice with pity; he respects her tears;
His stubborn features half admit a smile,
And his tone softens—"Well! I'll wait awhile."
Pity! a man so good, so mild, so meek,
At such an age, should have his bread to seek;
And all those rude and fierce attacks to dread.
That are more harrowing than the want of bread;
Ah! who shall whisper to that misery peace!
And say that want and insolence shall cease?
    "But why not publish?"—those who know too well,
Dealers in Greek, are fearful 'twill not sell;
Then he himself is timid, troubled, slow,
Nor likes his labours nor his griefs to show;
The hope of fame may in his heart have place,
But he has dread and horror of disgrace;
Nor has he that confiding, easy way,

That might his learning and himself display;
But to his work he from the world retreats,
And frets and glories o'er the favourite sheets.
        But see! the Man himself; and sure I trace
Signs of new joy exulting in that face
O'er care that sleeps—we err, or we discern
Life in thy looks—the reason may we learn?
        "Yes," he replied, "I'm happy, I confess,
To learn that some are pleased with happiness
Which others feel—there are who now combine
The worthiest natures in the best design,
To aid the letter'd poor, and soothe such ills as mine.
We who more keenly feel the world's contempt,
And from its miseries are the least exempt;
Now Hope shall whisper to the wounded breast
And Grief, in soothing expectation, rest.
        "Yes, I am taught that men who think, who feel,
Unite the pains of thoughtful men to heal;
Not with disdainful pride, whose bounties make
The needy curse the benefits they take;
Not with the idle vanity that knows
Only a selfish joy when it bestows;
Not with o'erbearing wealth, that, in disdain,
Hurls the superfluous bliss at groaning pain;
But these are men who yield such blest relief,
That with the grievance they destroy the grief;
Their timely aid the needy sufferers find,
Their generous manner soothes the suffering mind;
There is a gracious bounty, form'd to raise
Him whom it aids; their charity is praise;
A common bounty may relieve distress,
But whom the vulgar succour they oppress;
This though a favour is an honour too,
Though Mercy's duty, yet 'tis Merit's due;
When our relief from such resources rise,
All painful sense of obligation dies;
And grateful feelings in the bosom wake,
For 'tis their offerings, not their alms we take.
        "Long may these founts of Charity remain,
And never shrink, but to be fill'd again;
True! to the Author they are now confined,
To him who gave the treasure of his mind,
His time, his health,—and thankless found mankind:
But there is hope that from these founts may flow
A side-way stream, and equal good bestow;

Good that may reach us, whom the day's distress
Keeps from the fame and perils of the Press;
Whom Study beckons from the Ills of Life,
And they from Study; melancholy strife!
Who then can say, but bounty now so free,
And so diffused, may find its way to me?
    "Yes! I may see my decent table yet
Cheer'd with the meal that adds not to my debt;
May talk of those to whom so much we owe,
And guess their names whom yet we may not know;
Blest, we shall say, are those who thus can give,
And next who thus upon the bounty live;
Then shall I close with thanks my humble meal.
And feel so well—Oh, God! how shall I feel!" [2]

LETTER IV.

............But cast your eyes again
And view those errors which new sects maintain,
Or which of old disturbed the Church's peaceful reign;
And we can point each period of the time
When they began and who begat the crime;
Can calculate how long th' eclipse endured;
Who interposed; what digits were obscured;
Of all which are already passed away
We knew the rise, the progress, and decay.

DRYDEN, Hind and Panther

Oh, said the Hind, how many sons have you
Who call you mother, whom you never knew!
But most of them who that relation plead
Are such ungracious youths as wish you dead;
They gape at rich revenues which you hold,
And fain would nibble at your grandame gold.

ibid.

SECTS AND PROFESSIONS IN RELIGION.

Sects and Professions in Religion are numerous and successive—
General effect of false Zeal—Deists—Fanatical Idea of Church
Reformers—The Church of Rome—Baptists—Swedenborgians—
Univerbalists—Jews—Methodists of two Kinds: Calvinistic and
Arminian—The Preaching of a Calvinistic Enthusiast—His contempt of
Learning—Dislike to sound Morality: why—His Ideas of Conversion—
His Success and Pretensions to Humility. The Arminian Teacher of the
older Flock—Their Notions of the operations and power of Satan—
Description of his Devices—Their opinion of regular Ministers—
Comparison of these with the Preacher himself—A Rebuke to his
Hearers; introduces a description of the powerful Effects of the Word
in the early and awakening Days of Methodism.

"SECTS in Religion?"—Yes of every race
We nurse some portion in our favour'd place;
Not one warm preacher of one growing sect
Can say our Borough treats him with neglect:
Frequent as fashions they with us appear,
And you might ask, "how think we for the year?"
They come to us as riders in a trade,
And with much art exhibit and persuade.

Minds are for Sects of various kinds decreed,
As diff'rent soils are formed for diff'rent seed;
Some when converted sigh in sore amaze,
And some are wrapt in joy's ecstatic blaze;
Others again will change to each extreme,
They know not why—as hurried in a dream;
Unstable, they, like water, take all forms,
Are quick and stagnant; have their calms and storms;
High on the hills, they in the sunbeams glow,
Then muddily they move debased and slow;
Or cold and frozen rest, and neither rise nor flow.

Yet none the cool and prudent Teacher prize.
On him ther dote who wakes their ectasies;
With passions ready primed such guide they meet,
And warm and kindle with th' imparted heat;
'Tis he who wakes the nameless strong desire,
The melting rapture and the glowing fire;
'Tis he who pierces deep the tortured breast,
And stirs the terrors never more to rest.

Opposed to these we have a prouder kind,
Rash without heat, and without raptures blind;
These our Glad Tidings unconcern'd peruse,
Search without awe, and without fear refuse;
The truths, the blessings found in Sacred Writ,
Call forth their spleen, and exercise their wit;
Respect from these nor saints nor martyrs gain,
The zeal they scorn, and they deride the pain:
And take their transient, cool, contemptuous view,
Of that which must be tried, and doubtless may be true.

Friends of our Faith we have, whom doubts like these,
And keen remarks, and bold objections please;
They grant such doubts have weaker minds oppress'd,
Till sound conviction gave the troubled rest.
"But still," they cry, "let none their censures spare.
They but confirm the glorious hopes we share;
From doubt, disdain, derision, scorn, and lies,
With five-fold triumph sacred Truth shall rise."

Yes! I allow, so Truth shall stand at last,
And gain fresh glory by the conflict past:—
As Solway-Moss (a barren mass and cold,
Death to the seed, and poison to the fold),
The smiling plain and fertile vale o'erlaid,
Choked the green sod, and kill'd the springing blade;
That, changed by culture, may in time be seen
Enrich'd by golden grain and pasture green;

And these fair acres rented and enjoy'd
May those excel by Solway-Moss destroy'd.

 Still must have mourn'd the tenant of the day,
For hopes destroy'd, and harvests swept away;
To him the gain of future years unknown,
The instant grief and suffering were his own:
So must I grieve for many a wounded heart,
Chill'd by those doubts which bolder minds impart:
Truth in the end shall shine divinely clear,
But sad the darkness till those times appear;
Contests for truth, as wars for freedom, yield
Glory and joy to those who gain the field:
But still the Christian must in pity sigh
For all who suffer, and uncertain die.

 Here are, who all the Church maintains approve,
But yet the Church herself they will not love;
In angry speech, they blame the carnal tie
Which pure Religion lost her spirit by;
What time from prisons, flames, and tortures led,
She slumber'd careless in a royal bed;
To make, they add, the Church's glory shine,
Should Diocletian reign, not Constantine.

 "In pomp," they cry, "is "England's Church array'd,
Her cool Reformers wrought like men afraid;
We would have pull'd her gorgeous temples down,
And spurn'd her mitre, and defiled her gown:
We would have trodden low both bench and stall,
Nor left a tithe remaining, great or small."

 Let us be serious—Should such trials come.
Are they themselves prepared for martyrdom?
It seems to us that our reformers knew
Th' important work they undertook to do;
An equal priesthood they were loth to try,
Lest zeal and care should with ambition die;
To them it seem'd that, take the tenth away,
Yet priests must eat, and you must feed or pay:
Would they indeed, who hold such pay in scorn,
Put on the muzzle when they tread the corn?
Would they all, gratis, watch and tend the fold,
Nor take one fleece to keep them from the cold?

 Men are not equal, and 'tis meet and right
That robes and titles our respect excite;
Order requires it; 'tis by vulgar pride
That such regard is censured and denied;
Or by that false enthusiastic zeal,

That thinks the Spirit will the priest reveal,
And show to all men, by their powerful speech,
Who are appointed and inspired to teach:
Alas! could we the dangerous rule believe,
Whom for their teacher should the crowd receive?
Since all the varying kinds demand respect,
All press you on to join their chosen sect,
Although but in this single point agreed,
"Desert your churches and adopt our creed."
    We know full well how much our forms offend
The burthen'd Papist and the simple Friend:
Him, who new robes for every service takes,
And who in drab and beaver sighs and shakes;
He on the priest, whom hood and band adorn,
Looks with the sleepy eye of silent scorn;
But him I would not for my friend and guide,
Who views such things with spleen, or wears with pride.
    See next our several Sects,—but first behold
The Church of Rome, who here is poor and old:
Use not triumphant raillery, or, at least,
Let not thy mother be a whore and beast;
Great was her pride indeed in ancient times,
Yet shall we think of nothing but her crimes?
Exalted high above all earthly things,
She placed her foot upon the neck of kings;
But some have deeply since avenged the crown,
And thrown her glory and her honours down;
Nor neck nor ear can she of kings command,
Nor place a foot upon her own fair land.
    Among her sons, with us a quiet few,
Obscure themselves, her ancient state review,
And fond and melancholy glances cast
On power insulted, and on triumph past:
They look, they can but look, with many a sigh,
On sacred buildings doom'd in dust to lie;
"On seats," they tell, "where priests mid tapers dim
Breathed the warm prayer, or tuned the midnight hymn;
Where trembling penitents their guilt confessed,
Where want had succour, and contrition rest;
There weary men from trouble found relief,
There men in sorrow found repose from grief.
To scenes like these the fainting soul retired;
Revenge and anger in these cells expired;
By Pity soothed, Remorse lost half her fears,
And soften'd Pride dropp'd penitential tears.

"Then convent walls and nunnery spires arose,
In pleasant spots which monk or abbot chose;
When counts and barons saints devoted fed,
And making cheap exchange, had pray'r for bread.
  "Now all is lost, the earth where abbeys stood
Is layman's land, the glebe, the stream, the wood:
His oxen low where monks retired to eat,
His cows repose upon the prior's seat:
And wanton doves within the cloisters bill,
Where the chaste votary warr'd with wanton will."
  Such is the change they mourn, but they restrain
The rage of grief, and passively complain.
  We've Baptists old and new; forbear to ask
What the distinction—I decline the task;
This I perceive, that when a sect grows old,
Converts are few, and the converted cold:
First comes the hotbed heat, and while it glows
The plants spring up, and each with vigour grows:
Then comes the cooler day, and though awhile
The verdure prospers and the blossoms smile,
Yet poor the fruit, and form'd by long delay,
Nor will the profits for the culture pay;
The skilful gard'ner then no longer stops,
But turns to other beds for bearing crops.
  Some Swedenborgians in our streets are found,
Those wandering walkers on enchanted ground,
Who in our world can other worlds survey,
And speak with spirits though confin'd in clay:
Of Bible-mysteries they the keys possess,
Assured themselves, where wiser men but guess:
'Tis theirs to see around, about, above,—
How spirits mingle thoughts, and angels move;
Those whom our grosser views from us exclude,
To them appear—a heavenly multitude;
While the dark sayings, seal'd to men like us,
Their priests interpret, and their flocks discuss.
  But while these gifted men, a favour'd fold,
New powers exhibit and new worlds behold;
Is there not danger lest their minds confound
The pure above them with the gross around?
May not these Phaetons, who thus contrive
'Twixt heaven above and earth beneath to drive,
When from their flaming chariots they descend,
The worlds they visit in their fancies blend?
Alas! too sure on both they bring disgrace,

Their earth is crazy, and their heaven is base.
  We have, it seems, who treat, and doubtless well,
Of a chastising not awarding Hell;
Who are assured that an offended God
Will cease to use the thunder and the rod;
A soul on earth, by crime and folly stain'd,
When here corrected has improvement gain'd;
In other state still more improved to grow,
And nobler powers in happier world to know;
New strength to use in each divine employ,
And more enjoying, looking to more joy.
  A pleasing vision! could we thus be sure
Polluted souls would be at length so pure;
The view is happy, we may think it just,
It may be true—but who shall add, it must?
To the plain words and sense of Sacred Writ,
With all my heart I reverently submit;
But where it leaves me doubtful, I'm afraid
To call conjecture to my reason's aid;
Thy thoughts, thy ways, great God! are not as mine,
And to thy mercy I my soul resign.
  Jews are with us, but far unlike to those,
Who, led by David, warr'd with Israels foes;
Unlike to those whom his imperial son
Taught truths divine—the Preacher Solomon;
Nor war nor wisdom yield our Jews delight;
They will not study, and they dare not fight.
  These are, with us, a slavish, knavish crew,
Shame and dishonour to the name of Jew;
The poorest masters of the meanest arts,
With cunning heads, and cold and cautious hearts;
They grope their dirty way to petty gains,
While poorly paid for their nefarious pains.
Amazing race! deprived of land and laws,
A general language and a public cause;
With a religion none can now obey,
With a reproach that none can take away:
A people still, whose common ties are gone;
Who, mix'd with every race, are lost in none.
  What said their Prophet?—"Shouldst thou disobey,
The Lord shall take thee from thy land away;
Thou shalt a by-word and a proverb be,
And all shall wonder at thy woes and thee;
Daughter and son, shalt thou, while captive, have,
And see them made the bond-maid and the slave;

He, whom thou leav'st, the Lord thy God, shall bring
War to thy country on an eagle-wing.
A people strong and dreadful to behold,
Stern to the young, remorseless to the old;
Masters whose speech thou canst not understand
By cruel signs shall give the harsh command:
Doubtful of life shalt thou by night, by day,
For grief, and dread, and trouble pine away;
Thy evening wish,—Would God I saw the sun
Thy morning sigh,—Would God the day were done!
Thus shalt thou suffer, and to distant times
Regret thy misery, and lament thy crimes."

    A part there are, whom doubtless man might trust,
Worthy as wealthy, pure, religious, just;
They who with patience, yet with rapture, look
On the strong promise of the Sacred Book:
As unfulfill'd th' endearing words they view,
And blind to truth, yet own their prophets true;
Well pleased they look for Sion's coming state,
Nor think of Julian's boast and Julian's fate.

    More might I add: I might describe the flocks
Made by Seceders from the ancient stocks;
Those who will not to any guide submit,
Nor find one creed to their conceptions fit—
Each sect, they judge, in something goes astray,
And every church has lost the certain way!
Then for themselves they carve out creed and laws,
And weigh their atoms, and divide their straws.

    A Sect remains, which, though divided long
In hostile parties, both are fierce and strong,
And into each enlists a warm and zealous throng.
Soon as they rose in fame, the strife arose,
The Calvinistic these, th' Arminian those;
With Wesley some remain'd, the remnant Whitfield chose.
Now various leaders both the parties take,
And the divided hosts their new divisions make.

    See yonder Preacher! to his people pass,
Borne up and swell'd by tabernacle-gas:
Much he discourses, and of various points,
All unconnected, void of limbs and joints;
He rails, persuades, explains, and moves the will
By fierce bold words, and strong mechanic skill.

    "That Gospel, Paul with zeal and love maintain'd,
To others lost, to you is now explain'd;
No worldly learning can these points discuss,

Books teach them not as they are taught to us.
Illiterate call us!—let their wisest man
Draw forth his thousands as your Teacher can:
They give their moral precepts: so, they say,
Did Epictetus once, and Seneca;
One was a slave, and slaves we all must be,
Until the Spirit comes and sets us free.
Yet hear you nothing from such man but works;
They make the Christian service like the Turks.

    "Hark to the Churchman: day by day he cries,
'Children of Men, be virtuous and be wise:
Seek patience, justice, temp'rance, meekness, truth;
In age be courteous, be sedate in youth.'—
So they advise, and when such things be read,
How can we wonder that their flocks are dead?
The Heathens wrote of Virtue: they could dwell
On such light points: in them it might be well;
They might for virtue strive; but I maintain,
Our strife for virtue would be proud and vain.
When Samson carried Gaza's gates so far,
Lack'd he a helping hand to bear the bar?
Thus the most virtuous must in bondage groan:
Samson is grace, and carries all alone.

    "Hear you not priests their feeble spirits spend,
In bidding Sinners turn to God, and mend;
To check their passions and to walk aright,
To run the Race, and fight the glorious Fight?
Nay more—to pray, to study, to improve,
To grow in goodness, to advance in love?

    "Oh! Babes and Sucklings, dull of heart and slow,
Can Grace be gradual? Can Conversion grow?
The work is done by instantaneous call;
Converts at once are made, or not at all;
Nothing is left to grow, reform, amend,
The first emotion is the Movement's end:
If once forgiven, Debt can be no more;
If once adopted, will the heir be poor?
The man who gains the twenty-thousand prize,
Does he by little and by little rise?
There can no fortune for the Soul be made,
By peddling cares and savings in her trade.

    "Why are our sins forgiven?—Priests reply,
—Because by Faith on Mercy we rely;
'Because, believing, we repent and pray.'
Is this their doctrine?—then they go astray;

We're pardon'd neither for belief nor deed,
For faith nor practice, principle nor creed;
Nor for our sorrow for our former sin,
Nor for our fears when better thoughts begin;
Nor prayers nor penance in the cause avail,
All strong remorse, all soft contrition fail:
It is the Call! till that proclaims us free,
In darkness, doubt, and bondage we must be;
Till that assures us, we've in vain endured,
And all is over when we're once assured.

    "This is Conversion:—First there comes a cry
Which utters, 'Sinner, thou'rt condemned to die;'
Then the struck soul to every aid repairs,
To church and altar, ministers and prayers;
In vain she strives,—involved, ingulf'd in sin,
She looks for hell, and seems already in:
When in this travail, the New Birth comes on,
And in an instant every pang is gone;
The mighty work is done without our pains,—
Claim but a part, and not a part remains.

    "All this experience tells the Soul, and yet
These moral men their pence and farthings set
Against the terrors of the countless Debt;
But such compounders, when they come to jail,
Will find that Virtues never serve as bail.

    "So much to duties: now to Learning look,
And see their priesthood piling book on book;
Yea, books of infidels, we're told, and plays,
Put out by heathens in the wink'd-on days;
The very letters are of crooked kind,
And show the strange perverseness of their mind.
Have I this Learning? When the Lord would speak;
Think ye he needs the Latin or the Greek?
And lo! with all their learning, when they rise
To preach, in view the ready sermon lies;
Some low-prized stuff they purchased at the stalls,
And more like Seneca's than mine or Paul's:
Children of Bondage, how should they explain
The Spirit's freedom, while they wear a chain?
They study words, for meanings grow perplex d,
And slowly hunt for truth from text to text,
Through Greek and Hebrew:—we the meaning seek
Of that within, who every tongue can speak:
This all can witness; yet the more I know,
The more a meek and humble mind I show.

"No; let the Pope, the high and mighty priest,
Lord to the poor, and servant to the Beast;
Let bishops, deans, and prebendaries swell
With pride and fatness till their hearts rebel:
I'm meek and modest:—if I could be proud,
This crowded meeting, lo! th' amazing crowd!
Your mute attention, and your meek respect,
My spirit's fervour, and my words' effect,
Might stir th' unguarded soul; and oft to me
The Tempter speaks, whom I compel to flee;
He goes in fear, for he my force has tried,—
Such is my power! but can you call it pride?

"No, Fellow-Pilgrims! of the things I've shown
I might be proud, were they indeed my own!
But they are lent: and well you know the source
Of all that's mine, and must confide of course:
Mine! no, I err; 'tis but consigned to me,
And I am nought but steward and trustee."

FAR other Doctrines yon Arminian speaks;
"Seek Grace," he cries, "for he shall find who seeks."
This is the ancient stock by Wesley led;
They the pure body, he the reverend head:
All innovation they with dread decline,
Their John the elder was the John divine.
Hence, still their moving prayer, the melting hymn,
The varied accent, and the active limb:
Hence that implicit faith in Satan's might,
And their own matchless prowess in the fight.
In every act they see that lurking foe,
Let loose awhile, about the world to go;
A dragon flying round the earth, to kill
The heavenly hope, and prompt the carnal will;
Whom sainted knights attack in sinners' cause,
And force the wounded victim from his paws;
Who but for them would man's whole race subdue,
For not a hireling will the foe pursue.

"Show me one Churchman who will rise and pray
Through half the night, though lab'ring all the day,
Always abounding—show me him, I say:"—
Thus cries the Preacher, and he adds, "Their sheep
Satan devours at leisure as they sleep.
Not so with us; we drive him from the fold,

For ever barking and for ever bold:
While they securely slumber, all his schemes
Take full effect,—the Devil never dreams:
Watchful and changeful through the world he goes,
And few can trace this deadliest of their foes;
But I detect, and at his work surprise
The subtle Serpent under all disguise.

 "Thus to Man's soul the Foe of Souls will speak,
—'A Saint elect, you can have nought to seek;
Why all this labour in so plain a case,
Such care to run, when certain of the race?'
All this he urges to the carnal will,
He knows you're slothful, and would have you still:
Be this your answer,—'Satan, I will keep
Still on the watch till you are laid asleep.'
Thus too the Christian's progress he'll retard:—
'The gates of mercy are for ever barr'd;
And that with bolts so driven and so stout,
Ten thousand workmen cannot wrench them out.'
To this deceit you have but one reply,—
Give to the Father of all Lies the lie.

 "A Sister's weakness he'll by fits surprise,
His her wild laughter, his her piteous cries;
And should a pastor at her side attend,
He'll use her organs to abuse her friend:
These are possessions—unbelieving wits
Impute them all to Nature: 'They're her fits,
Caused by commotions in tne nerves and brains;'—
Vain talk! but they'll be fitted for their pains.

 "These are in part the ills the Foe has wrought,
And these the Churchman thinks not worth his thought;
They bid the troubled try for peace and rest,
Compose their minds, and be no more distress'd;
As well might they command the passive shore
To keep secure, and be o'erflow'd no more;
To the wrong subject is their skill applied,—
To act like workmen, they should stem the tide.

 "These are the Church-Physicians: they are paid
With noble fees for their advice and aid;
Yet know they not the inward pulse to feel,
To ease the anguish, or the wound to heal.
With the sick Sinner, thus their work begins:
'Do you repent you of your former sins?
Will you amend if you revive and live?
And, pardon seeking, will you pardon give?

Have you belief in what your Lord has done,
And are you thankful?—all is well my son.'
    "A way far different ours—we thus surprise
A soul with questions, and demand replies:
'How dropp'd you first,' I ask, 'the legal Yoke?
What the first word the living Witness spoke?
Perceived you thunders roar and lightnings shine,
And tempests gathering ere the Birth divine?
Did fire, and storm, and earthquake all appear
Before that still small voice, What dost thou here?
Hast thou by day and night, and soon and late,
Waited and watch'd before Admission-gate;
And so a pilgrim and a soldier pass'd
To Sion's hill through battle and through blast?
Then in thy way didst thou thy foe attack,
And mad'st thou proud Apollyon turn his back?'
    "Heart-searching things are these, and shake the mind,
Yea, like the rustling of a mighty wind.
    "Thus would I ask: 'Nay, let me question now,
How sink my sayings in your bosoms? how?
Feel you a quickening? drops the subject deep?
Stupid and stony, no! you're all asleep;
Listless and lazy, waiting for a close,
As if at church;—do I allow repose?
Am I a legal minister? do I
With form or rubric, rule or rite comply?
Then whence this quiet, tell me, I beseech?
One might believe you heard your Rector preach,
Or his assistant dreamer:—Oh! return,
Ye times of burning, when the heart would burn;
Now hearts are ice, and you, my freezing fold,
Have spirits sunk and sad, and bosoms stony-cold.
    "Oh! now again for those prevailing powers,
Which, once began this mighty work of ours;
When the wide field, God's Temple, was the place,
And birds flew by to catch a breath of grace;
When 'mid his timid friends and threat'ning foes,
Our zealous chief as Paul at Athens rose:
When with infernal spite and knotty clubs
The Ill-One arm'd his scoundrels and his scrubs;
And there were flying all around the spot
Brands at the Preacher, but they touch'd him not:
Stakes brought to smite him, threaten'd in his cause,
And tongues, attuned to curses, roar'd applause;
Louder and louder grew his awful tones,

Sobbing and sighs were heard, and rueful groans;
Soft women fainted, prouder man express'd
Wonder and woe, and butchers smote the breast;
Eyes wept, ears tingled; stiff'ning on each head,
The hair drew back, and Satan howl'd and fled.
    "In that soft season when the gentle breeze
Rises all round, and swells by slow degrees;
Till tempests gather, when through all the sky
The thunders rattle, and the lightnings fly;
When rain in torrents wood and vale deform,
And all is horror, hurricane, and storm:
    "So, when the Preacher in that glorious time,
Than clouds more melting, more than storm sublime,
Dropp'd the new Word, there came a charm around;
Tremors and terrors rose upon the sound;
The stubborn spirits by his force he broke,
As the fork'd lightning rives the knotted oak:
Fear, hope, dismay, all signs of shame or grace,
Chain'd every foot, or featured every face;
Then took his sacred trump a louder swell,
And now they groan'd, they sicken'd, and they fell;
Again he sounded, and we heard the cry
Of the Word-wounded, as about to die;
Further and further spread the conquering word,
As loud he cried—'The Battle of the Lord.'
E'en those apart who were the sound denied,
Fell down instinctive, and in spirit died.
Nor stay'd he yet—his eye, his frown, his speech,
His very gesture, had a power to teach:
With outstretch'd arms, strong voice, and piercing call,
He won the field, and made the Dagons fall;
And thus in triumph took his glorious way,
Through scenes of horror, terror, and dismay."

LETTER V.

Say then which class to greater folly stoop,
The great in promise, or the poor in hope?

Be brave, for your leader is brave, and vows reformation; there shall be in England seven halfpenny loaves sold for a penny; and the three-hooped pot shall have ten hoops. I will make it felony to drink small beer: all shall eat and drink on my score, and I will apparel them all in one livery,that they may agree like brothers; and they shall all worship me as their lord.

SHAKSPEARE, Henry VI.

THE ELECTION.

The Evils of the Contest, and how in part to be avoided—The Miseries endured by a Friend of the Candidate—The various Liberties taken with him who has no Personal Interest in the Success—The unreasonable Expectations of Voters—The Censures of the opposing Party—The Vices as well as Follies shown in such Time of Contest—Plans and Cunning of Electors—Evils which remain after the Decision, opposed in vain by the Efforts of the Friendly, and of the Successful; among whom is the Mayor—Story of his Advancement till he was raised to the Government of the Borough—These Evils not to be placed in Balance with the Liberty of the People, but are yet Subjects of just Complaint.

YES, our Election's past, and we've been free,
Somewhat as madmen without keepers be;
And such desire of Freedom has been shown,
That both the parties wish'd her all their own:
All our free smiths and cobblers in the town
Were loth to lay such pleasant freedom down;
To put the bludgeon and cockade aside,
And let us pass unhurt and undefied.
   True! you might then your party's sign produce,
And so escape with only half th' abuse:
With half the danger as you walk'd along,
With rage and threat'ning but from half the throng.
This you might do, and not your fortune mend,
For where you lost a foe you gain'd a friend;
And to distress you, vex you, and expose,
Election-friends are worse than any foes;
The party-curse is with the canvass past,
But party-friendship, for jour grief, will last.

Friends of all kinds; the civil and the rude,
Who humbly wish, or boldly dare t'intrude:
These beg or take a liberty to come
(Friends should be free), and make your house their home;
They know that warmly you their cause espouse,
And come to make their boastings and their bows;
You scorn their manners, you their words mistrust,
But you must hear them, and they know you must.

One plainly sees a friendship firm and true,
Between the noble candidate and you;
So humbly begs (and states at large the case),
"You'll think of Bobby and the little place."

Stifling his shame by drink, a wretch will come,
And prate your wife and daughter from the room:
In pain you hear him, and at heart despise,
Yet with heroic mind your pangs disguise;
And still in patience to the sot attend,
To show what man can bear to serve a friend.

One enters hungry—not to be denied,
And takes his place and jokes—"We're of a side."
Yet worse, the proser who, upon the strength
Of his one vote, has tales of three hours' length;
This sorry rogue you bear, yet with surprise
Start at his oaths, and sicken at his lies.

Then comes there one, and tells in friendly way
What the opponents in their anger say;
All that through life has vex'd you, all abuse,
Will this kind friend in pure regard produce;
And having through your own offences run,
Adds (as appendage) what your friends have done,

Has any female cousin made a trip
To Gretna Green, or more vexatious slip?
Has your wife's brother, or your uncle's son,
Done aught amiss, or is he thought t'have done?
Is there of all your kindred some who lack
Vision direct, or have a gibbous back?
From your unlucky name may quips and puns
Be made by these upbraiding Goths and Huns?
To some great public character have you
Assigned the fame to worth and talents due,
Proud of your praise?—In this, in any case,
Where the brute-spirit may affix disgrace,
These friends will smiling bring it, and the while
You silent sit, and practise for a smile.

Vain of their power, and of their value sure,

They nearly guess the tortures you endure;
Nor spare one pang—for they perceive your heart
Goes with the cause; you'd die before you'd start;
Do what they may, they're sure you'll not offend
Men who have pledged their honours to your friend.

 Those friends indeed, who start as in a race,
May love the sport, and laugh at this disgrace;
They have in view the glory and the prize,
Nor heed the dirty steps by which they rise:
But we their poor associates lose the fame,
Though more than partners in the toil and shame.

 Were this the whole; and did the time produce
But shame and toil, but riot and abuse;
We might be then from serious griefs exempt,
And view the whole with pity and contempt.
Alas! but here the vilest passions rule;
It is Seduction's, is Temptation's school;
Where vices mingle in the oddest ways,
The grossest slander and the dirtiest praise;
Flattery enough to make the vainest sick,
And clumsy stratagem, and scoundrel trick:
Nay more, your anger and contempt to cause,
These, while they fish for profit, claim applause;
Bribed, bought, and bound, they banish shame and fear;
Tell you they're staunch, and have a soul sincere;
Then talk of honour, and, if doubt's express'd,
Show where it lies, and smite upon the breast.

 Among these worthies, some at first declare
For whom they vote: he then has most to spare;
Others hang off—when coming to the post
Is spurring time, and then he'll spare the most:
While some demurring, wait, and find at last
The bidding languish, and the market past;
These will affect all bribery to condemn,
And be it Satan laughs, he laughs at them.

 Some too are pious—One desired the Lord
To teach him where "to drop his little word;
To lend his vote where it will profit best;
Promotion came not from the east or west;
But as their freedom had promoted some,
He should be glad to know which way 'twould come.
It was a naughty world, and where to sell
His precious charge, was more than he could tell."

 "But you succeeded?"—True, at mighty cost,
And our good friend, I fear, will think he's lost:

Inns, horses, chaises, dinners, balls, and notes;
What fill'd their purses, and what drench'd their throats;
The private pension, and indulgent lease,—
Have all been granted to these friends who fleece;
Friends who will hang like burs upon his coat,
And boundless judge the value of a vote.

    And though the terrors of the time be pass'd,
There still remain the scatterings of the blast;
The boughs are parted that entwined before,
And ancient harmony exists no more;
The gusts of wrath our peaceful seats deform,
And sadly flows the sighing of the storm:
Those who have gain'd are sorry for the gloom,
But they who lost, unwilling peace should come;
There open envy, here suppress'd delight,
Yet live till time shall better thoughts excite,
And so prepare us, by a six-years' truce,
Again for riot, insult, and abuse.

    Our worthy Mayor, on the victorious part,
Cries out for peace, and cries with all his heart;
He, civil creature! ever does his best
To banish wrath from every voter's breast;
"For where," says he, with reason strong and plain,
"Where is the profit? what will anger gain?"
His short stout person he is wont to brace
In good brown broad-cloth, edg'd with two-inch lace,
When in his seat; and still the coat seems new,
Preserved by common use of seaman's blue.

    He was a fisher from his earliest day,
And placed his nets within the Borough's bay;
Where, by his skates, his herrings, and his soles,
He lived, nor dream'd of Corporation-Doles;
But toiling saved, and saving, never ceased
Till he had box'd up twelvescore pounds at least:
He knew not money's power, but judged it best
Safe in his trunk to let his treasure rest;
Yet to a friend complain'd: "Sad charge, to keep
So many pounds; and then I cannot sleep:"
"Then put it out," replied the friend:—"What, give
My money up? why then I could not live:"
"Nay, but for interest place it in his hands
Who'll give you mortgage on his house or lands."
"Oh but," said Daniel, "that's a dangerous plan;
He may be robb'd like any other man:"
"Still he is bound, and you may be at rest,

More safe the money than within your chest;
And you'll receive, from all deductions clear,
Five pounds for every hundred, every year."
"What good in that?" quoth Daniel, "for 'tis plain,
If part I take, there can but part remain:"
"What! you, my friend, so skill'd in gainful things,
Have you to learn what Interest money brings?"
"Not so," said Daniel, "perfectly I know,
He's the most interest who has most to show."
"True! and he'll show the more the more he lends;
Thus he his weight and consequence extends;
For they who borrow must restore each sum,
And pay for use. What, Daniel, art thou dumb?"
For much amazed was that good man.—"Indeed!"
Said he with gladd'ning eye, "will money breed?
How have I lived ? I grieve, with all my heart,
For my late knowledge in this precious art:—
Five pounds for every hundred will he give?
And then the hundred?—I begin to live."—
So he began, and other means he found,
As he went on, to multiply a pound:
Though blind so long to Interest, all allow
That no man better understands it now:
Him in our Body-Corporate we chose,
And once among us, he above us rose;
Stepping from post to post, he reach'd the Chair,
And there he now reposes—that's the Mayor.

    But 'tis not he, 'tis not the kinder few,
The mild, the good, who can our peace renew;
A peevish humour swells in every eye,
The warm are angry, and the cool are shy;
There is no more the social board at whist,
The good old partners are with scorn dismiss'd;
No more with dog and lantern comes the maid,
To guide the mistress when the rubber's play'd;
Sad shifts are made lest ribands blue and green
Should at one table, at one time, be seen:
On care and merit none will now rely,
'Tis Party sells what party-friends must buy;
The warmest burgess wears a bodger's coat,
And fashion gains less int'rest than a vote;
Uncheck'd the vintner still his poison vends,
For he too votes, and can command his friends.

    But this admitted; be it still agreed,
These ill effects from noble cause proceed;

Though like some vile excrescences they be,
The tree they spring from is a sacred tree,
And its true produce, Strength and Liberty.
      Yet if we could th' attendant ills suppress,
If we could make the sum of mischief less;
If we could warm and angry men persuade
No more man's common comforts to invade;
And that old ease and harmony re-seat,
In all our meetings, so in joy to meet;
Much would of glory to the Muse ensue,
And our good Vicar would have less to do.

LETTER VI.

Quid leges sine moribus
Vanae proficiunt?
                    HORACE.

Vae! misero mihi, mea nunc facinora
Aperiuntur, clam quae speravi fore.
                    MANILIUS.

Trades and Professions of every kind to be found in the Borough—Its Seamen and Soldiers—Law, the Danger of the Subject—Coddrington's Offence—Attorneys increased; their splendid Appearance, how supported—Some worthy Exceptions—Spirit of Litigation, how stirred up—A Boy articled as a Clerk; his Ideas—How this Profession perverts the Judgement—Actions appear through this medium in a false Light—Success from honest Application—Archer, a worthy Character—Swallow, a character of a different kind—His Origin, Progress, Success &c.

PROFESSIONS—LAW.

"TRADES and Professions"—these are themes the Muse,
Left to her freedom, would forbear to choose;
But to our Borough they in truth belong,
And we, perforce, must take them in our song.
    Be it then known that we can boast of these
In all denominations, ranks, degrees;
All who our numerous wants through life supply,
Who soothe us sick, attend us when we die,
Or for the dead their various talents try.
Then have we those who live by secret arts,
By hunting fortunes, and by stealing hearts;
Or who by nobler means themselves advance,
Or who subsist by charity and chance.
    Say, of our native heroes shall I boast,
Born in our streets, to thunder on our coast,
Our Borough-seamen? Could the timid Muse
More patriot ardour in their breasts infuse;
Or could she paint their merit or their skill,
She wants not love, alacrity, or will:
But needless all; that ardour is their own,
And for their deeds, themselves have made them known.
    Soldiers in arms! Defenders of our soil!

Who from destruction save us; who from spoil
Protect the sons of peace, who traffic, or who toil;
Would I could duly praise you; that each deed
Your foes might honour, and your friends might read:
This too is needless; you've imprinted well
Your powers, and told what I should feebly tell:
Beside, a Muse like mine, to satire prone,
Would fail in themes where there is praise alone.
—Law shall I sing, or what to Law belongs?
Alas! there may be danger in such songs;
A foolish rhyme, 'tis said, a trifling thing,
The law found treason, for it touch'd the King.
But kings have mercy, in these happy times.
Or surely One had suffered for his rhymes;
Our glorious Edwards and our Henrys bold,
So touch'd, had kept the reprobate in hold;
But he escap'd,—nor fear, thank Heav'n, have I,
Who love my king, for such offence to die.
But I am taught the danger would be much,
If these poor lines should one attorney touch—
(One of those Limbs of Law who're always here;
The Heads come down to guide them twice a year.)
I might not swing, indeed, but he in sport
Would whip a rhymer on from court to court;
Stop him in each, and make him pay for all
The long proceedings in that dreaded Hall:—
Then let my numbers flow discreetly on,
Warn'd by the fate of luckless Coddrington, {3}
Lest some attorney (pardon me the name)
Should wound a poor solicitor for fame.

One Man of Law in George the Second's reign
Was all our frugal fathers would maintain;
He too was kept for forms; a man of peace,
To frame a contract, or to draw a lease:
He had a clerk, with whom he used to write
All the day long, with whom he drank at night,
Spare was his visage, moderate his bill,
And he so kind, men doubted of his skill.

Who thinks of this, with some amazement sees,
For one so poor, three flourishing at ease;
Nay, one in splendour! see that mansion tall,
That lofty door, the far-resounding hall;
Well-furnish'd rooms, plate shining on the board,
Gay liveried lads, and cellar proudly stored:
Then say how comes it that such fortunes crown

These sons of strife, these terrors of the town?
    Lo! that small Office! there th' incautious guest
Goes blindfold in, and that maintains the rest;
There in his web, th' observant spider lies,
And peers about for fat intruding flies;
Doubtful at first, he hears the distant hum,
And feels them fluttering as they nearer come;
They buzz and blink, and doubtfully they tread
On the strong bird-lime of the utmost thread;
But when they're once entangled by the gin,
With what an eager clasp he draws them in;
Nor shall they 'scape, till after long delay,
And all that sweetens life is drawn away.
    "Nay, this," you cry, "is common-place, the tale
Of petty tradesmen o'er their evening ale;
There are who, living by the legal pen,
Are held in honour,—'Honourable men'"
    Doubtless—there are who hold manorial courts,
Or whom the trust of powerful friends supports,
Or who, by labouring through a length of time,
Have pick'd their way, unsullied by a crime.
These are the few: in this, in every place,
Fix the litigious rupture-stirring race;
Who to contention as to trade are led,
To whom dispute and strife are bliss and bread.
    There is a doubtful Pauper, and we think
'Tis not with us to give him meat and drink;
There is a Child; and 'tis not mighty clear
Whether the mother lived with us a year:
A Road's indicted, and our seniors doubt
If in our proper boundary or without:
But what says our attorney? He, our friend,
Tells us 'tis just and manly to contend.
    "What! to a neighbouring parish yield your cause,
While you have money, and the nation laws?
What! lose without a trial, that which, tried,
May—nay it must—be given on our side?
All men of spirit would contend; such men
Than lose a pound would rather hazard ten.
What! be imposed on? No! a British soul
Despises imposition, hates control:
The law is open; let them, if they dare,
Support their cause; the Borough need not spare.
All I advise is vigour and good-will:
Is it agreed then—Shall I file a bill?"

The trader, grazier, merchant, priest, and all,
Whose sons aspiring, to professions call,
Choose from their lads some bold and subtle boy,
And judge him fitted for this grave employ:
Him a keen old practitioner admits,
To write five years and exercise his wits:
The youth has heard—it is in fact his creed—
Mankind dispute, that Lawyers may be fee'd:
Jails, bailiffs, writs, all terms and threats of Law,
Grow now familiar as once top and taw;
Rage, hatred, fear, the mind's severer ills,
All bring employment, all augment his bills:
As feels the surgeon for the mangled limb,
The mangled mind is but a job for him;
Thus taught to think, these legal reasoners draw
Morals and maxims from their views of Law;
They cease to judge by precepts taught in schools,
By man's plain sense, or by religious rules;
No! nor by law itself, in truth discern'd,
But as its statutes may be warp'd and turn'd:
How they should judge of man, his word and deed,
They in their books and not their bosoms read:
Of some good act you speak with just applause;
"No, no!" says he, "'twould be a losing cause:
Blame you some tyrant's deed?—he answers "Nay,
He'll get a verdict; heed you what you say."
Thus to conclusions from examples led,
The heart resigns all judgment to the head;
Law, law alone for ever kept in view,
His measures guides, and rules his conscience too;
Of ten commandments, he confesses three
Are yet in force, and tells you which they be,
As Law instructs him, thus: "Your neighbour's wife
You must not take, his chattles, nor his life;
Break these decrees, for damage you must pay;
These you must reverence, and the rest—you may."
   Law was design'd to keep a state in peace;
To punish robbery, that wrong might cease;
To be impregnable: a constant fort,
To which the weak and injured might resort:
But these perverted minds its force employ,
Not to protect mankind, but to annoy;
And long as ammunition can be found,
Its lightning flashes and its thunders sound.
   Or Law with lawyers is an ample still,

Wrought by the passions' heat with chymic skill:
While the fire burns, the gains are quickly made,
And freely flow the profits of the trade;
Nay, when the fierceness fails, these artists blow
The dying fire, and make the embers glow,
As long as they can make the smaller profits flow:
At length the process of itself will stop,
When they perceive they've drawn out every drop.
Yet, I repeat, there are who nobly strive
To keep the sense of moral worth alive;
Men who would starve, ere meanly deign to live
On what deception and chican'ry give;
And these at length succeed; they have their strife,
Their apprehensions, stops, and rubs in life;
But honour, application, care, and skill,
Shall bend opposing fortune to their will.

    Of such is Archer, he who keeps in awe
Contending parties by his threats of law:
He, roughly honest, has been long a guide
In Borough-business, on the conquering side;
And seen so much of both sides, and so long,
He thinks the bias of man's mind goes wrong:
Thus, though he's friendly, he is still severe,
Surly, though kind, suspiciously sincere:
So much he's seen of baseness in the mind,
That, while a friend to man, he scorns mankind;
He knows the human heart, and sees with dread,
By slight temptation, how the strong are led;
He knows how interest can asunder rend
The bond of parent, master, guardian, friend,
To form a new and a degrading tie
'Twixt needy vice and tempting villainy.
Sound in himself, yet when such flaws appear,
He doubts of all, and learns that self to fear:
For where so dark the moral view is grown,
A timid conscience trembles for her own;
The pitchy-taint of general vice is such
As daubs the fancy, and you dread the touch.

    Far unlike him was one in former times,
Famed for the spoil he gather'd by his crimes;
Who, while his brethren nibbling held their prey,
He like an eagle seized and bore the whole away.

    Swallow, a poor Attorney, brought his boy
Up at his desk, and gave him his employ;
He would have bound him to an honest trade,

Could preparations have been duly made.
The clerkship ended, both the sire and son
Together did what business could be done;
Sometimes they'd luck to stir up small disputes
Among their friends, and raise them into suits:
Though close and hard, the father was content
With this resource, now old and indolent:
But his young Swallow, gaping and alive
To fiercer feelings, was resolved to thrive:—
"Father," he said, "but little can they win,
Who hunt in couples where the game is thin;
Let's part in peace, and each pursue his gain,
Where it may start—our love may yet remain."
The parent growl'd, he couldn't think that love
Made the young cockatrice his den remove;
But, taught by habit, he the truth suppress "d,
Forced a frank look, and said he "thought it best."
Not long they'd parted ere dispute arose;
The game they hunted quickly made them foes.
Some house the father by his art had won
Seem'd a fit cause of contest to the son,
Who raised a claimant, and then found a way
By a staunch witness to secure his prey.
The people cursed him, but in times of need
Trusted in one so certain to succeed:
By Law's dark by-ways he had stored his mind
With wicked knowledge, how to cheat mankind.
Few are the freeholds in our ancient town;
A copyright from heir to heir came down,
From whence some heat arose, when there was doubt
In point of heirship; but the fire went out,
Till our attorney had the art to raise
The dying spark, and blow it to a blaze:
For this he now began his friends to treat;
His way to starve them was to make them eat,
And drink oblivious draughts—to his applause,
It must be said, he never starved a cause;
He'd roast and boil'd upon his board; the boast
Of half his victims was his boil'd and roast;
And these at every hour:—he seldom took
Aside his client, till he'd praised his cook;
Nor to an office led him, there in pain
To give his story and go out again;
But first the brandy and the chine where seen,
And then the business came by starts between.

"Well, if 'tis so, the house to you belongs;
But have you money to redress these wrongs?
Nay, look not sad, my friend; if you're correct,
You'll find the friendship that you'd not expect."
    If right the man, the house was Swallow's own;
If wrong, his kindness and good-will were shown:
"Rogue!" "Villain!" "Scoundrel!" cried the losers all:
He let them cry, for what would that recall?
At length he left us, took a village seat,
And like a vulture look'd abroad for meat;
The Borough-booty, give it all its praise,
Had only served the appetite to raise;
But if from simple heirs he drew their land,
He might a noble feast at will command;
Still he proceeded by his former rules,
His bait their pleasures, when he fished for fools—
Flagons and haunches on his board were placed,
And subtle avarice look'd like thoughtless waste:
Most of his friends, though youth from him had fled,
Were young, were minors, of their sires in dread;
Or those whom widow'd mothers kept in bounds,
And check'd their generous rage for steeds and hounds;
Or such as travell'd 'cross the land to view
A Christian's conflict with a boxing Jew:
Some too had run upon Newmarket heath
With so much speed that they were out of breath;
Others had tasted claret, till they now
To humbler port would turn, and knew not how.
All these for favours would to Swallow run,
Who never sought their thanks for all he'd done;
He kindly took them by the hand, then bow'd
Politely low, and thus his love avow'd—
(For he'd a way that many judged polite,
A cunning dog—he'd fawn before he'd bite)—
    "Observe, my friends, the frailty of our race
When age unmans us—let me state a case:
There's our friend Rupert—we shall soon redress
His present evil—drink to our success—
I flatter not; but did you ever see
Limbs better turn'd? a prettier boy than he?
His senses all acute, his passions such
As Nature gave—she never does too much;
His the bold wish the cup of joy to drain,
And strength to bear it without qualm or pain.
    "Now view his father as he dozing lies,

Whose senses wake not when he opes his eyes;
Who slips and shuffles when he means to walk,
And lisps and gabbles if he tries to talk;
Feeling he's none—he could as soon destroy
The earth itself, as aught it holds enjoy;
A nurse attends him to lay straight his limbs,
Present his gruel, and respect his whims:
Now shall this dotard from our hero hold
His lands and lordships? Shall he hide his gold!
That which he cannot use, and dare not show,
And will not give—why longer should he owe?
Yet, t'would be murder should we snap the locks,
And take the thing he worships from the box;
So let him dote and dream: but, till he die,
Shall not our generous heir receive supply?
For ever sitting on the river's brink?
And ever thirsty, shall he fear to drink?
The means are simple, let him only wish,
Then say he's willing, and I'll fill his dish."

    They all applauded, and not least the boy,
Who now replied, "It fill'd his heart with joy
To find he needed not deliv'rance crave
Of death, or wish the Justice in the grave;
Who, while he spent, would every art retain,
Of luring home the scatter'd gold again;
Just as a fountain gaily spirts and plays
With what returns in still and secret ways."

    Short was the dream of bliss; he quickly found
His father's acres all were Swallow's ground.
Yet to those arts would other heroes lend
A willing ear, and Swallow was their friend;
Ever successful, some began to think
That Satan help'd him to his pen and ink;
And shrewd suspicions ran about the place,
"There was a compact"—I must leave the case.
But of the parties, had the fiend been one,
The business could not have been speedier done:
Still when a man has angled day and night,
The silliest gudgeons will refuse to bite:
So Swallow tried no more: but if they came
To seek his friendship, that remain'd the same:
Thus he retired in peace, and some would say
He'd balk'd his partner, and had learn'd to pray.
To this some zealots lent an ear, and sought
How Swallow felt, then said "a change is wrought."

'Twas true there wanted all the signs of grace,
But there were strong professions in their place;
Then, too, the less that men from him expect,
The more the praise to the converting sect;
He had not yet subscribed to all their creed,
Nor own'd a Call, but he confess'd the need:
His aquiescent speech, his gracious look,
That pure attention, when the brethren spoke,
Was all contrition,—he had felt the wound,
And with confession would again be sound.

　　True, Swallow's board had still the sumptuous treat;
But could they blame? the warmest zealots eat:
He drank—'twas needful his poor nerves to brace;
He swore—'twas habit; he was grieved—'twas grace:
What could they do a new-born zeal to nurse?
"His wealth's undoubted—let him hold our purse;
He'll add his bounty, and the house we'll raise
Hard by the church, and gather all her strays:
We'll watch her sinners as they home retire,
And pluck the brands from the devouring fire."

　　Alas! such speech was but an empty boast;
The good men reckon'd, but without their host;
Swallow, delighted, took the trusted store,
And own'd the sum; they did not ask for more,
Till more was needed; when they call'd for aid—
And had it?—No, their agent was afraid:
"Could he but know to whom he should refund
He would most gladly—nay, he'd go beyond;
But when such numbers claim'd, when some were gone.
And others going—he must hold it on;
The Lord would help them."—Loud their anger grew,
And while they threat'ning from his door withdrew,
He bow'd politely low, and bade them all adieu,

　　But lives the man by whom such deeds are done!
Yes, many such—But Swallow's race is run;
His name is lost,—for though his sons have name,
It is not his, they all escape the shame;
Nor is there vestige now of all he had,
His means are wasted, for his heir was mad:
Still we of Swallow as a monster speak,
A hard bad man, who prey'd upon the weak.

LETTER VII.

Finirent multi letho mala; credula vitam
Spes alit, et melius cras fore semper ait.
>   TIBULLUS.

He fell to juggle, cant, and cheat...
For as those fowls that live in water
Are never wet, he did but smatter;
Whate'er he labour'd to appear,
His understanding still was clear.
A paltry wretch he had, half starved,
That him in place of zany served.
>   BUTLER, Hudibras.

PROFESSIONS—PHYSIC.

The Worth and Excellence of the true Physician—Merit, not the sole
Cause of Success—Modes of advancing Reputation—Motives of
medical Men for publishing their Works—The great Evil of Quackery—
Present State of advertising Quacks—Their Hazard—Some fail, and
why—Causes of Success—How Men of understanding are prevailed
upon to have recourse to Empirics, and to permit their Names to be
advertised—Evils of Quackery: to nervous Females; to Youth; to
Infants—History of an advertising Empiric, &c.

NEXT, to a graver tribe we turn our view,
And yield the praise to worth and science due,
But this with serious words and sober style,
For these are friends with whom we seldom smile.
Helpers of men they're call'd, and we confess
Theirs the deep study, theirs the lucky guess;
We own that numbers join with care and skill,
A temperate judgment, a devoted will:
Men who suppress their feelings, but who feel
The painful symptoms they delight to heal;
Patient in all their trials, they sustain
The starts of passion, the reproach of pain;
With hearts affected, but with looks serene,
Intent they wait through all the solemn scene;
Glad if a hope should rise from nature's strife,
To aid their skill and save the lingering life;
But this must virtue's generous effort be,
And spring from nobler motives than a fee:

To the Physician of the Soul, and these,
Turn the distress'd for safety, hope, and ease.
    But as physicians of that nobler kind
Have their warm zealots, and their sectaries blind;
So among these for knowledge most renowned,
Are dreamers strange, and stubborn bigots found:
Some, too, admitted to this honourd name,
Have, without learning, found a way to fame;
And some by learning—young physicians write,
To set their merit in the fairest light;
With them a treatise in a bait that draws
Approving voices—'tis to gain applause,
And to exalt them in the public view,
More than a life of worthy toil could do.
When 'tis proposed to make the man renown'd,
In every age, convenient doubts abound;
Convenient themes in every period start,
Which he may treat with all the pomp of art;
Curious conjectures he may always make,
And either side of dubious questions take;
He may a system broach, or, if he please,
Start new opinions of an old disease:
Or may some simple in the woodland trace,
And be its patron, till it runs its race;
As rustic damsels from their woods are won,
And live in splendour till their race be run;
It weighs not much on what their powers be shown,
When all his purpose is to make them known.
    To show the world what long experience gains,
Requires not courage, though it calls for pains;
But at life's outset to inform mankind
Is a bold effort of a valiant mind.
    The great, good man, for noblest cause displays
What many labours taught, and many days;
These sound instruction from experience give,
The others show us how they mean to live.
That they have genius, and they hope mankind
Will to its efforts be no longer blind.
    There are, beside, whom powerful friends advance,
Whom fashion favours, person, patrons, chance:
And merit sighs to see a fortune made
By daring rashness or by dull parade.
    But these are trifling evils; there is one
Which walks uncheck'd, and triumphs in the sun:
There was a time, when we beheld the Quack,

On public stage, the licensed trade attack;
He made his laboured speech with poor parade,
And then a laughing zany lent him aid:
Smiling we pass'd him, but we felt the while
Pity so much, that soon we ceased to smile;
Assured that fluent speech and flow'ry vest
Disguised the troubles of a man distress'd;—

 But now our Quacks are gamesters, and they play
With craft and skill to ruin and betray;
With monstrous promise they delude the mind,
And thrive on all that tortures human-kind.

 Void of all honour, avaricious, rash,
The daring tribe compound their boasted trash—
Tincture of syrup, lotion, drop, or pill;
All tempt the sick to trust the lying bill;
And twenty names of cobblers turn'd to squires,
Aid the bold language of these blushless liars.
There are among them those who cannot read,
And yet they'll buy a patent, and succeed;
Will dare to promise dying sufferers aid,
For who, when dead, can threaten or upbraid?
With cruel avarice still they recommend
More draughts, more syrup, to the journey's end:
"I feel it not;"—"Then take it every hour:"
"It makes me worse;"—"Why then it shows its power;"
"I fear to die;"—"Let not your spirits sink,
You're always safe, while you believe and drink."

 How strange to add, in this nefarious trade,
That men of parts are dupes by dunces made:
That creatures, nature meant should clean our streets,
Have purchased lands and mansions, parks and seats:
Wretches with conscience so obtuse, they leave
Their untaught sons their parents to deceive;
And when they're laid upon their dying bed,
No thought of murder comes into their head,
Nor one revengeful ghost to them appears,
To fill the soul with penitential fears.

 Yet not the whole of this imposing train
Their gardens, seats, and carriages obtain:
Chiefly, indeed, they to the robbers fall,
Who are most fitted to disgrace them all;
But there is hazard—patents must be bought,
Venders and puffers for the poison sought;
And then in many a paper through the year,
Must cures and cases, oaths and proofs appear;

Men snatch'd from graves, as they were dropping in,
Their lungs cough'd up, their bones pierced through their skin
Their liver all one schirrus, and the frame
Poison'd with evils which they dare not name;
Men who spent all upon physicians' fees,
Who never slept, nor had a moment's ease,
Are now as roaches sound, and all as brisk as bees,
　　If the sick gudgeons to the bait attend,
And come in shoals, the angler gains his end:
But should the advertising cash be spent,
Ere yet the town has due attention lent,
Then bursts the bubble, and the hungry cheat
Pines for the bread he ill deserves to eat;
It is a lottery, and he shares perhaps
The rich man's feast, or begs the pauper's scraps.
　　From powerful causes spring th' empiric's gains,
Man's love of life, his weakness, and his pains;
These first induce him the vile trash to try,
Then lend his name, that other men may buy:
This love of life, which in our nature rules,
To vile imposture makes us dupes and tools;
Then pain compels th' impatient soul to seize
On promised hopes of instantaneous ease;
And weakness too with every wish complies,
Worn out and won by importunities.
　　Troubled with something in your bile or blood,
You think your doctor does you little good;
And grown impatient, you require in haste
The nervous cordial, nor dislike the taste;
It comforts, heals, and strengthens; nay, you think
It makes you better every time you drink;
"Then lend your name "you're loth, but yet confess
Its powers are great, and so you acquiesce:
Yet think a moment, ere your name you lend,
With whose 'tis placed, and what you recommend;
Who tipples brandy will some comfort feel,
But will he to the med'cine set his seal?
Wait, and you'll find the cordial you admire
Has added fuel to your fever's fire:
Say, should a robber chance your purse to spare,
Would you the honour of the man declare?
Would you assist his purpose? swell his crime?
Besides, he might not spare a second time.
　　Compassion sometimes sets the fatal sign,
The man was poor, and humbly begg'd a line;

Else how should noble names and titles back
The spreading praise of some advent'rous quack?
But he the moment watches, and entreats
Your honour's name,—your honour joins the cheats;
You judged the med'cine harmless, and you lent
What help you could, and with the best intent;
But can it please you, thus to league with all
Whom he can beg or bribe to swell the scrawl?
Would you these wrappers with your name adorn
Which hold the poison for the yet unborn?

    No class escapes them—from the poor man's pay,
The nostrum takes no trifling part away:
See! those square patent bottles from the shop,
Now decoration to the cupboard's top;
And there a favourite hoard you'll find within,
Companions meet! the julep and the gin.

    Time too with cash is wasted; 'tis the fate
Of real helpers to be call'd too late;
This find the sick, when (time and patience gone)
Death with a tenfold terror hurries on.

    Suppose the case surpasses human skill,
There comes a quack to flatter weakness still;
What greater evil can a flatterer do,
Than from himself to take the sufferer's view?
To turn from sacred thoughts his reasoning powers,
And rob a sinner of his dying hours?
Yet this they dare, and craving to the last,
In hope's strong bondage hold their victim fast:
For soul or body no concern have they,
All their inquiry, "Can the patient pay?
"And will he swallow draughts until his dying day?"

    Observe what ills to nervous females flow,
When the heart flutters, and the pulse is low;
If once induced these cordial sips to try,
All feel the ease, and few the danger fly;
For, while obtain'd, of drams they've all the force,
And when denied, then drams are the resource.

    Nor these the only evils—there are those
Who for the troubled mind prepare repose;
They write: the young are tenderly address'd,
Much danger hinted, much concern express'd;
They dwell on freedoms lads are prone to take,
Which makes the doctor tremble for their sake;
Still if the youthful patient will but trust
In one so kind, so pitiful, and just;

If he will take the tonic all the time,
And hold but moderate intercourse with crime;
The sage will gravely give his honest word,
That strength and spirits shall be both restored;
In plainer English—if you mean to sin,
Fly to the drops, and instantly begin.

    Who would not lend a sympathizing sigh,
To hear yon infant's pity-moving cry?
That feeble sob, unlike the new-born note
Which came with vigour from the op'ning throat,
When air and light first rush'd on lungs and eyes,
And there was life and spirit in the cries;
Now an abortive, faint attempt to weep
Is all we hear; sensation is asleep:
The boy was healthy, and at first express'd
His feelings loudly when he fail'd to rest;
When cramm'd with food, and tighten'd every limb,
To cry aloud was what pertain'd to him;
Then the good nurse (who, had she borne a brain,
Had sought the cause that made her babe complain)
Has all her efforts, loving soul! applied
To set the cry, and not the cause, aside;
She gave her powerful sweet without remorse
The sleeping cordial—she had tried its force,
Repeating oft: the infant, freed from pain,
Rejected food, but took the dose again,
Sinking to sleep; while she her joy express'd,
That her dear charge could sweetly take his rest:
Soon may she spare her cordial; not a doubt
Remains, but quickly he will resfc without.

    This moves our grief and pity, and we sigh
To think what numbers from these causes die;
But what contempt and anger should we show,
Did we the lives of these impostors know!

    Ere for the world's I left the cares of school,
One I remember who assumed the fool;
A part well suited—when the idler boys
Would shout around him, and he loved the noise;
They called him Neddy;—Neddy had the art
To play with skill his ignominious part;
When he his trifles would for sale display,
And act the mimic for a schoolboy's pay.
For many years he plied his humble trade,
And used his tricks and talents to persuade;
The fellow barely read, but chanced to look

Among the fragments of a tatter'd book;
Where, after many efforts made to spell
One puzzling word, he found it—oxymel;
A potent thing, 'twas said to cure the ills
Of ailing lungs—the oxymel of squills:
Squills he procured, but found the bitter strong
And most unpleasant; none would take it long;
But the pure acid and the sweet would make
A med'cine numbers would for pleasure take.
There was a fellow near, an artful knave,
Who knew the plan, and much assistance gave;
He wrote the puffs, and every talent plied
To make it sell: it sold, and then he died.

    Now all the profit fell to Ned's control,
And Pride and Avarice quarrell'd for his soul;
When mighty profits by the trash were made,
Pride built a palace, Avarice groan'd and paid;
Pride placed the signs of grandeur all about,
And Avarice barr'd his friends and children out.

    Now see him Doctor! yes, the idle fool,
The butt, the robber of the lads at school;
Who then knew nothing, nothing since acquired,
Became a doctor, honour'd and admired;
His dress, his frown, his dignity were such,
Some who had known him thought his knowledge much;
Nay, men of skill, of apprehension quick,
Spite of their knowledge, trusted him when sick;
Though he could neither reason, write, nor spell,
They yet had hope his trash would make them well;
And while they scorn'd his parts, they took his oxymel.

    Oh! when his nerves had once received a shock,
Sir Isaac Newton might have gone to Rock:
Hence impositions of the grossest kind,
Hence thought is feeble, understanding blind;
Hence sums enormous by those cheats are made,
And deaths unnumber'd by their dreadful trade.

    Alas! in vain is my contempt express'd,
To stronger passions are their words address'd;
To pain, to fear, to terror, their appeal,
To those who, weakly reasoning, strongly feel.

    What then our hopes?—perhaps there may by law
Be method found these pests to curb and awe;
Yet in this land of freedom law is slack
With any being to commence attack;
Then let us trust to science—there are those

Who can their falsehoods and their frauds disclose,
All their vile trash detect, and their low tricks expose;
Perhaps their numbers may in time confound
Their arts—as scorpions give themselves the wound;
For when these curers dwell in every place,
While of the cured we not a man can trace,
Strong truth may then the public mind persuade,
And spoil the fruits of this nefarious trade.

LETTER VIII.

Non possidentem multa vocaveris
Recte beatum: rectius occupat
Nomen Beati, qui Deorum
Muneribus sapienter uti,
Duramque callet pauperiem pati.
HORACE, Ode 9.

Non propter vitam faciunt patrimonia quidam,
Sed vitio caeci propter patrimonia vivunt.
JUVENAL, Satire 12.

Non uxor salvum te vult, non filius; omnes
Vicini oderunt; noti pueri atque puellae;
Miraris cum tu argento post omnia ponas,
Si nemo praestet, quem non merearis, amorem.
HORACE, Satires.

TRADES.

No extensive manufactories in the Borough; yet considerable Fortunes made there—Ill Judgment of Parents in disposing of their Sons—The best educated not the most likely to succeed—Instance—Want of Success compensated by the lenient Power of some Avocations—The Naturalist—The Weaver an Entomologist, &c.—A Prize Flower—Story of Walter and William.

OF manufactures, trade, inventions rare,
Steam-towers and looms, you'd know our Borough's share—
'Tis small: we boast not these rich subjects here,
Who hazard thrice ten thousand pounds a-year;
We've no huge buildings, where incessant noise
Is made by springs and spindles, girls and boys;
Where, 'mid such thundering sounds, the maiden's song
Is "Harmony in Uproar" all day long.
 Still common minds with us in common trade,
Have gain'd more wealth than ever student made;
And yet a merchant, when he gives his son
His college-learning, thinks his duty done;
A way to wealth he leaves his boy to find,
Just when he's made for the discovery blind.
 Jones and his wife perceived their elder boy
Took to his learning, and it gave them joy;

This they encouraged, and were bless'd to see
Their son a fellow with a high degree;
A living fell, he married, and his sire
Declared 'twas all a father could require;
Children then bless'd them, and when letters came,
The parents proudly told each grandchild's name.

Meantime the sons at home in trade were placed,
Money their object—just the father's taste;
Saving he lived and long, and when he died,
He gave them all his fortune to divide:
"Martin," said he, "at vast expense was taught;
He gain'd his wish, and has the ease he sought."

Thus the good priest (the Christian scholar!) finds
"What estimate is made by vulgar minds;
He sees his brothers, who had every gift
Of thriving, now assisted in their thrift;
While he, whom learning, habits, all prevent,
Is largely mulct for each impediment.

Yet let us own that Trade has much of chance,
Not all the careful by their care advance;
With the same parts and prospects, one a seat
Builds for himself; one finds it in the Fleet.
Then to the wealthy you will see denied
Comforts and joys that with the poor abide:
There are who labour through the year, and yet
No more have gain'd than—not to be in debt:
Who still maintain the same laborious course,
Yet pleasure hails them from some favourite source,
And health, amusements, children, wife, or friend,
With life's dull views their consolations blend.

Nor these alone possess the lenient power
Of soothing life in the desponding hour;
Some favourite studies, some delightful care,
The mind with trouble and distresses share;
And by a coin, a flower, a verse, a boat,
The stagnant spirits have been set afloat;
They pleased at first, and then the habit grew,
Till the fond heart no higher pleasure knew;
Till, from all cares and other comforts freed,
Th' important nothing took in life the lead.

With all his phlegm, it broke a Dutchman's heart,
At a vast price, with one loved root to part;
And toys like these fill many a British mind,
Although their hearts are found of firmer kind.

Oft have I smiled the happy pride to see

Of humble tradesmen, in their evening glee;
When of some pleasing fancied good possess'd,
Each grew alert, was busy, and was bless'd:
Whether the call-bird yield the hour's delight,
Or, magnified in microscope the mite;
Or whether tumblers, croppers, carriers seize
The gentle mind, they rule it and they please.

    There is my friend the Weaver: strong desires
Reign in his breast; 'tis beauty he admires:
See! to the shady grove he wings his way,
And feels in hope the raptures of the day—
Eager he looks: and soon, to glad his eyes,
From the sweet bower, by nature form'd, arise
Bright troops of virgin moths and fresh-born butterflies;
Who broke that morning from their half-year's sleep,
To fly o'er flowers where they were wont to creep.

    Above the sovereign oak, a sovereign skims,
The purple Emp'ror, strong in wing and limbs:
There fair Camilla takes her flight serene,
Adonis blue, and Paphia silver-queen;
With every filmy fly from mead or bower,
And hungry Sphinx who threads the honey'd flower;
She o'er the Larkspur's bed, where sweets abound.
Views ev'ry bell, and hums th' approving sound;
Poised on her busy plumes, with feeling nice
She draws from every flower, nor tries a floret twice.

    He fears no bailiff's wrath, no baron's blame,
His is untax'd and undisputed game:
Nor less the place of curious plant he knows;
He both his Flora and his Fauna shows;
For him is blooming in its rich array
The glorious flower which bore the palm away;
In vain a rival tried his utmost art,
His was the prize, and joy o'erflow'd his heart.

    "This, this! is beauty; cast, I pray, your eyes
On this my glory! see the grace! the size!
Was ever stem so tall, so stout, so strong,
Exact in breadth, in just proportion long?
These brilliant hues are all distinct and clean,
No kindred tint, no blending streaks between:
This is no shaded, run-off, pin-eyed thing;
A king of flowers, a flower for England's king:
I own my pride, and thank the favouring star
Which shed such beauty on my fair Bizarre."

    Thus may the poor the cheap indulgence seize,

While the most wealthy pine and pray for ease;
Content not always waits upon success,
And more may he enjoy who profits less.

    Walter and William took (their father dead)
Jointly the trade to which they both were bred;
When fix'd, they married, and they quickly found
With due success their honest labours crown'd;
Few were their losses, but although a few,
Walter was vex'd and somewhat peevish grew:
"You put your trust in every pleading fool,"
Said he to William, and grew strange and cool.
"Brother forbear," he answer'd; "take your due,
Nor let my lack of caution injure you:"
Half friends they parted,—better so to close,
Than longer wait to part entirely foes.

    Walter had knowledge, prudence, jealous care;
He let no idle views his bosom share;
He never thought nor felt for other men—
"Let one mind one, and all are minded then."
Friends he respected, and believed them just,
But they were men, and he would no man trust;
He tried and watch'd his people day and night,—
The good it harm'd not; for the bad 'twas right:
He could their humours bear, nay disrespect,
But he could yield no pardon to neglect;
That all about him were of him afraid
"Was right," he said—"so should we be obey'd."

    These merchant-maxims, much good fortune too,
And ever keeping one grand point in view,
To vast amount his once small portion drew.

    William was kind and easy; he complied
With all requests, or grieved when he denied;
To please his wife he made a costly trip,
To please his child he let a bargain slip;
Prone to compassion, mild with the distress'd,
He bore with all who poverty profess'd,
And some would he assist, nor one would he arrest.
He had some loss at sea, bad debts at land,
His clerk absconded with some bills in hand,
And plans so often fail'd, that he no longer plann'd.
To a small house (his brother's) he withdrew,
At easy rent—the man was not a Jew;
And there his losses and his cares he bore,
Nor found that want of wealth could make him poor.

    No, he in fact was rich! nor could he move,

But he was follow'd by the looks of love;
All he had suffer'd, every former grief,
Made those around more studious in relief;
He saw a cheerful smile in every face,
And lost all thoughts of error and disgrace.
Pleasant it was to see them in their walk
Round their small garden, and to hear them talk;
Free are their children, but their love refrains
From all offence—none murmurs, none complains;
Whether a book amused them, speech or play,
Their looks were lively, and their hearts were gay;
There no forced efforts for delight were made,
Joy came with prudence, and without parade;
Their common comforts they had all in view,
Light were their troubles, and their wishes few:
Thrift made them easy for the coming day,
Religion took the dread of death away;
A cheerful spirit still ensured content,
And love smiled round them wheresoe'er they went.
    Walter, meantime, with all his wealth's increase,
Gain'd many points, but could not purchase peace;
When he withdrew from business for an hour,
Some fled his presence, all confess'd his power;
He sought affection, but received instead
Fear undisguised, and love-repelling dread;
He look'd around him—"Harriet, dost thou love?"
"I do my duty," said the timid dove;
"Good Heav'n, your duty! prithee, tell me now—
To love and honour—was not that your vow?
Come, my good Harriet, I would gladly seek
Your inmost thought—Why can't the woman speak?
Have you not all things?"—"Sir, do I complain?"—
"No, that's my part, which I perform in vain;
I want a simple answer, and direct—
But you evade; yes! 'tis as I suspect.
Come then, my children! Watt! upon your knees
Vow that you love me."—"Yes, sir, if you please."
"Again! By Heav'n, it mads me; I require
Love, and they'll do whatever I desire:
Thus too my people shun me; I would spend
A thousand pounds to get a single friend;
I would be happy—I have means to pay
For love and friendship, and you run away:
Ungrateful creatures! why, you seem to dread
My very looks; I know you wish me dead.

Come hither, Nancy! you must hold me dear;
Hither, I say; why! what have you to fear?
You see I'm gentle—Come, you trifler, come:
My God! she trembles!—Idiot, leave the room!
Madam; your children hate me; I suppose
They know their cue; you make them all my foes:
I've not a friend in all the world—not one:
I'd be a bankrupt sooner; nay, 'tis done;
In every better hope of life I fail,
You're all tormentors, and my house a jail.
Out of my sight! I'll sit and make my will—
What, glad to go? stay, devils, and be still;
'Tis to your Uncle's cot you wish to run,
To learn to live at ease and be undone;
Him you can love, who lost his whole estate,
And I, who gain you fortunes, have your hate;
'Tis in my absence you yourselves enjoy:
Tom! are you glad to lose me? tell me, boy:
Yes! does he answer?—Yes! upon my soul;
No awe, no fear, no duty, no control!
Away! away! ten thousand devils seize
All I possess, and plunder where they please!
What's wealth to me?—yes, yes! it gives me sway,
And you shall feel it—Go! begone, I say." {4}

LETTER IX.

Interpone tuis interdum gaudia curis
Ut possis animo quemvis sufferre laborem.
CATULLUS

......Nostra fatiscat
Laxaturque chelys, vires instigat alitque
Tempestiva quies, major post otia virtus.
STATIUS, Sylvae.

Jamque mare et tellus nullum discremen habebant;
Omnia pontus erant: deerant quoque littora ponto.
OVID, Metamophoses.

AMUSEMENTS.

Common Amusements of a Bathing-place—Morning Rides, Walks,
&c.—Company resorting to the Town—Different Choice of
Lodgings—Cheap Indulgences—Seaside Walks—Wealthy Invalid—
Summer evening on the Sands—Sea Productions—"Water parted from
the Sea"—Winter Views serene—In what cases to be avoided—Sailing
upon the River—A small Islet of Sand off the Coast—Visited by
Company—Covered by the Flowing of the Tide—Adventure in that
place.

OF our Amusements ask you?—We amuse
Ourselves and friends with seaside walks and views,
Or take a morning ride, a novel, or the news;
Or, seeking nothing, glide about the street,
And so engaged, with various parties meet;
Awhile we stop, discourse of wind and tide
Bathing and books, the raffle, and the ride;
Thus, with the aid which shops and sailing give,
Life passes on; 'tis labour, but we live.
    When evening comes, our invalids awake,
Nerves cease to tremble, heads forbear to ache;
Then cheerful meals the sunken spirits raise,
Cards or the dance, wine, visiting, or plays.
    Soon as the season comes, and crowds arrive,
To their superior rooms the wealthy drive;
Others look round for lodging snug and small,
Such is their taste—they've hatred to a hall:
Hence one his fav'rite habitation gets,

The brick-floor'd parlour which the butcher lets;
Where, through his single light, he may regard
The various business of a common yard,
Bounded by backs of buildings form'd of clay,
By stable, sties, and coops, et caetera.
    The needy-vain, themselves awhile to shun,
For dissipation to these dog-holes run;
Where each (assuming petty pomp) appears,
And quite forgets the shopboard and the shears.
    For them are cheap amusements: they may slip
Beyond the town and take a private dip;
When they may urge that, to be safe they mean,
They've heard there's danger in a light machine;
They too can gratis move the quays about,
And gather kind replies to every doubt;
There they a pacing, lounging tribe may view,
The stranger's guides, who've little else to do;
The Borough's placemen, where no more they gain
Than keeps them idle, civil, poor, and vain.
Then may the poorest with the wealthy look
On ocean, glorious page of Nature's book!
May see its varying views in every hour,
All softness now, then rising with all power,
As sleeping to invite, or threat'ning to devour:
'Tis this which gives us all our choicest views;
Its waters heal us, and its shores amuse.
    See! those fair nymphs upon that rising strand,
Yon long salt lake has parted from the land;
Well pleased to press that path, so clean, so pure,
To seem in danger, yet to feel secure;
Trifling with terror, while they strive to shun
The curling billows; laughing as they run;
They know the neck that joins the shore and sea,
Or, ah! how changed that fearless laugh would be.
    Observe how various Parties take their way,
By seaside walks, or make the sand-hills gay;
There group'd are laughing maids and sighing swains,
And some apart who feel unpitied pains;
Pains from diseases, pains which those who feel,
To the physician, not the fair, reveal:
For nymphs (propitious to the lover's sigh)
Leave these poor patients to complain and die.
    Lo! where on that huge anchor sadly leans
That sick tall figure, lost in other scenes;
He late from India's clime impatient sail'd,

There, as his fortune grew, his spirits fail'd;
For each delight, in search of wealth he went,
For ease alone, the wealth acquired is spent—
And spent in vain; enrich'd, aggrieved, he sees
The envied poor possess'd of joy and ease:
And now he flies from place to place, to gain
Strength for enjoyment, and still flies in vain:
Mark! with what sadness, of that pleasant crew,
Boist'rous in mirth, he takes a transient view;
And fixing then his eye upon the sea,
Thinks what has been and what must shortly be:
Is it not strange that man should health destroy,
For joys that come when he is dead to joy?

Now is it pleasant in the Summer-eve,
When a broad shore retiring waters leave,
Awhile to wait upon the firm fair sand,
When all is calm at sea, all still at land;
And there the ocean's produce to explore,
As floating by, or rolling on the shore:
Those living jellies which the flesh inflame,
Fierce as a nettle, and from that its name;
Some in huge masses, some that you may bring
In the small compass of a lady's ring;
Figured by hand divine—there's not a gem
Wrought by man's art to be compared to them;
Soft, brilliant, tender, through the wave they glow,
And make the moonbeam brighter where they flow.
Involved in sea-wrack, here you find a race
Which science, doubting, knows not where to place;
On shell or stone is dropp'd the embryo-seed,
And quickly vegetates a vital breed.

While thus with pleasing wonder you inspect
Treasures the vulgar in their scorn reject,
See as they float along th' entangled weeds
Slowly approach, upborne on bladdery beads;
Wait till they land, and you shall then behold
The fiery sparks those tangled fronds infold,
Myriads of living points; th' unaided eye
Can but the fire and not the form descry.
And now your view upon the ocean turn,
And there the splendour of the waves discern;
Cast but a stone, or strike them with an oar,
And you shall flames within the deep explore;
Or scoop the stream phosphoric as you stand,
And the cold flames shall flash along your hand;

When, lost in wonder, you shall walk and gaze
On weeds that sparkle, and on waves that blaze.

  The ocean too has Winter views serene,
When all you see through densest fog is seen;
When you can hear the fishers near at hand
Distinctly speak, yet see not where they stand;
Or sometimes them and not their boat discern;
Or half-conceal'd some figure at the stern;
The view's all bounded, and from side to side
Your utmost prospect but a few ells wide;
Boys who, on shore, to sea the pebble cast,
Will hear it strike against the viewless mast;
While the stern boatman growls his fierce disdain,
At whom he knows not, whom he threats in vain.

  Tis pleasant then to view the nets float past,
Net after net till you have seen the last:
And as you wait till all beyond you slip,
A boat comes gliding from an anchor'd ship,
Breaking the silence with the dipping oar,
And their own tones, as labouring for the shore;
Those measured tones which with the scene agree,
And give a sadness to serenity.

  All scenes like these the tender Maid should shun,
Nor to a misty beach in autumn run;
Much should she guard against the evening cold,
And her slight shape with fleecy warmth infold;
This she admits, but not with so much ease
Gives up the night-walk when th' attendants please:
Her have I seen, pale, vapour'd through the day,
With crowded parties at the midnight play;
Faint in the morn, no powers could she exert;
At night with Pam delighted and alert;
In a small shop she's raffled with a crowd,
Breath'd the thick air, and cough'd and laugh'd aloud;
She who will tremble if her eye explore
"The smallest monstrous mouse that creeps on floor;"
Whom the kind doctor charged, with shaking head,
At early hour to quit the beaux for bed;
She has, contemning fear, gone down the dance,
Till she perceived the rosy morn advance;
Then has she wonder'd, fainting o'er her tea,
Her drops and julep should so useless be:
Ah! sure her joys must ravish every sense,
Who buys a portion at such vast expense.

  Among those joys, 'tis one at eve to sail

On the broad River with a favourite gale;
When no rough waves upon the bosom ride,
But the keel cuts, nor rises on the tide;
Safe from the stream the nearer gunwale stands,
Where playful children trail their idle hands:
Or strive to catch long grassy leaves that float
On either side of the impeded boat;
What time the moon arising shows the mud,
A shining border to the silver flood:
When, by her dubious light, the meanest views,
Chalk, stones, and stakes, obtain the richest hues;
And when the cattle, as they gazing stand,
Seem nobler objects than when view'd from land:
Then anchor'd vessels in the way appear,
And sea-boys greet them as they pass—"What cheer?"
The sleeping shell-ducks at the sound arise,
And utter loud their unharmonious cries;
Fluttering they move their weedy beds among,
Or instant diving, hide their plumeless young.

    Along the wall, returning from the town,
The weary rustic homeward wanders down:
Who stops and gazes at such joyous crew,
And feels his envy rising at the view;
He the light speech and laugh indignant hears,
And feels more press'd by want, more vex'd by fears.

    Ah! go in peace, good fellow, to thine home,
Nor fancy these escape the general doom:
Gay as they seem, be sure with them are hearts
With sorrow tried; there's sadness in their parts:
If thou couldst see them when they think alone,
Mirth, music, friends, and these amusements gone;
Couldst thou discover every secret ill
That pains their spirit, or resists their will;
Couldst thou behold forsaken Love's distress,
Or Envy's pang at glory and success,
Or Beauty, conscious of the spoils of Time,
Or Guilt alarm'd when Memory shows the crime;
All that gives sorrow, terror, grief, and gloom;
Content would cheer thee trudging to thine home.

    There are, 'tis true, who lay their cares aside,
And bid some hours in calm enjoyment glide;
Perchance some fair one to the sober night
Adds (by the sweetness of her song) delight;
And as the music on the water floats,
Some bolder shore returns the soften'd notes;

Then, youth, beware, for all around conspire
To banish caution and to wake desire;
The day's amusement, feasting, beauty, wine,
These accents sweet and this soft hour combine,
When most unguarded, then to win that heart of thine:
But see, they land! the fond enchantment flies,
And in its place life's common views arise.

Sometimes a Party, row'd from town will land
On a small islet form'd of shelly sand,
Left by the water when the tides are low,
But which the floods in their return o'erflow:
There will they anchor, pleased awhile to view
The watery waste, a prospect wild and new;
The now receding billows give them space,
On either side the growing shores to pace;
And then returning, they contract the scene,
Till small and smaller grows the walk between;
As sea to sea approaches, shore to shores,
Till the next ebb the sandy isle restores.

Then what alarm! what danger and dismay,
If all their trust, their boat, should drift away;
And once it happen'd—Gay the friends advanced,
They walk'd, they ran, they play'd, they sang, they danced;
The urns were boiling, and the cups went round,
And not a grave or thoughtful face was found;
On the bright sand they trod with nimble feet,
Dry shelly sand that made the summer-seat;
The wondering mews flew fluttering o'er the head,
And waves ran softly up their shining bed.
Some form'd a party from the rest to stray,
Pleased to collect the trifles in their way;
These to behold they call their friends around,
No friends can hear, or hear another sound;
Alarm'd, they hasten, yet perceive not why,
But catch the fear that quickens as they fly.

For lo! a lady sage, who paced the sand
With her fair children, one in either hand,
Intent on home, had turn'd, and saw the boat
Slipp'd from her moorings, and now far afloat;
She gazed, she trembled, and though faint her call,
It seem'd, like thunder, to confound them all.
Their sailor-guides, the boatman and his mate,
Had drank, and slept regardless of their state:
"Awake!" they cried aloud; "Alarm the shore!
Shout all, or never shall we reach it more!"

Alas! no shout the distant land can reach,
Nor eye behold them from the foggy beach:
Again they join in one loud powerful cry,
Then cease, and eager listen for reply;
None came—the rising wind blew sadly by:
They shout once more, and then they turn aside,
To see how quickly flow'd the coming tide;
Between each cry they find the waters steal
On their strange prison, and new horrors feel;
Foot after foot on the contracted ground
The billows fall, and dreadful is the sound;
Less and yet less the sinking isle became,
And there was wailing, weeping, wrath, and blame.

 Had one been there, with spirit strong and high,
Who could observe, as he prepared to die,
He might have seen of hearts the varying kind,
And traced the movement of each different mind:
He might have seen, that not the gentle maid
Was more than stern and haughty man afraid;
Such, calmly grieving, will their fears suppress,
And silent prayers to Mercy's throne address;
While fiercer minds, impatient, angry, loud,
Force their vain grief on the reluctant crowd:
The party's patron, sorely sighing, cried,
"Why would you urge me? I at first denied."
Fiercely they answer'd, "Why will you complain,
Who saw no danger, or was warn'd in vain?"
A few essay'd the troubled soul to calm,
But dread prevail'd, and anguish and alarm.

 Now rose the water through the lessening sand,
And they seem'd sinking while they yet could stand.
The sun went down, they look'd from side to side,
Nor aught except the gathering sea descried;
Dark and more dark, more wet, more cold it grew,
And the most lively bade to hope adieu:
Children by love then lifted from the seas,
Felt not the waters at the parent's knees,
But wept aloud; the wind increased the sound,
And the cold billows as they broke around.

 "Once more, yet once again, with all our strength,
Cry to the land—we may be heard at length."
Vain hope if yet unseen! but hark! an oar,
That sound of bliss! comes dashing to their shore;
Still, still the water rises; "Haste!" they cry,
"Oh! hurry, seamen; in delay we die;"

(Seamen were these, who in their ship perceived
The drifted boat, and thus her crew relieved.)
And now the keel just cuts the cover'd sand,
Now to the gunwale stretches every hand:
With trembling pleasure all confused embark,
And kiss the tackling of their welcome ark;
While the most giddy, as they reach the shore,
Think of their danger, and their GOD adore.

LETTER X.

Non iter lances mensasque nitentes,
Cum stupet insanis acies fulgoribus, et cum
Acclinis falsis animus meliora recusat:
Verum hic impransi mecum disquirite.
HORACE, Satires.

O prodiga rerum
Luxuries, nunquam parvo contenta paratu,
Est quaesitorum terra pelagoque ciborum
Ambitiosa fames, et lautae gloria mensae.
LUCAN, Pharsalia.

CLUBS AND SOCIAL MEETINGS.

Desire of Country Gentlemen for Town Associations—Book Clubs—
Too much of literary Character expected from them—Literary
Conversation prevented; by Feasting, by Cards—Good,
notwithstanding, results—Card Club with Eagerness resorted to—
Players—Umpires at the Whist Table—Petulances of Temper there
discovered—Free and Easy Club; not perfectly easy or free—Freedom,
how interrupted—The superior Member—Termination of the
Evening—Drinking and Smoking Clubs—The Midnight Conversation
of the delaying Members—Society of the poorer Inhabitants; its Use;
gives Pride and Consequence to the humble Character—Pleasant
Habitations of the frugal Poor—Sailor returning to his Family—
Freemasons' Club—The Mystery—What its Origin—Its professed
Advantages—Griggs and Gregorians—A kind of Masons—Reflections
on these various Societies.

YOU say you envy in your calm retreat
Our social Meetings;—'tis with joy we meet.
In these our parties you are pleased to find
Good sense and wit, with intercourse of mind;
Composed of men who read, reflect, and write,
Who, when they meet, must yield and share delight.
To you our Book-club has peculiar charm,
For which you sicken in your quiet farm;
Here you suppose us at our leisure placed,
Enjoying freedom, and displaying taste:
With wisdom cheerful, temperately gay,
Pleased to enjoy, and willing to display.
    If thus your envy gives your ease its gloom,

Give wings to fancy, and among us come.
We're now assembled; you may soon attend—
I'll introduce you—"Gentlemen, my friend."
　　"Now are you happy? you have pass'd a night
In gay discourse, and rational delight."
　　"Alas! not so: for how can mortals think,
Or thoughts exchange, if thus they eat and drink?
No! I confess when we had fairly dined,
That was no time for intercourse of mind;
There was each dish prepared with skill t'invite,
And to detain the struggling appetite;
On such occasions minds with one consent
Are to the comforts of the body lent;
There was no pause—the wine went quickly round,
Till struggling Fancy was by Bacchus bound;
Wine is to wit as water thrown on fire,
By duly sprinkling both are raised the higher;
Thus largely dealt, the vivid blaze they choke,
And all the genial flame goes off in smoke."
　　"But when no more your boards these loads contain,
When wine no more o'erwhelms the labouring brain,
But serves, a gentle stimulus; we know
How wit must sparkle, and how fancy flow."
It might be so, but no such club-days come;
We always find these dampers in the room:
If to converse were all that brought us here,
A few odd members would in turn appear;
Who, dwelling nigh, would saunter in and out,
O'erlook the list, and toss the books about;
Or yawning read them, walking up and down,
Just as the loungers in the shops in town;
Till fancying nothing would their minds amuse,
They'd push them by, and go in search of news.
　　But our attractions are a stronger sort,
The earliest dainties and the oldest port;
All enter then with glee in every look,
And not a member thinks about a book.
　　Still, let me own, there are some vacant hours,
When minds might work, and men exert their powers:
Ere wine to folly spurs the giddy guest,
But gives to wit its vigour and its zest;
Then might we reason, might in turn display
Our several talents, and be wisely gay;
We might—but who a tame discourse regards,
When Whist is named, and we behold the Cards?

We from that time are neither grave nor gay;
Our thought, our care, our business is to play:
Fix'd on these spots and figures, each attends
Much to his partners, nothing to his friends.

Our public cares, the long, the warm debate,
That kept our patriots from their beds so late;
War, peace, invasion, all we hope or dread,
Vanish like dreams when men forsake their bed;
And groaning nations and contending kings
Are all forgotten for these painted things;
Paper and paste, vile figures and poor spots,
Level all minds, philosophers and sots;
And give an equal spirit, pause, and force,
Join'd with peculiar diction, to discourse:
"Who deals?—you led—we're three by cards—had you
Honour in hand?"—"Upon my honour, two."
Hour after hour, men thus contending sit,
Grave without sense, and pointed without wit.

Thus it appears these envied Clubs possess
No certain means of social happiness;
Yet there's a good that flows from scenes like these—
Man meets with man at leisure and at ease;
We to our neighbours and our equals come,
And rub off pride that man. contracts at home;
For there, admitted master, he is prone
To claim attention and to talk alone:
But here he meets with neither son nor spouse;
No humble cousin to his bidding bows;
To his raised voice his neighbours' voices rise,
To his high look as lofty look replies;
When much he speaks, he finds that ears are closed,
And certain signs inform him when he's prosed;
Here all the value of a listener know,
And claim, in turn, the favour they bestow.

No pleasure gives the speech, when all would speak,
And all in vain a civil hearer seek.
To chance alone we owe the free discourse,
In vain you purpose what you cannot force;
'Tis when the favourite themes unbidden spring,
That fancy soars with such unwearied wing;
Then may you call in aid the moderate glass,
But let it slowly and unprompted pass;
So shall there all things for the end unite,
And give that hour of rational delight.

Men to their Clubs repair, themselves to please,

To care for nothing, and to take their ease;
In fact, for play, for wine, for news they come:
Discourse is shared with friends or found at home.

But Cards with Books are incidental things;
We've nights devoted to these queens and kings:
Then if we choose the social game, we may;
Now 'tis a duty, and we're bound to play;
Nor ever meeting of the social kind
Was more engaging, yet had less of mind.

Our eager parties, when the lunar light
Throws its full radiance on the festive night,
Of either sex, with punctual hurry come,
And fill, with one accord, an ample room;
Pleased, the fresh packs on cloth of green they see,
And seizing, handle with preluding glee;
They draw, they sit, they shuffle, cut, and deal;
Like friends assembled, but like foes to feel:
But yet not all,—a happier few have joys
Of mere amusement, and their cards are toys;
No skill nor art, nor fretful hopes have they,
But while their friends are gaming, laugh and play.

Others there are, the veterans of the game,
Who owe their pleasure to their envied fame;
Through many a year with hard-contested strife,
Have they attain'd this glory of their life:
Such is that ancient burgess, whom in vain
Would gout and fever on his couch detain;
And that large lady, who resolves to come,
Though a first fit has warn'd her of her doom!
These are as oracles: in every cause
They settle doubts, and their decrees are laws;
But all are troubled, when, with dubious look,
Diana questions what Apollo spoke.

Here avarice first, the keen desire of gain,
Rules in each heart, and works in every brain:
Alike the veteran-dames and virgins feel,
Nor care what graybeards or what striplings deal;
Sex, age, and station, vanish from their view,
And gold, their sov'reign good, the mingled crowd pursue.

Hence they are jealous, and as rivals, keep
A watchful eye on the beloved heap;
Meantime discretion bids the tongue be still,
And mild good-humour strives with strong ill-will
Till prudence fails; when, all impatient grown,
They make their grief by their suspicions known,

"Sir, I protest, were Job himself at play,
He'd rave to see you throw your cards away;
Not that I care a button—not a pin
For what I lose; but we had cards to win:
A saint in heaven would grieve to see such hand
Cut up by one who will not understand."

"Complain of me! and so you might indeed
If I had ventured on that foolish lead,
That fatal heart—but I forgot your play—
Some folk have ever thrown their hearts away."

"Yes, and their diamonds; I have heard of one
Who made a beggar of an only son."

"Better a beggar, than to see him tied
To art and spite, to insolence and pride."

"Sir, were I you, I'd strive to be polite,
Against my nature, for a single night."

"So did you strive, and, madam! with success;
I knew no being we could censure less!"

Is this too much? Alas! my peaceful Muse
Cannot with half their virulence abuse.
And hark! at other tables discord reigns,
With feign'd contempt for losses and for gains;
Passions awhile are bridled: then they rage,
In waspish youth, and in resentful age;
With scraps of insult—"Sir, when next you play,
Reflect whose money 'tis you throw away.
No one on earth can less such things regard,
But when one's partner doesn't know a card—
I scorn suspicion, ma'am, but while you stand
Behind that lady, pray keep down your hand."

"Good heav'n, revoke: remember, if the set
Be lost, in honour you should pay the debt."

"There, there's your money; but, while I have life,
I'll never more sit down with man and wife;
They snap and snarl indeed, but in the heat
Of all their spleen, their understandings meet;
They are Freemasons, and have many a sign,
That we, poor devils! never can divine:
May it be told, do ye divide th' amount,
Or goes it all to family account?"

Next is the Club, where to their friends in town
Our country neighbours once a month come down;

We term it Free-and-Easy, and yet we
Find it no easy matter to be free:
E'en in our small assembly, friends among,
Are minds perverse, there's something will be wrong;
Men are not equal; some will claim a right
To be the kings and heroes of the night;
Will their own favourite themes and notions start,
And you must hear, offend them, or depart.

 There comes Sir Thomas from his village-seat,
Happy, he tells us, all his friends to meet;
He brings the ruin'd brother of his wife,
Whom he supports, and makes him sick of life;
A ready witness whom he can produce
Of all his deeds—a butt for his abuse;
Soon as he enters, has the guests espied,
Drawn to the fire, and to the glass applied—
"Well, what's the subject?—what are you about?
The news, I take it—come, I'll help you out:"—
And then, without one answer he bestows
Freely upon us all he hears and knows;
Gives us opinions, tells us how he votes,
Recites the speeches, adds to them his notes;
And gives old ill-told tales for new-born anecdotes:
Yet cares he nothing what we judge or think,
Our only duty's to attend and drink:
At length, admonish'd by his gout he ends
The various speech, and leaves at peace his friends;
But now, alas! we've lost the pleasant hour,
And wisdom flies from wine's superior power.

 Wine like the rising sun, possession gains,
And drives the mist of dulness from the brains;
The gloomy vapour from the spirit flies,
And views of gaiety and gladness rise:
Still it proceeds; till from the glowing heat,
The prudent calmly to their shades retreat:—
Then is the mind o'ercast—in wordy rage
And loud contention angry men engage;
Then spleen and pique, like fireworks thrown in spite,
To mischief turn the pleasures of the night;
Anger abuses, Malice loudly rails,
Revenge awakes, and Anarchy prevails;
Till wine, that raised the tempest, makes its cease,
And maudlin Love insists on instant peace;
He, noisy mirth and roaring song commands,
Gives idle toasts, and joins unfriendly bands:

Till fuddled Friendship vows esteem and weeps,
And jovial Folly drinks and sings and sleeps.

A Club there is of Smokers—Dare you come
To that close, clouded, hot, narcotic room?
When, midnight past, the very candles seem
Dying for air, and give a ghastly gleam;
When curling fumes in lazy wreaths arise,
And prosing topers rub their winking eyes;
When the long tale, renew'd when last they met,
Is spliced anew, and is unfinish'd yet;
When but a few are left the house to tire,
And they half sleeping by the sleepy fire;
E'en the poor ventilating vane that flew
Of late so fast, is now grown drowsy too;
When sweet, cold, clammy punch its aid bestows,
Then thus the midnight conversation flows:—
    "Then, as I said, and—mind me—as I say,
At our last meeting—you remember"—"Ay?"
"Well, very well—then freely as I drink
I spoke my thought—you take me—what I think.
And, sir, said I, if I a Freeman be,
It is my bounden duty to be free."
    "Ay, there you posed him: I respect the Chair,
But man is man, although the man's a mayor;
If Muggins live—no, no!—if Muggins die,
He'll quit his office—neighbour, shall I try?"
    "I'll speak my mind, for here are none but friends:
They're all contending for their private ends;
No public spirit—once a vote would bring,
I say a vote—was then a pretty thing;
It made a man to serve his country and his king:
But for that place, that Muggins must resign,
You've my advice—'tis no affair of mine."

    The Poor Man has his Club: he comes and spends
His hoarded pittance with his chosen friends;
Nor this alone,—a monthly dole he pays,
To be assisted when his health decays;
Some part his prudence, from the day's supply,
For cares and troubles in his age, lays by;
The printed rules he guards with painted frame,

And shows his children where to read his name;
Those simple words his honest nature move,
That bond of union tied by laws of love;
This is his pride, it gives to his employ
New value, to his home another joy;
While a religious hope its balm applies
For all his fate inflicts, and all his state denies.
    Much would it please you, sometimes to explore
The peaceful dwellings of our Borough poor:
To view a sailor just return'd from sea,
His wife beside; a child on either knee,
And others crowding near, that none may lose
The smallest portions of the welcome news;
What dangers pass'd, "When seas ran mountains high,
When tempest raved, and horrors veil'd the sky;
When prudence fail'd, when courage grew dismay'd,
When the strong fainted, and the wicked pray'd,—
Then in the yawning gulf far down we drove,
And gazed upon the billowy mount above;
Till up that mountain, swinging with the gale,
We view'd the horrors of the watery vale."
    The trembling children look with steadfast eyes,
And, panting, sob involuntary sighs:
Soft sleep awhile his torpid touch delays,
And all is joy and piety and praise.

    Masons are ours, Freemasons—but, alas!
To their own bards I leave the mystic class;
In vain shall one, and not a gifted man,
Attempt to sing of this enlightened clan:
I know no Word, boast no directing Sign,
And not one Token of the race is mine;
Whether with Hiram, that wise widow's son,
They came from Tyre to royal Solomon,
Two pillars raising by their skill profound,
Boaz and Jachin through the east renown'd:
Whether the sacred Books their rise express,
Or books profane, 'tis vain for me guess:
It may be lost in date remote and high,
They know not what their own antiquity:
It may be, too, derived from cause so low,
They have no wish their origin to show:
If, as Crusaders, they combine to wrest

From heathen lords the land they long possess'd;
Or were at first some harmless club, who made
Their idle meetings solemn by parade;
Is but conjecture—for the task unfit,
Awe-struck and mute, the puzzling theme I quit:
Yet, if such blessings from their Order flow,
We should be glad their moral code to know;
Trowels of silver are but simple things,
And Aprons worthless as their apron-strings;
But if indeed you have the skill to teach
A social spirit, now beyond our reach;
If man's warm passions you can guide and bind,
And plant the virtues in the wayward mind;
If you can wake to Christian love the heart,—
In mercy, something of your powers impart.

    But, as it seems, we Masons must become
To know the Secret, and must then be dumb;
And as we venture for uncertain gains,
Perhaps the profit is not worth the pains.

    When Bruce, that dauntless traveller, thought he stood
On Nile's first rise, the fountain of the flood,
And drank exulting in the sacred spring,
The critics told him it was no such thing;
That springs unnumber'd round the country ran,
But none could show him where the first began:
So might we feel, should we our time bestow,
To gain these Secrets and these Signs to know;
Might question still if all the truth we found,
And firmly stood upon the certain ground;
We might our title to the Mystery dread,
And fear we drank not at the river-head.

    Griggs and Gregorians here their meeting hold,
Convivial Sects, and Bucks alert and bold;
A kind of Masons, but without their sign;
The bonds of union—pleasure, song, and wine.
Man, a gregarious creature, loves to fly
Where he the trackings of the herd can spy;
Still to be one with many he desires,
Although it leads him through the thorns and briers.

    A few! but few there are, who in the mind
Perpetual source of consolation find:
The weaker many to the world will come,

For comforts seldom to be found from home.
When the faint hands no more a brimmer hold,
When flannel-wreaths the useless limbs infold,
The breath impeded, and the bosom cold;
When half the pillow'd man the palsy chains,
And the blood falters in the bloated veins,—
Then, as our friends no further aid supply
Than hope's cold phrase and courtesy's soft sigh,
We should that comfort for ourselves ensure,
Which friends could not, if we could friends procure.

    Early in life, when we can laugh aloud,
There's something pleasant in a social crowd,
Who laugh with us—but will such joy remain
When we lie struggling on the bed of pain?
When our physician tells us with a sigh,
No more on hope and science to rely,
Life's staff is useless then; with labouring breath
We pray for Hope divine—the staff of Death;—
This is a scene which few companions grace,
And where the heart's first favourites yield their place.

    Here all the aid of man to man must end,
Here mounts the soul to her eternal Friend:
The tenderest love must here its tie resign,
And give th' aspiring heart to love divine.

    Men feel their weakness, and to numbers run,
Themselves to strengthen, or themselves to shun;
But though to this our weakness may be prone,
Let's learn to live, for we must die, alone.

LETTER XI.

All the comforts of life in a Tavern are known,
'Tis his home who possesses not one of his own;
And to him who has rather too much of that one,
'Tis the house of a friend where he's welcome to run;
The instant you enter my door you're my Lord,
With whose taste and whose pleasure I'm proud to accord,
And the louder you call, and the longer you stay,
The more I am happy to serve and obey.

To the house of a friend if you're pleased to retire,
You must all things admit, you must all tilings admire;
You must pay with observance the price of your treat,
You must eat what is praised, and must praise what you eat,
But here you may come, and no tax we require,
You may loudly condemn what you greatly admire;
You may growl at our wishes and pains to excel,
And may snarl at the rascals who please you so well.

At your wish we attend, and confess that your speech
On the nation's affairs might the minister teach;
His views you may blame, and his measures oppose,
There's no Tavern-treason—you're under the Rose;
Should rebellions arise in your own little state,
With me you may safely their consequence wait;
To recruit your lost spirits 'tis prudent to come,
And to fly to a friend when the devil's at home.

That I've faults is confess'd; but it won't be denied,
'Tis my interest the faults of my neighbours to hide;
If I've sometimes lent Scandal occasion to prate,
I've often conceal'd what she lov'd to relate;
If to Justice's bar some have wander'd from mine,
'Twas because the dull rogues wouldn't stay by their wine;
And for brawls at my house, well the poet explains,
That men drink shallow draughts, and so madden their brains.

INNS.

A difficult Subject for Poetry—Invocation of the Muse—Description of
the principal Inn and those of the first Class—The large deserted
Tavern—Those of a second Order—Their Company—One of
particular Description—A lower kind of Public-Houses; yet

distingushed among themselves—Houses on the Quays for Sailors—
The Green Man; its Landlord, and the Adventure of his Marriage, &c.

MUCH do I need, and therefore will I ask,
A Muse to aid me in my present task;
For then with special cause we beg for aid,
When of our subject we are most afraid:
INNS are this subject—'tis an ill-drawn lot,
So, thou who gravely triflest, fail me not;
Fail not, but haste, and to my memory bring
Scenes yet unsung, which few would choose to sing;
Thou mad'st a Shilling splendid; thou hast thrown
On humble themes the graces all thine own;
By thee the Mistress of a Village-school
Became a queen enthroned upon her stool;
And far beyond the rest thou gav'st to shine
Belinda's Lock—that deathless work was thine.
    Come, lend thy cheerful light, and give to please,
These seats of revelry, these scenes of ease;
Who sings of Inns much danger has to dread,
And needs assistance from the fountain-head.
    High in the street, o'erlooking all the place,
The rampant Lion shows his kingly face;
His ample jaws extend from side to side,
His eyes are glaring, and his nostrils wide;
In silver shag the sovereign form is dress'd,
A mane horrific sweeps his ample chest;
Elate with pride, he seems t'assert his reign,
And stands the glory of his wide domain.
    Yet nothing dreadful to his friends the sight,
But sign and pledge of welcome and delight.
To him the noblest guest the town detains
Flies for repast, and in his court remains;
Him too the crowd with longing looks admire,
Sigh for his joys, and modestly retire;
Here not a comfort shall to them be lost
Who never ask or never feel the cost.
    The ample yards on either side contain
Buildings where order and distinction reign;—
The splendid carriage of the wealthier guest,
The ready chaise and driver smartly dress'd;
Whiskeys and gigs and curricles are there,
And high-fed prancers many a raw-boned pair.
On all without a lordly host sustains
The care of empire, and observant reigns;

The parting guest beholds him at his side,
With pomp obsequious, bending in his pride;
Round all the place his eyes all objects meet,
Attentive, silent, civil, and discreet.
O'er all within the lady-hostess rules,
Her bar she governs, and her kitchen schools;
To every guest th' appropriate speech is made,
And every duty with distinction paid;
Respectful, easy, pleasant, or polite—
"Your honour's servant"—"Mister Smith, good night."
    Next, but not near, yet honour'd through the town,
There swing, incongruous pair! the Bear and Crown:
That Crown suspended gems and ribands deck,
A golden chain hangs o'er that furry neck:
Unlike the nobler beast, the Bear is bound,
And with the Crown so near him, scowls uncrown'd;
Less his dominion, but alert are all
Without, within, and ready for the call;
Smart lads and light run nimbly here and there,
Nor for neglected duties mourns the Bear.
    To his retreats, on the Election-day,
The losing party found their silent way;
There they partook of each consoling good,
Like him uncrown'd, like him in sullen mood—
Threat'ning, but bound.—Here meet a social kind,
Our various clubs for various cause combined;
Nor has he pride, but thankful takes as gain
The dew-drops shaken from the Lion's mane:
A thriving couple here their skill display,
And share the profits of no vulgar sway.
    Third in our Borough's list appears the sign
Of a fair queen—the gracious Caroline;
But in decay—each feature in the face
Has stain of Time, and token of disgrace.
The storm of winter, and the summer-sun,
Have on that form their equal mischief done;
The features now are all disfigured seen,
And not one charm adorns th' insulted queen.
To this poor face was never paint applied,
Th' unseemly work of cruel Time to hide;
Here we may rightly such neglect upbraid,
Paint on such faces is by prudence laid.
Large the domain, but all within combine
To correspond with the dishonoured sign;
And all around dilapidates; you call—

But none replies—they're inattentive all:
At length a ruin'd stable holds your steed,
While you through large and dirty rooms proceed,
Spacious and cold; a proof they once had been
In honour,—now magnificently mean;
Till in some small half-furnish'd room you rest,
Whose dying fire denotes it had a guest.
In those you pass'd, where former splendour reign'd,
You saw the carpets torn, the paper stain'd;
Squares of discordant glass in windows fix'd,
And paper oil'd in many a space betwixt;
A soil'd and broken sconce, a mirror crack'd,
With table underpropp'd, and chairs new back'd;
A marble side-slab with ten thousand stains,
And all an ancient Tavern's poor remains.

    With much entreaty, they your food prepare,
And acid wine afford, with meagre fare;
Heartless you sup; and when a dozen times
You've read the fractured window's senseless rhymes,
Have been assured that Phoebe Green was fair,
And Peter Jackson took his supper there;
You reach a chilling chamber, where you dread
Damps, hot or cold, from a tremendous bed;
Late comes your sleep, and you are waken'd soon
By rustling tatters of the old festoon.

    O'er this large building, thus by time defaced,
A servile couple has its owner placed,
Who not unmindful that its style is large,
To lost magnificence adapt their charge:
Thus an old beauty, who has long declined,
Keeps former dues and dignity in mind;
And wills that all attention should be paid
For graces vanish'd and for charms decay'd.

    Few years have pass'd, since brightly 'cross the way,
Lights from each window shot the lengthen'd ray,
And busy looks in every face were seen,
Through the warm precincts of the reigning Queen;
There fires inviting blazed, and all around
Was heard the tinkling bells' seducing sound;
The nimble waiters to that sound from far
Sprang to the call, then hasteri'd to the bar,
Where a glad priestess of the temple sway'd,
The most obedient, and the most obey'd;
Rosy and round, adorn'd in crimson vest,
And flaming ribands at her ample breast:

She, skill'd like Circe, tried her guests to move,
With looks of welcome and with words of love;
And such her potent charms, that men unwise
Were soon transform'd and fitted for the sties.

 Her port in bottles stood, a well-stain'd row,
Drawn for the evening from the pipe below;
Three powerful spirits filled a parted case,
Some cordial bottles stood in secret place;
Fair acid-fruits in nets above were seen,
Her plate was splendid, and her glasses clean;
Basins and bowls were ready on the stand,
And measures clatter'd in her powerful hand.

 Inferior Houses now our notice claim,
But who shall deal them their appropriate fame?
Who shall the nice, yet known distinction, tell,
Between the peal complete and single Bell?

 Determine ye, who on your shining nags
Wear oil-skin beavers, and bear seal-skin bags;
Or ye, grave topers, who with coy delight
Snugly enjoy the sweetness of the night;
Ye travellers all, superior Inns denied
By moderate purse, the low by decent pride;
Come and determine,—will you take your place
At the full Orb, or half the lunar Face?
With the Black-Boy or Angel will ye dine?
Will ye approve the Fountain or the Vine?
Horses the white or black will ye prefer?
The Silver-Swan or Swan opposed to her—
Rare bird! whose form the raven-plumage decks,
And graceful curve her three alluring necks?
All these a decent entertainment give,
And by their comforts comfortably live.

 Shall I pass by the Boar?—there are who cry,
"Beware the Boar," and pass determined by:
Those dreadful tusks, those little peering eyes
And churning chaps, are tokens to the wise.
There dwells a kind old Aunt, and there you see
Some kind young Nieces in her company;
Poor village nieces, whom the tender dame
Invites to town, and gives their beauty Fame;
The grateful sisters feel th' important aid,
And the good Aunt is flatter'd and repaid.

 What, though it may some cool observers strike,
That such fair sisters should be so unlike;
That still another and another comes,

And at the matron's tables smiles and blooms;
That all appear as if they meant to stay
Time undefined, nor name a parting day;
And yet, though all are valued, all are dear,
Causeless, they go, and seldom more appear.

    Yet let Suspicion hide her odious head,
And Scandal vengeance from a burgess dread;
A pious friend, who with the ancient dame
At sober cribbage takes an evening game;
His cup beside him, through their play he quaffs,
And oft renews, and innocently laughs;
Or growing serious, to the text resorts,
And from the Sunday-sermon makes reports;
While all, with grateful glee, his wish attend,
A grave protector and a powerful friend:
But Slander says, who indistinctly sees,
Once he was caught with Sylvia on his knees;—
A cautious burgess with a careful wife
To be so caught!—'tis false, upon my life.

    Next are a lower kind, yet not so low
But they, among them, their distinctions know;
And when a thriving landlord aims so high,
As to exchange the Chequer for the Pye,
Or from Duke William to the Dog repairs,
He takes a finer coat and fiercer airs.

    Pleased with his power, the poor man loves to say
What favourite Inn shall share his evening's pay;
Where he shall sit the social hour, and lose
His past day's labours and his next day's views.
Our Seamen too have choice; one takes a trip
In the warm cabin of his favourite Ship;
And on the morrow in the humbler Boat
He rows till fancy feels herself afloat;
Can he the sign—Three Jolly Sailors—pass,
Who hears a fiddle and who sees a lass?
The Anchor too affords the seaman joys,
In small smoked room, all clamour, crowd, and noise;
Where a curved settle half surrounds the fire,
Where fifty voices purl and punch require;
They come for pleasure in their leisure hour,
And they enjoy it to their utmost power;
Standing they drink, they swearing smoke, while all
Call, or make ready for a second call:
There is no time for trifling—"Do ye see?
We drink and drub the French extempore."

See! round the room, on every beam and balk,
Are mingled scrolls of hieroglyphic chalk;
Yet nothing heeded—would one stroke suffice
To blot out all, here honour is too nice,—
"Let knavish landsmen think such dirty things,
We're British tars, and British tars are kings."

But the Green-Man shall I pass by unsung,
Which mine own James upon his sign-post hung?
His sign his image,—for he was once seen
A squire's attendant, clad in keeper's green;
Ere yet, with wages more and honour less,
He stood behind me in a graver dress.

James in an evil hour went forth to woo
Young Juliet Hart, and was her Romeo:
They'd seen the play, and thought it vastly sweet
For two young lovers by the moon to meet;
The nymph was gentle, of her favours free,
E'en at a word—no Rosalind was she;
Nor, like that other Juliet, tried his truth
With—"Be thy purpose marriage, gentle youth?"
But him received, and heard his tender tale,
When sang the lark, and when the nightingale;
So in few months the generous lass was seen
I' the way that all the Capulets had been.

Then first repentance seized the amorous man,
And—shame on love!—he reason'd and he ran;
The thoughtful Romeo trembled for his purse,
And the sad sounds, "for better and for worse."

Yet could the Lover not so far withdraw,
But he was haunted both by Love and Law;
Now Law dismay'd him as he view'd its fangs,
Now Pity seized him for his Juliet's pangs;
Then thoughts of justice and some dread of jail,
Where all would blame him, and where none might bail;
These drew him back, till Juliet's hut appear'd,
Where love had drawn him when he should have fear'd.

There sat the father in his wicker throne,
Uttering his curses in tremendous tone:
With foulest names his daughter he reviled,
And look'd a very Herod at the child:
Nor was she patient, but with equal scorn,
Bade him remember when his Joe was born:
Then rose the mother, eager to begin
Her plea for frailty, when the swain came in.

To him she turn'd, and other theme began,

Show'd him his boy, and bade him be a man;
"An honest man, who, when he breaks the laws,
Will make a woman honest if there's cause."
With lengthen'd speech she proved what came to pass
Was no reflection on a loving lass:
"If she your love as wife and mother claim,
What can it matter which was first the name?
But 'tis most base, 'tis perjury and theft,
When a lost girl is like a widow left;
The rogue who ruins .. " here the father found
His spouse was treading on forbidden ground.
    "That's not the point," quoth he, "I don't suppose
My good friend Fletcher to be one of those;
What's done amiss he'll mend in proper time—
I hate to hear of villany and crime:
'Twas my misfortune, in the days of youth,
To find two lasses pleading for my truth;
The case was hard, I would with all my soul
Have wedded both, but law is our control;
So one I took, and when we gain'd a home,
Her friend agreed—what could she more?—to come;
And when she found that I'd a widow'd bed,
Me she desired—what could I less?—to wed.
An easier case is yours: you've not the smart
That two fond pleaders cause in one man's heart.
You've not to wait from year to year distress'd,
Before your conscience can be laid at rest;
There smiles your bride, there sprawls your new-born son,
A ring, a licence, and the thing is done."—
    "My loving James,"—the Lass began her plea,
I'll make thy reason take a part with me;
Had I been froward, skittish, or unkind,
Or to thy person or thy passion blind;
Had I refused, when 'twas thy part to pray,
Or put thee off with promise and delay;
Thou might'st in justice and in conscience fly,
Denying her who taught thee to deny:
But, James, with me thou hadst an easier task,
Bonds and conditions I forbore to ask;
I laid no traps for thee, no plots or plans,
Nor marriage named by licence or by banns;
Nor would I now the parson's aid employ,
But for this cause,"—and up she held her boy.
    Motives like these could heart of flesh resist?
James took the infant and in triumph kiss'd;

Then to his mother's arms the child restored,
Made his proud speech and pledged his worthy word.
    "Three times at church our banns shall publish'd be,
Thy health be drunk in bumpers three times three;
And thou shalt grace (bedeck'd in garments gay)
The christening-dinner on the wedding-day."
    James at my door then made his parting bow,
Took the Green-Man, and is a master now.

LETTER XII.

These are monarchs none respect,
Heroes, yet an humbled crew,
Nobles, whom the crowd correct,
Wealthy men, whom duns pursue;
Beauties shrinking from the view
Of the day's detecting eye;
Lovers, who with much ado
Long-forsaken damsels woo,
And heave the ill-feign'd sigh.

These are misers, craving means
Of existence through the day,
Famous scholars, conning scenes
Of a dull bewildering play;
Ragged beaux and misses gray,
Whom the rabble praise and blame,
Proud and mean, and sad and gay,
Toiling after ease, are they,
Infamous, and boasting fame.

PLAYERS.

They arrive in the Borough—Welcomed by their former Friends—Are
better fitted for Comic than Tragic Scenes: yet better approved in the
latter by one Part of their Audience—Their general Character and
Pleasantry—Particular Distresses and Labours—Their Fortitude and
Patience—A private rehearsal—The Vanity of the aged Actress—A
Heroine from the Milliner's Shop—A deluded Tradesman—Of what
Persons the Company is composed—Character and Adventures of
Frederick Thompson.

DRAWN by the annual call, we now behold
Our Troop Dramatic, heroes known of old,
And those, since last they march'd, enlisted and enrolled:
Mounted on hacks or borne in waggons some,
The rest on foot (the humbler brethren) come.
Three favour'd places, an unequal time,
Join to support this company sublime:
Ours for the longer period—see how light
Yon parties move, their former friends in sight,
Whose claims are all allow'd, and friendship glads the night.
Now public rooms shall sound with words divine,

And private lodgings hear how heroes shine;
No talk of pay shall yet on pleasure steal,
But kindest welcome bless the friendly meal;
While o'er the social jug and decent cheer,
Shall be described the fortunes of the year.
  Peruse these bills, and see what each can do,—
Behold! the prince, the slave, the monk, the Jew;
Change but the garment, and they'll all engage
To take each part, and act in every age:
Cull'd from all houses, what a house are they!
Swept from all barns, our Borough-critics say;
But with some portion of a critic's ire,
We all endure them; there are some admire:
They might have praise, confined to farce alone;
Full well they grin, they should not try to groan;
But then our servants' and our seamen's wives
Love all that rant and rapture as their lives;
He who 'Squire Richard's part could well sustain,
Finds as King Richard he must roar amain—
"My horse! my horse!"—Lo! now to their abodes,
Come lords and lovers, empresses and gods.
The master-mover of these scenes has made
No trifling gain in this adventurous trade;
Trade we may term it, for he duly buys
Arms out of use and undirected eyes:
These he instructs, and guides them as he can,
And vends each night the manufactured man:
Long as our custom lasts they gladly stay,
Then strike their tents, like Tartars! and away!
The place grows bare where they too long remain,
But grass will rise ere they return again.
  Children of Thespes, welcome; knights and queens!
Counts! barons! beauties! when before your scenes,
And mighty monarchs thund'ring from your throne;
Then step behind, and all your glory's gone:
Of crown and palace, throne and guards bereft,
The pomp is vanish'd and the care is left.
Yet strong and lively is the joy they feel,
When the full house secures the plenteous meal;
Flatt'ring and flatter'd, each attempts to raise
A brother's merits for a brother's praise:
For never hero shows a prouder heart,
Than he who proudly acts a hero's part;
Nor without cause; the boards, we know, can yield
Place for fierce contest, like the tented field.

Graceful to tread the stage, to be in turn
The prince we honour, and the knave we spurn;
Bravely to bear the tumult of the crowd,
The hiss tremendous, and the censure loud:
These are their parts,—and he who these sustains,
Deserves some praise and profit for his pains.
Heroes at least of gentler kind are they,
Against whose swords no weeping widows pray,
No blood their fury sheds, nor havoc marks their way.

Sad happy race! soon raised and soon depress'd,
Your days all pass'd in jeopardy and jest;
Poor without prudence, with afflictions vain,
Not warn'd by misery, not enrich'd by gain;
Whom Justice, pitying, chides from place to place,
A wandering, careless, wretched, merry race,
Whose cheerful looks assume, and play the parts
Of happy rovers with repining hearts;
Then cast off care, and in the mimic pain
Of tragic woe feel spirits light and vain,
Distress and hope—the mind's the body's wear,
The man's affliction, and the actor's tear:
Alternate times of fasting and excess
Are yours, ye smiling children of distress.

Slaves though ye be, your wandering freedom seems,
And with your varying views and restless schemes,
Your griefs are transient, as your joys are dreams.

Yet keen those griefs—ah! what avail thy charms,
Fair Juliet! what that infant in thine arms;
What those heroic lines thy patience learns,
What all the aid thy present Romeo earns,
Whilst thou art crowded in that lumbering wain
With all thy plaintive sisters to complain?

Nor is there lack of labour—To rehearse,
Day after day, poor scraps of prose and verse;
To bear each other's spirit, pride, and spite;
To hide in rant the heart ache of the night;
To dress in gaudy patchwork, and to force
The mind to think on the appointed course;—
This is laborious, and may be defined
The bootless labour of the thriftless mind.

There is a veteran Dame: I see her stand
Intent and pensive with her book in hand;
Awhile her thoughts she forces on her part,
Then dwells on objects nearer to the heart;
Across the room she paces, gets her tone,

And fits her features for the Danish throne;
To-night a queen—I mark her motion slow,
I hear her speech, and Hamlet's mother know.
    Methinks 'tis pitiful to see her try
For strength of arms and energy of eye;
With vigour lost, and spirits worn away,
Her pomp and pride she labours to display;
And when awhile she's tried her part to act,
To find her thoughts arrested by some fact;
When struggles more and more severe are seen,
In the plain actress than the Danish queen,—
At length she feels her part, she finds delight,
And fancies all the plaudits of the night;
Old as she is, she smiles at every speech,
And thinks no youthful part beyond her reach,
But as the mist of vanity again
Is blown away, by press of present pain,
Sad and in doubt she to her purse applies
For cause of comfort, where no comfort lies;
Then to her task she sighing turns again—
"Oh! Hamlet, thou hast cleft my heart in twain!"
    And who that poor, consumptive, wither'd thing,
Who strains her slender throat and strives to sing?
Panting for breath and forced her voice to drop,
And far unlike the inmate of the shop,
Where she, in youth and health, alert and gay,
Laugh'd off at night the labours of the day;
With novels, verses, fancy's fertile powers,
And sister-converse pass'd the evening hours:
But Cynthia's soul was soft, her wishes strong,
Her judgment weak, and her conclusions wrong;
The morning-call and counter were her dread,
And her contempt the needle and the thread:
But when she read a gentle damsel's part,
Her woe, her wish! she had them all by heart.
    At length the hero of the boards drew nigh,
Who spake of love till sigh re-echo'd sigh;
He told in honey'd words his deathless flame,
And she his own by tender vows became;
Nor ring nor licence needed souls so fond,
Alfonso's passion was his Cynthia's bond:
And thus the simple girl, to shame betray'd,
Sinks to the grave forsaken and dismay'd.
    Sick without pity, sorrowing without hope,
See her! the grief and scandal of the troop;

A wretched martyr to a childish pride,
Her woe insulted, and her praise denied:
Her humble talents, though derided, used,
Her prospects lost, her confidence abused;
All that remains—for she not long can brave
Increase of evils—is an early grave.
　　Ye gentle Cynthias of the shop, take heed
What dreams you cherish, and what books ye read!
　　A decent sum had Peter Nottage made,
By joining bricks—to him a thriving trade:
Of his employment master and his wife,
This humble tradesman led a lordly life;
The house of kings and heroes lack'd repairs,
And Peter, though reluctant, served the Players:
Connected thus, he heard in way polite,—
"Come, Master Nottage, see us play to night,"
At first 'twas folly, nonsense, idle stuff,
But seen for nothing it grew well enough;
And better now—now best, and every night,
In this fool's paradise he drank delight;
And as he felt the bliss, he wish'd to know
Whence all this rapture and these joys could flow;
For if the seeing could such pleasure bring,
What must the feeling?—feeling like a king?
　　In vain his wife, his uncle, and his friend,
Cried—"Peter! Peter! let such follies end;
'Tis well enough these vagabonds to see,
But would you partner with a showman be?"
　　"Showman!" said Peter, "did not Quin and Clive,
And Roscius-Garrick, by the science thrive?
Showman!—'tis scandal; I'm by genius led
To join a class who've Shakspeare at their head."
　　Poor Peter thus by easy steps became
A dreaming candidate for scenic fame,
And, after years consumed, infirm and poor,
He sits and takes the tickets at the door.
　　Of various men these marching troops are made,—
Pen-spurning clerks, and lads contemning trade;
Waiters and servants by confinement teased,
And youths of wealth by dissipation eased;
With feeling nymphs, who, such resource at hand,
Scorn to obey the rigour of command;
Some, who from higher views by vice are won,
And some of either sex by love undone;
The greater part lamenting as their fall,

What some an honour and advancement call.

There are who names in shame or fear assume,
And hence our Bevilles and our Savilles come;
It honours him, from tailor's board kick'd down,
As Mister Dormer to amuse the town;
Falling, he rises: but a kind there are
Who dwell on former prospects, and despair;
Justly but vainly they their fate deplore,
And mourn their fall, who fell to rise no more.

Our merchant Thompson, with his sons around,
Most mind and talent in his Frederick found:
He was so lively, that his mother knew,
If he were taught, that honour must ensue;
The father's views were in a different line,—
But if at college he were sure to shine.
Then should he go—to prosper who could doubt?
When schoolboy stigmas would be all wash'd out,
For there were marks upon his youthful face,
'Twixt vice and error—a neglected case—
These would submit to skill; a little time,
And none could trace the error or the crime;
Then let him go, and once at college, he
Might choose his station—what would Frederick be.

'Twas soon determined—He could not descend
To pedant-laws and lectures without end;
And then the chapel—night and morn to pray,
Or mulct and threaten'd if he kept away;
No! not to be a bishop—so he swore,
And at his college he was seen no more.

His debts all paid, the father, with a sigh,
Placed him in office—"Do, my Frederick, try:
Confine thyself a few short months and then—"
He tried a fortnight, and threw down the pen.
Again demands were hush'd: "My son, you're free,
But you're unsettled; take your chance at sea:"
So in few days the midshipman, equipp'd
Received the mother's blessing, and was shipp'd.

Hard was her fortune! soon compell'd to meet
The wretched stripling staggering through the street;
For, rash, impetuous, insolent, and vain,
The Captain sent him to his friends again:
About the Borough roved th' unnappy boy,
And ate the bread of every chance-employ!
Of friends he borrow'd, and the parents yet
In secret fondness authorized the debt;

The younger sister, still a child, was taught
To give with feign'd affright the pittance sought;
For now the father cried—"It is too late
For trial more—I leave him to his fate,"—
Yet left him not: and with a kind of joy,
The mother heard of her desponding boy;
At length he sicken'd, and he found, when sick,
All aid was ready, all attendance quick;
A fever seized him, and at once was lost
The thought of trespass, error, crime, and cost:
Th' indulgent parents, knelt beside the youth,
They heard his promise and believed his truth;
And when the danger lessen'd on their view,
They cast off doubt, and hope assurance grew;—
Nursed by his sisters, cherish'd by his sire,
Begg'd to be glad, encouraged to aspire,
His life, they said, would now all care repay,
And he might date his prospects from that day;
A son, a brother to his home received,
They hoped for all things, and in all believed.

    And now will pardon, comfort, kindness draw
The youth from vice? will honour, duty, law?
Alas! not all: the more the trials lent,
The less he seem'd to ponder and repent;
Headstrong, determined in his own career,
He thought reproof unjust and truth severe;
The soul's disease was to its crisis come,
He first abused and then abjured his home;
And when he chose a vagabond to be,
He made his shame his glory—"I'll be free."

    Friends, parents, relatives, hope, reason, love,
With anxious ardour for that empire strove;
In vain their strife, in vain the means applied,
They had no comfort, but that all were tried;
One strong vain trial made, the mind to move,
Was the last effort of parental love.

    E'en then he watch'd his father from his home,
And to his mother would for pity come,
Where, as he made her tender terrors rise,
He talk'd of death, and threaten'd for supplies.
Against a youth so vicious and undone,
All hearts were closed, and every door but one:
The Players received him; they with open heart
Gave him his portion and assign'd his part;
And ere three days were added to his life,

He found a home, a duty, and a wife.

    His present friends, though they were nothing nice,
Nor ask'd how vicious he, or what his vice,
Still they expected he should now attend
To the joint duty as a useful friend;
The leader too declared, with frown severe,
That none should pawn a robe that kings might wear;
And much it moved him, when he Hamlet play'd,
To see his Father's Ghost so drunken made:
Then too the temper, the unbending pride
Of this ally, would no reproof abide:—
So leaving these, he march'd away and join'd
Another troop, and other goods purloin'd;
And other characters, both gay and sage,
Sober and sad, made stagger on the stage.
Then to rebuke with arrogant disdain,
He gave abuse, and sought a home again.

    Thus changing scenes, but with unchanging vice,
Engaged by many, but with no one twice:
Of this, a last and poor resource, bereft,
He to himself, unhappy guide! was left—
And who shall say where guided? to what seats
Of starving villany? of thieves and cheats?

    In that sad time of many a dismal scene
Had he a witness, not inactive, been;
Had leagued with petty pilferers, and had crept
Where of each sex degraded numbers slept:
With such associates he was long allied,
Where his capacity for ill was tried,
And that once lost, the wretch was cast aside,
For now, though willing with the worst to act,
He wanted powers for an important fact;
And while he felt as lawless spirits feel,
His hand was palsied, and he couldn't steal.

    By these rejected, is their lot so strange,
So low! that he could suffer by the change?
Yes! the new station as a fall we judge,—
He now became the harlots' humble drudge,
Their drudge in common; they combined to save
Awhile from starving their submissive slave;
For now his spirit left him, and his pride,
His scorn, his rancour, and resentment died;
Few were his feelings—but the keenest these,
The rage of hunger, and the sigh for ease;
He who abused indulgence, now became

By want subservient, and by misery tame;
A slave, he begg'd forbearance; bent with pain,
He shunn'd the blow,—"Ah! strike me not again,"
    Thus was he found: the master of a hoy
Saw the sad wretch whom he had known a boy;
At first in doubt, but Frederick laid aside
All shame, and humbly for his aid applied:
He, tamed and smitten with the storms gone by,
Look'd for compassion through one living eye,
And stretch'd th' unpalsied hand: the seaman felt
His honest heart with gentle pity melt,
And his small boon with cheerful frankness dealt;
Then made inquiries of th' unhappy youth,
Who told, nor shame forbade him, all the truth.
    "Young Frederick Thompson, to a chandler's shop
By harlots order'd, and afraid to stop!—
What! our good merchant's favourite to be seen
In state so loathsome and in dress so mean?"—
So thought the seaman as he bade adieu,
And, when in port, related all he knew.
    But time was lost, inquiry came too late,
Those whom he served knew nothing of his fate;
No! they had seized on what the sailor gave,
Nor bore resistance from their abject slave.
The spoil obtain'd they cast him from the door,
Robb'd, beaten, hungry, pain'd, diseas'd, and poor.
    Then nature, pointing to the only spot
Which still had comfort for so dire a lot,
Although so feeble, led him on the way,
And hope look'd forward to a happier day:
He thought, poor prodigal! a father yet
His woes would pity and his crimes forget;
Nor had he brother who with speech severe
Would check the pity or refrain the tear:
A lighter spirit in his bosom rose,
As near the road he sought an hour's repose.
    And there he found it: he had left the town,
But buildings yet were scatter'd up and down;
To one of these, half-ruin'd and half-built,
Was traced this child of wretchedness and guilt;
There, on the remnant of a beggar's vest,
Thrown by in scorn, the sufferer sought for rest;
There was this scene of vice and woe to close,
And there the wretched body found repose. [5]

LETTER XIII.

Do good by stealth, and blush to find it fame.
                    POPE, Satires.

There are a sort of men whose visages
Do cream and mantle like a standing pool,
And do a wilful stillness entertain;
With purpose to be dress'd in an opinion,
As who should say, "I am Sir Oracle,
"And when I ope my lips let no dog bark."
                    SHAKESPEARE, Merchant of Venice.

Sum felix; quis enim neget? felixque manebo:
Hoc quoque quis dubitet? Tutum me copia fecit.

THE ALMS-HOUSE AND TRUSTEES.

The frugal Merchant—Rivalship in Modes of Frugality—Private Exceptions to the general Manners—Alms-house built—Its Description—Founder dies—Six Trustees—Sir Denys Brand, a Principal—His Eulogium in the Chronicles of the day—Truth reckoned invidious on these Occasions—An explanation of the Magnanimity and Wisdom of Sir Denys—His kinds of Moderation and Humility—Laughton, his Successor, a planning, ambitious, wealthy Man—Advancement in Life his perpetual Object, and all things make the means of it—His Idea of Falsehood—His Resentment dangerous; how removed—Success produces Love of Flattery: his daily Gratification—His Merits and Acts of Kindness—His proper Choice of Almsmen—In this respect meritorious—His Predecessor not so cautious.

LEAVE now our streets, and in yon plain behold
Those pleasant Seats for the reduced and old;
A merchant's gift, whose wife and children died,
When he to saving all his powers applied;
He wore his coat till bare was every thread,
And with the meanest fare his body fed.
He had a female cousin, who with care
Walk'd in his steps, and learn'd of him to spare;
With emulation and success they strove,
Improving still, still seeking to improve,
As if that useful knowledge they would gain—
How little food would human life sustain:
No pauper came their table's crumbs to crave;

Scraping they lived, but not a scrap they gave:
When beggars saw the frugal Merchant pass,
It moved their pity, and they said, "Alas!
Hard is thy fate my brother," and they felt
A beggar's pride as they that pity dealt.
The dogs, who learn of man to scorn the poor,
Bark'd him away from every decent door;
While they who saw him bare, but thought him rich,
To show respect or scorn, they knew not which.
    But while our Merchant seemed so base and mean,
He had his wanderings, sometimes "not unseen;"
To give in secret was a favourite act,
Yet more than once they took him in the fact
To scenes of various woe he nightly went,
And serious sums in healing misery spent;
Oft has he cheer'd the wretched at a rate
For which he daily might have dined on plate;
He has been seen—his hair all silver-white,
Shaking and shining—as he stole by night,
To feed unenvied on his still delight.
A twofold taste he had; to give and spare,
Both were his duties, and had equal care;
It was his joy to sit alone and fast,
Then send a widow and her boys repast:
Tears in his eyes would spite of him appear,
But he from other eyes has kept the tear:
All in a wint'ry night from far he came,
To soothe the sorrows of a suffering dame;
Whose husband robb'd him, and to whom he meant
A ling'ring, but reforming punishment:
Home then he walked, and found his anger rise
When fire and rushlight met his troubled eyes;
But these extinguish'd, and his prayer address'd
To Heaven in hope, he calmly sank to rest.
    His seventieth year was pass'd and then was seen
A building rising on the northern green;
There was no blinding all his neighbours' eyes,
Or surely no one would have seen it rise:
Twelve rooms contiguous stood, and six were near,
There men were placed, and sober matrons here:
There were behind small useful gardens made,
Benches before, and trees to give them shade;
In the first room were seen above, below,
Some marks of taste, a few attempts at show.
The founder's picture and his arms were there

(Not till he left us), and an elbow'd chair;
There, 'mid these signs of his superior place,
Sat the mild ruler of this humble race.

 Within the row are men who strove in vain,
Through years of trouble, wealth and ease to gain;
Less must they have than an appointed sum,
And freemen been, or hither must not come;
They should be decent, and command respect,
(Though needing fortune), whom these doors protect,
And should for thirty dismal years have tried
For peace unfelt and competence denied.

 Strange! that o'er men thus train'd in sorrow's school,
Power must be held, and they must live by rule;
Infirm, corrected by misfortunes, old,
Their habits settled and their passions cold;
Of health, wealth, power, and worldly cares bereft,
Still must they not at liberty be left;
There must be one to rule them, to restrain
And guide the movements of his erring train.

 If then control imperious, check severe,
Be needed where such reverend men appear;
To what would youth, without such checks, aspire,
Free the wild wish, uncurb'd the strong desire?
And where (in college or in camp) they found
The heart ungovern'd and the hand unbound?

 His house endow'd, the generous man resign'd
All power to rule, nay power of choice declined;
He and the female saint survived to view
Their work complete, and bade the world adieu!

 Six are the Guardians of this happy seat,
And one presides when they on business meet;
As each expires, the five a brother choose;
Nor would Sir Denys Brand the charge refuse;
True, 'twas beneath him, "but to do men good
Was motive never by his heart withstood:"
He too is gone, and they again must strive
To find a man in whom his gifts survive.
Now, in the various records of the dead,
Thy worth, Sir Denys, shall be weigh'd and read;
There we the glory of thy house shall trace,
With each alliance of thy noble race.

 Yes! here we have him!—"Came in William's reign,
The Norman Brand; the blood without a stain;
From the fierce Dane and ruder Saxon clear,
Pict, Irish, Scot, or Cambrian mountaineer:

But the pure Norman was the sacred spring,
And he, Sir Denys, was in heart a king:
Erect in person and so firm in soul,
Fortune he seem'd to govern and control:
Generous as he who gives his all away,
Prudent as one who toils for weekly pay;
In him all merits were decreed to meet,
Sincere though cautious, frank and yet discreet,
Just all his dealings, faithful every word,
His passions' master, and his temper's lord."

 Yet more, kind dealers in decaying fame?
His magnanimity you next proclaim;
You give him learning, join'd with sound good sense,
And match his wealth with his benevolence;
What hides the multitude of sins, you add,
Yet seem to doubt if sins he ever had.

 Poor honest Truth! thou writ'st of living men,
And art a railer and detractor then;
They die, again to be described, and now
A foe to merit and mankind art thou!

 Why banish Truth? It injures not the dead,
It aids not them with flattery to be fed;
And when mankind such perfect pictures view,
They copy less, the more they think them true.
Let us a mortal as he was behold,
And see the dross adhering to the gold;
When we the errors of the virtuous state,
Then erring men their worth may emulate.

 View then this picture of a noble mind,
Let him be wise, magnanimous, and kind;
What was the wisdom? Was it not the frown
That keeps all question, all inquiry down?
His words were powerful and decisive all,
But his slow reasons came for no man's call.
"'Tis thus," he cried, no doubt with kind intent,
To give results and spare all argument:—

 "Let it be spared—all men at least agree
Sir Denys Brand had magnanimity:
His were no vulgar charities; none saw
Him like the Merchant to the hut withdraw;
He left to meaner minds the simple deed,
By which the houseless rest, the hungry feed
His was a public bounty vast and grand,
'Twas not in him to work with viewless hand;
He raised the Room that towers above the street,

A public room where grateful parties meet;
He first the Life-boat plann'd; to him the place
Is deep in debt—'twas he revived the Race;
To every public act this hearty friend
Would give with freedom or with frankness lend;
His money built the Jail, nor prisoner yet
Sits at his ease, but he must feel the debt;
To these let candour add his vast display;
Around his mansion all is grand and gay,
And this is bounty with the name of pay."

    I grant the whole, nor from one deed retract,
But wish recorded too the private act:
All these were great, but still our hearts approve
Those simpler tokens of the Christian love;
'Twould give me joy some gracious deed to meet
That has not call'd for glory through the street:
Who felt for many, could not always shun,
In some soft moment, to be kind to one;
And yet they tell us, when Sir Denys died,
That not a widow in the Borough sigh'd;
Great were his gifts, his mighty heart I own,
But why describe what all the world has known?

    The rest is petty pride, the useless art
Of a vain mind to hide a swelling heart:
Small was his private room: men found him there
By a plain table, on a paltry chair;
A wretched floor-cloth, and some prints around,
The easy purchase of a single pound:
These humble trifles and that study small
Make a strong contrast with the servants' hall;
There barely comfort, here a proud excess,
The pompous seat of pamper'd idleness,
Where the sleek rogues with one consent declare,
They would not live upon his honour's fare;
He daily took but one half hour to dine,
On one poor dish and some three sips of wine;
Then he'd abuse them for their sumptuous feasts,
And say, "My friends! you make yourselves like beasts;
One dish suffices any man to dine,
But you are greedy as a herd of swine;
Learn to be temperate."—Had they dared t'obey,
He would have praised and turn'd them all away.

    Friends met Sir Denys riding in his ground,
And there the meekness of his spirit found:
For that gray coat, not new for many a year,

Hides all that would like decent dress appear;
An old brown pony 'twas his will to ride,
Who shuffled onward, and from side to side;
A five-pound purchase, but so fat and sleek,
His very plenty made the creature weak.

    "Sir Denys Brand! and on so poor a steed!"
"Poor! it may be—such things I never heed:"
And who that youth behind, of pleasant mien,
Equipped as one who wishes to be seen,
Upon a horse, twice victor for a plate,
A noble hunter, bought at dearest rate?—
Him the lad fearing yet resolved to guide,
He curbs his spirit while he strokes his pride.

    "A handsome youth, Sir Denys; and a horse
Of finer figure never trod the course,—
Yours, without question?"—"Yes! I think a groom
Bought me the beast; I cannot say the sum
I ride him not; it is a foolish pride
Men have in cattle—but my people ride;
The boy is—hark ye, sirrah! what's your name?
Ay, Jacob, yes! I recollect—the same;
As I bethink me now, a tenant's son—
I think a tenant,—is your father one?"

    There was an idle boy who ran about,
And found his master's humble spirit out;
He would at awful distance snatch a look,
Then run away and hide him in some nook;
"For oh!" quoth he, "I dare not fix my sight
On him, his grandeur puts me in a fright;
Oh! Mister Jacob, when you wait on him,
Do you not quake and tremble every limb?"

    The Steward soon had orders—"Summers, see
That Sam be clothed, and let him wait on me."

Sir Denys died, bequeathing all affairs
In trust to Laughton's long-experienced cares;
Before a Guardian, and Sir Denys dead,
All rule and power devolved upon his head,
Numbers are call'd to govern, but in fact
Only the powerful and assuming act.

    Laughton, too wise to be a dupe to fame,
Cared not a whit of what descent he came,
Till he was rich; he then conceived the thought

To fish for pedigree, but never caught:
All his desire, when he was young and poor,
Was to advance; he never cared for more:
"Let me buy, sell, be factor, take a wife,
Take any road, to get along in life."
    Was he a miser then? a robber? foe
To those who trusted? a deceiver?—No!
He was ambitious; all his powers of mind
Were to one end controll'd, improved, combined;
Wit, learning, judgment, were, by his account,
Steps for the ladder he design'd to mount;
Such step was money: wealth was but his slave,
For power he gain'd it, and for power he gave:
Full well the Borough knows that he'd the art
Of bringing money to the surest mart;
Friends too were aids,—they led to certain ends,
Increase of power and claim on other friends.
A favourite step was marriage: then he gain'd
Seat in our Hall, and o'er his party reign'd;
Houses and land he bought, and long'd to buy,
But never drew the springs of purchase dry,
And thus at last they answer'd every call,
The failing found him ready for their fall:
He walks along the street, the mart, the quay,
And looks and mutters, "This belongs to me."
His passions all partook the general bent;
Interest inform'd him when he should resent,
How long resist, and on what terms relent:
In points where he determined to succeed,
In vain might reason or compassion plead;
But gain'd his point, he was the best of men,
'Twas loss of time to be vexatious then:
Hence he was mild to all men whom he led,
Of all who dared resist, the scourge and dread.
    Falsehood in him was not the useless lie
Of boasting pride or laughing vanity:
It was the gainful, the persuading art,
That made its way and won the doubting heart,
Which argued, soften'd, humbled, and prevail'd,
Nor was it tried till ev'ry truth had fail'd;
No sage on earth could more than he despise
Degrading, poor, unprofitable lies.
    Though fond of gain, and grieved by wanton waste,
To social parties he had no distaste;
With one presiding purpose in his view,

He sometimes could descend to trifle too!
Yet, in these moments, he had still the art
To ope the looks and close the guarded heart;
And, like the public host, has sometimes made
A grand repast, for which the guests have paid.

    At length, with power endued and wealthy grown,
Frailties and passions, long suppress'd, were shown:
Then to provoke him was a dangerous thing,
His pride would punish, and his temper sting;
His powerful hatred sought th' avenging hour,
And his proud vengeance struck with all his power,
Save when th' offender took a prudent way
The rising storm of fury to allay:
This might he do, and so in safety sleep,
By largely casting to the angry deep;
Or, better yet (its swelling force t'assuage),
By pouring oil of flattery on its rage.

    And now, of all the heart approved, possess'd,
Fear'd, favour'd, follow'd, dreaded, and caress'd,
He gently yields to one mellifluous joy,
The only sweet that is not found to cloy,
Bland adulation!—other pleasures pall
On the sick taste, and transient are they all;
But this one sweet has such enchanting power,
The more we take, the faster we devour:
Nauseous to those who must the dose apply,
And most disgusting to the standers-by;
Yet in all companies will Laughton feed,
Nor care how grossly men perform the deed.

    As gapes the nursling, or, what comes more near,
Some Friendly-Island chief, for hourly cheer;
When wives and slaves, attending round his seat,
Prepare by turns the masticated meat;
So for this master, husband, parent, friend,
His ready slaves their various efforts blend,
And, to their lord still eagerly inclined,
Pour the crude trash of a dependent mind.

    But let the Muse assign the man his due,
Worth he possess'd, nor were his virtues few:—
He sometimes help'd the injured in their cause;
His power and purse have back'd the failing laws;
He for religion has a due respect,
And all his serious notions, are correct;
Although he pray'd and languish'd for a son,
He grew resign'd when Heaven denied him one;

He never to this quiet mansion sends
Subject unfit, in compliment to friends;
Not so Sir Denys, who would yet protest
He always chose the worthiest and the best:
Not men in trade by various loss brought down,
But those whose glory once amazed the town,
Who their last guinea in their pleasures spent,
Yet never fell so low as to repent:
To these his pity he could largely deal,
Wealth they had known, and therefore want could feel.
    Three seats were vacant while Sir Denys reign'd,
And three such favourites their admission gain'd;
These let us view, still more to understand
The moral feelings of Sir Denys Brand. [6]

LETTER XIV.

INHABITANTS OF THE ALMS-HOUSE.

Sed quia caecus inest vitiis amor, omne futurum
Despicitur; suadent brevem praesentia fructum,
Et ruit in vetitum damni secura libido.
CLAUD.

Nunquam parvo contenta paratu,
Et quaesitorum terra pelagoque ciborum
Ambitiosa fames, et lautae gloria mensae.
LUCAN.

Et Luxus, populator Opum, tibi semper adhaerens,
Infelix humili gressu comitatur Egestas.
CLAUD.

Behold what blessing wealth to life can lend.
POPE.

LIFE OF BLANEY.

Blaney, a wealthy Heir, dissipated, and reduced to Poverty—His fortune restored by Marriage; again consumed—His Manner of Living in the West Indies—Recalled to a larger Inheritance—His more refined and expensive Luxuries—His method of quieting Conscience—Death of his Wife—Again become poor—His method of supporting Existence—His Ideas of Religion—His Habits and Connections when old—Admitted into the Alms-house.

OBSERVE that tall pale Veteran! what a look
Of shame and guilt!—who cannot read that book?
Misery and mirth are blended in his face,
Much innate vileness and some outward grace;
There wishes strong and stronger griefs are seen,
Looks ever changed, and never one serene:
Show not that manner, and these features all,
The serpent's cunning, and the sinner's fall?
　　Hark to that laughter!—'tis the way he takes
To force applause for each vile jest he makes;
Such is yon man, by partial favour sent
To these calm seats to ponder and repent.
　　Blaney, a wealthy heir at twenty-one,

At twenty-five was ruin'd and undone,
These years with grievous crimes we need not load,
He found his ruin in the common road!—
Gamed without skill, without inquiry bought,
Lent without love, and borrow'd without thought.
But, gay and handsome, he had soon the dower
Of a kind wealthy widow in his power:
Then he aspired to loftier flights of vice,
To singing harlots of enormous price:
He took a jockey in his gig to buy
A horse so valued that a duke was shy:
To gain the plaudits of the knowing few,
Gamblers and grooms, what would not Blaney do?
His dearest friend, at that improving age,
Was Hounslow Dick, who drove the western stage.

    Cruel he was not—if he left his wife,
He left her to her own pursuits in life;
Deaf to reports, to all expenses blind,
Profuse, not just, and careless, but not kind.

    Yet, thus assisted, ten long winters pass'd
In wasting guineas ere he saw his last;
Then he began to reason, and to feel
He could not dig, nor had he learn'd to steal;
And should he beg as long as he might live,
He justly fear'd that nobody would give:
But he could charge a pistol, and at will
All that was mortal, by a bullet kill:
And he was taught, by those whom he would call
Man's surest guides, that he was mortal all.

    While thus he thought, still waiting for the day
When he should dare to blow his brains away,
A place for him a kind relation found,
Where England's monarch ruled, but far from English ground:
He gave employ that might for bread suffice,
Correct his habits and restrain his vice.

    Here Blaney tried (what such man's miseries teach)
To find what pleasures were within his reach;
These he enjoy'd, though not in just the style
He once possess'd them in his native isle;
Congenial souls he found in every place,
Vice in all soils, and charms in every race:
His lady took the same amusing way,
And laugh'd at Time till he had turn'd them gray;
At length for England once again they steer'd,
By ancient views and new designs endear'd;

His kindred died, and Blaney now became
An heir to one who never heard his name.

    What could he now?—The man had tried before
The joys of youth, and they were joys no more;
To vicious pleasure he was still inclined,
But vice must now be season'd and refined;
Then as a swine he would on pleasure seize,
Now common pleasures had no power to please:
Beauty alone has for the vulgar charms,
He wanted beauty trembling with alarms:
His was no more a youthful dream of joy,
The wretch desired to ruin and destroy;
He bought indulgence with a boundless price,
Most pleased when decency bow'd down to vice,
When a fair dame her husband's honour sold,
And a frail countess play'd for Blaney's gold.

    "But did not conscience in her anger rise?"
Yes! and he learn'd her terrors to despise;
When stung by thought, to soothing books he fled,
And grew composed and harden'd as he read;
Tales of Voltaire, and essays gay and slight.
Pleased him, and shone with their phosphoric light;
Which, though it rose from objects vile and base,
Where'er it came threw splendour on the place,
And was that light which the deluded youth,
And this gray sinner, deem'd the light of truth.

    He different works for different cause admired,
Some fix'd his judgment, some his passions fired;
To cheer the mind and raise a dormant flame,
He had the books, decreed to lasting shame,
Which those who read are careful not to name:
These won to vicious act the yielding heart,
And then the cooler reasoners soothed the smart.

    He heard of Blount, and Mandeville, and Chubb,
How they the doctors of their day would drub;
How Hume had dwelt on Miracles so well,
That none would now believe a miracle;
And though he cared not works so grave to read,
He caught their faith, and sign'd the sinner's creed.
Thus was he pleased to join the laughing side,
Nor ceased the laughter when his lady died;
Yet was he kind and careful of her fame,
And on her tomb inscribed a virtuous name;
"A tender wife, respected, and so forth,"
The marble still bears witness to the worth.

He has some children, but he knows not where;
Something they cost, but neither love nor care;
A father's feelings he has never known,
His joys, his sorrows, have been all his own.
　　He now would build, and lofty seat he built,
And sought, in various ways, relief from guilt.
Restless, for ever anxious to obtain
Ease for the heart by ramblings of the brain,
He would have pictures, and of course a Taste,
And found a thousand means his wealth to waste.
Newmarket steeds he bought at mighty cost;
They sometimes won, but Blaney always lost.
　　Quick came his ruin, came when he had still
For life a relish, and in pleasure skill:
By his own idle reckoning he supposed
His wealth would last him till his life was closed;
But no! he found this final hoard was spent,
While he had years to suffer and repent.
Yet, at the last, his noble mind to show,
And in his misery how he bore the blow,
He view'd his only guinea, then suppress'd,
For a short time, the tumults in his breast,
And mov'd by pride, by habit, and despair,
Gave it an opera-bird to hum an air.
　　Come ye! who live for Pleasure, come, behold
A man of pleasure when he's poor and old;
When he looks back through life, and cannot find
A single action to relieve his mind;
When he looks forward, striving still to keep
A steady prospect of eternal sleep;
When not one friend is left, of all the train
Whom 'twas his pride and boast to entertain,—
Friends now employ'd from house to house to run,
And say, "Alas! poor Blaney is undone!"—
Those whom he shook with ardour by the hand,
By whom he stood as long as he could stand,
Who seem'd to him from all deception clear,
And who, more strange! might think themselves sincere.
　　Lo! now the hero shuffling through the town,
To hunt a dinner and to beg a crown;
To tell an idle tale, that boys may smile;
To bear a strumpet's billet-doux a mile;
To cull a wanton for a youth of wealth
(With reverend view to both his taste and health);
To be a useful, needy thing between

Fear and desire—the pander and the screen;
To flatter pictures, houses, horses, dress,
The wildest fashion, or the worst excess;
To be the gray seducer, and entice
Unbearded folly into acts of vice:
And then, to level every fence which law
And virtue fix to keep the mind in awe,
He first inveigles youth to walk astray,
Next prompts and soothes them in their fatal way,
Then vindicates the deed, and makes the mind his prey.

 Unhappy man! what pains he takes to state—
(Proof of his fear!) that all below is fate;
That all proceed in one appointed track,
Where none can stop, or take their journey back:
Then what is vice or virtue?—Yet he'll rail
At priests till memory and quotation fail;
He reads, to learn the various ills they've done,
And calls them vipers, every mother's son.

 He is the harlot's aid, who wheedling tries
To move her friend for vanity's supplies;
To weak indulgence he allures the mind,
Loth to be duped, but willing to be kind;
And if successful—what the labour pays?
He gets the friend's contempt and Chloe's praise,
Who, in her triumph, condescends to say,
"What a good creature Blaney was to-day!"

 Hear the poor demon when the young attend,
And willing ear to vile experience lend;
When he relates (with laughing, leering eye)
The tale licentious, mix'd with blasphemy:
No genuine gladness his narrations cause,
The frailest heart denies sincere applause;
And many a youth has turn'd him half aside,
And laugh'd aloud, the sign of shame to hide.

 Blaney, no aid in his vile cause to lose,
Buys pictures, prints, and a licentious Muse;
He borrows every help from every art,
To stir the passions and mislead the heart:
But from the subject let us soon escape,
Nor give this feature all its ugly shape;
Some to their crimes escape from satire owe;
Who shall describe what Blaney dares to show?

 While thus the man, to vice and passion slave,
Was, with his follies, moving to the grave,
The ancient ruler of this mansion died,

And Blaney boldly for the seat applied:
Sir Denys Brand, then guardian, join'd his suit:
"'Tis true," said he, "the fellow's quite a brute—
A very beast; but yet, with all his sin,
He has a manner—let the devil in."
They half complied, they gave the wish'd retreat,
But raised a worthier to the vacant seat.

  Thus forced on ways unlike each former way,
Thus led to prayer without a heart to pray,
He quits the gay and rich, the young and free,
Among the badge-men with a badge to be:
He sees an humble tradesman rais'd to rule
The gray-beard pupils of this moral school;
Where he himself, an old licentious boy,
Will nothing learn, and nothing can enjoy;
In temp'rate measures he must eat and drink,
And, pain of pains! must live alone and think.

  In vain, by fortune's smiles, thrice affluent made,
Still has he debts of ancient date unpaid;
Thrice into penury by error thrown,
Not one right maxim has he made his own;
The old men shun him,—some his vices hate,
And all abhor his principles and prate;
Nor love nor care for him will mortal show,
Save a frail sister in the female row.

LETTER XV.

INHABITANTS OF THE ALMS-HOUSE.

She early found herself mistress of herself. All she did was right; all she said was admired. Early, very early, did she dismiss blushes from her cheek: she could not blush because she could not doubt; and silence, whatever was her subject, was as much a stranger to her as diffidence.

RICHARDSON.

Quo fugit Venus! heu! Quove color? decens
Quo motus? Quid habes illius, illius,
Quae spirabat amores,
Quae me surpuerat mihi?
HORACE, Odes.

CLELIA.

Her lively and pleasant Manners—Her Reading and Decision—Her Intercourse with different Classes of Society—Her kind of Character—The favoured Lover—Her Management of him: his of her—After one Period, Clelia with an Attorney; her Manner and Situation there—Another such Period, when her Fortune still declines—Mistress of an Inn—A Widow—Another such Interval: she becomes poor and infirm, but still vain and frivolous—The fallen Vanity—Admitted into the House: meets Blaney.

WE had a sprightly nymph—in every town
Are some such sprights, who wander up and down;
She had her useful arts, and could contrive,
In Time's despite, to stay at twenty-five;—
"Here will I rest; move on, thou lying year,
This is mine age, and I will rest me here."
    Arch was her look, and she had pleasant ways
Your good opinion of her heart to raise;
Her speech was lively, and with ease express'd,
And well she judged the tempers she address'd:
If some soft stripling had her keenness felt,
She knew the way to make his anger melt;
Wit was allow'd her, though but few could bring
Direct example of a witty thing;
'Twas that gay, pleasant, smart, engaging speech,
Her beaux admired, and just within their reach;

Not indiscreet, perhaps, but yet more free
Than prudish nymphs allow their wit to be.

    Novels and plays, with poems old and new,
Were all the books our nymph attended to;
Yet from the press no treatise issued forth,
But she would speak precisely of its worth.

    She with the London stage familiar grew,
And every actor's name and merit knew;
She told how this or that their part mistook,
And of the rival Romeos gave the look;
Of either house 'twas hers the strength to see,
Then judge with candour—"Drury Lane for me."
What made this knowledge, what this skill complete?
A fortnight's visit in Whitechapel Street.

    Her place in life was rich and poor between,
With those a favourite, and with these a queen;
She could her parts assume, and condescend
To friends more humble while an humble friend;
And thus a welcome, lively guest could pass,
Threading her pleasant way from class to class.

    "Her reputation?"—That was like her wit,
And seem'd her manner and her state to fit;
Sometking there was—what, none presumed to say;
Clouds lightly passing on a smiling day,—
Whispers and hints which went from ear to ear,
And mix'd reports no judge on earth could clear.
But of each sex a friendly number press'd
To joyous banquets this alluring guest:
There, if indulging mirth, and freed from awe,
If pleasing all, and pleased with all she saw,
Her speech was free, and such as freely dwelt
On the same feelings all around her felt;
Or if some fond presuming favourite tried
To come so near as once to be denied;
Yet not with brow so stern or speech so nice,
But that he ventured on denial twice:—
If these have been, and so has Scandal taught,
Yet Malice never found the proof she sought.

    But then came one, the Lovelace of his day,
Rich, proud, and crafty, handsome, brave, and gay;
Yet loved he not those labour'd plans and arts,
But left the business to the ladies' hearts,
And when he found them in a proper train
He thought all else superfluous and vain:
But in that training he was deeply taught,

And rarely fail'd of gaining all he sought;
He knew how far directly on to go,
How to recede and dally to and fro;
How to make all the passions his allies,
And, when he saw them in contention rise,
To watch the wrought-up heart, and conquer by surprise.
     Our heroine fear'd him not; it was her part
To make sure conquest of such gentle heart—
Of one so mild and humble; for she saw
In Henry's eye a love chastised by awe.
Her thoughts of virtue were not all sublime,
Nor virtuous all her thoughts; 'twas now her time
To bait each hook, in every way to please,
And the rich prize with dext'rous hand to seize.
She had no virgin-terrors; she could stray
In all love's maze, nor fear to lose her way;
Nay, could go near the precipiee, nor dread
A failing caution or a giddy head;
She'd fix her eyes upon the roaring flood,
And dance upon the brink where danger stood.
     'Twas nature all, she judged, in one so young,
To drop the eye and falter in the tongue;
To be about to take, and then command
His daring wish, and only view the hand:
Yes! all was nature; it became a maid
Of gentle soul t'encourage love afraid;—
He, so unlike the confident and bold,
Would fly in mute despair to find her cold:
The young and tender germ requires the sun
To make it spread; it must be smiled upon.
Thus the kind virgin gentle means devised,
To gain a heart so fond, a hand so prized;
More gentle still she grew, to change her way
Would cause confusion, danger, and delay:
Thus (an increase of gentleness her mode),
She took a plain, unvaried, certain road,
And every hour believed success was near,
Till there was nothing left to hope or fear.
     It must be own'd that, in this strife of hearts,
Man has advantage—has superior arts:
The lover's aim is to the nymph unknown,
Nor is she always certain of her own;
Or has her fears, nor these can so disguise,
But he who searches reads them in her eyes,
In the avenging frown, in the regretting sighs:

These are his signals, and he learns tb steer
The straighter course whenever they appear.

    "Pass we ten years, and what was Clelia's fate?"
At an attorney's board alert she sate,
Not legal mistress: he with other men
Once sought her hand, but other views were then;
And when he knew he might the bliss command,
He other blessing sought without the hand;
For still he felt alive the lambent flame,
And offer'd her a home,—and home she came.
    There, though her higher friendships lived no more,
She loved to speak of what she shared before—
"Of the dear Lucy, heiress of the hall,—
Of good Sir Peter,—of their annual ball,
And the fair countess!—Oh! she loved them all!"
The humbler clients of her friend would stare,
The knowing smile,—but neither caused her care;
She brought her spirits to her humble state,
And soothed with idle dreams her frowning fate.

    "Ten summers pass'd?, and how was Clelia then?"—
Alas! she suffer d' in this trying ten;
The pair had parted: who to him attend,
Must judge the nymph unfaithful to her friend;
But who on her would equal faith bestow,
Would think him rash,—and surely she must know.
    Then as a matron Clelia taught a school,
But nature gave not talents fit for rule:
Yet now, though marks of wasting years were seen,
Some touch of sorrow, some attack of spleen;
Still there was life, a spirit quick and gay,
And lively speech and elegant array.
    The Griffin's landlord these allured so far,
He made her mistress of his heart and bar;
He had no idle retrospective whim,
Till she was his, her deeds concern'd not him:
So far was well,—but Clelia thought not fit
(In all the Griffin needed) to submit:
Gaily to dress and in the bar preside,
Soothed the poor spirit of degraded pride;
But cooking, waiting, welcoming a crew

Of noisy guests, were arts she never knew:
Hence daily wars, with temporary truce,
His vulgar insult, and her keen abuse;
And as their spirits wasted in the strife,
Both took the Griffin's ready aid of life;
But she with greater prudence—Harry tried
More powerful aid, and in the trial died;
Yet drew down vengeance: in no distant time,
Th' insolvent Griffin struck his wings sublime;—
Forth from her palace walk'd th' ejected queen,
And show'd to frowning fate a look serene;
Gay spite of time, though poor, yet well attired,
Kind without love, and vain if not admired.

    Another term is past; ten other years
In various trials, troubles, views, and fears:
Of these some pass'd in small attempts at trade;
Houses she kept for widowers lately made;
For now she said, "They'll miss th' endearing friend,
And I'll be there the soften'd heart to bend:"
And true a part was done as Clelia plann'd—
The heart was soften'd, but she miss'd the hand;
She wrote a novel, and Sir Denys said
The dedication was the best he read;
But Edgeworths, Smiths, and Radcliffes so engross'd
The public ear, that all her pains were lost.
To keep a toy-shop was attempt the last,
There too she fail'd, and schemes and hopes were past.
    Now friendless, sick, and old, and wanting bread,
The first-born tears of fallen pride were shed—
True, bitter tears; and yet that wounded pride,
Among the poor, for poor distinctions sigh'd.
Though now her tales were to her audience fit;
Though loud her tones, and vulgar grown her wit,
Though now her dress—(but let me not explain
The piteous patchwork of the needy-vain,
The flirtish form to coarse materials lent,
And one poor robe through fifty fashions sent);
Though all within was sad, without was mean,—
Still 'twas her wish, her comfort, to be seen:
She would to plays on lowest terms resort,
Where once her box was to the beaux a court;
And, strange delight! to that same house where she

Join'd in the dance, all gaiety and glee,
Now with the menials crowding to the wall
She'd see, not share, the pleasures of the ball,
And with degraded vanity unfold,
How she too triumph'd in the years of old.
To her poor friends 'tis now her pride to tell,
On what a height she stood before she fell;
At church she points to one tall seat, and "There
We sat," she cries, "when my papa was mayor."
Not quite correct in what she now relates,
She alters persons, and she forges dates;
And finding memory's weaker help decay'd,
She boldly calls invention to her aid.

    Touch'd by the pity he had felt before,
For her Sir Denys oped the Alms-house door:
"With all her faults," he said, "the woman knew
How to distinguish—had a manner too;
And, as they say she is allied to some
In decent station—let the creature come."

    Here she and Blaney meet, and take their view
Of all the pleasures they would still pursue:
Hour after hour they sit, and nothing hide
Of vices past; their follies are their pride;
What to the sober and the cool are crimes,
They boast—exulting in those happy times;
The darkest deeds no indignation raise,
The purest virtue never wins their praise;
But still they on their ancient joys dilate,
Still with regret departed glories state,
And mourn their grievous fall, and curse their rigorous fate.

LETTER XVI.

INHABITANTS OF THE ALMS-HOUSE.

Thou art the Knight of the Burning Lamp: if thou wast any way given to virtue, I would swear by thy face; my oath should be by tnis fire. Oh! thou'rt a perpetual triumph, thou hast saved me a thousand marks in links and torches, walking in a night betwixt tavern and tavern.

SHAKESPEARE, Henry IV.

Ebrietas tibi fida comes, tibi Luxus, et atris
Circa te semper volitans Infamia pennis.

SILVIUS ITALICUS.

BENBOW.

SEE! yonder badgeman with that glowing face,
A meteor shining in this sober place!
Vast sums were paid, and many years were past,
Ere gems so rich around their radiance cast!
Such was the fiery front that Bardolph wore,
Guiding his master to the tavern door;
There first that meteor rose, and there alone,
In its due place, the rich effulgence shone:
But this strange fire the seat of peace invades
And shines portentous in these solemn shades.
    Benbow, a boon companion, long approved
By jovial sets, and (as he thought) beloved,
Was judged as one to joy and friendship prone,
And deem'd injurious to himself alone:
Gen'rous and free, he paid but small regard
To trade, and fail'd; and some declared "'twas hard:"
These were his friends—his foes conceived the case
Of common kind; he sought and found disgrace:
The reasoning few, who neither scorn'd nor loved,
His feelings pitied and his faults reproved.
    Benbow, the father, left possessions fair,
A worthy name and business to his heir;
Benbow, the son, those fair possessions sold,
And lost his credit, while he spent the gold:
He was a jovial trader: men enjoy'd
The night with him; his day was unemployed;
So when his credit and his cash were spent,
Here, by mistaken pity, he was sent;

Of late he came, with passions unsubdued,
And shared and cursed the hated solitude,
Where gloomy thoughts arise, where grievous cares intrude.
        Known but in drink,—he found an easy friend,
Well pleased his worth and honour to commend:
And thus inform'd, the guardian of the trust
Heard the applause, and said the claim was just,
A worthy soul! unfitted for the strife,
Care, and contention of a busy life;—
Worthy, and why?—that o'er the midnight bowl
He made his friend the partner of his soul,
And any man his friend:—then thus in glee,
"I speak my mind, I love the truth," quoth he;
Till 'twas his fate that useful truth to find,
'Tis sometimes prudent not to speak the mind.
        With wine inflated, man is all upblown,
And feels a power which he believes his own;
With fancy soaring to the skies, he thinks
His all the virtues all the while he drinks;
But when the gas from the balloon is gone,
When sober thoughts and serious cares come on,
Where then the worth that in himself he found?
Vanish'd—and he sank grov'lling on the ground.
        Still some conceit will Benbow's mind inflate,
Poor as he is,—'tis pleasant to relate
The joys he once possess'd—it soothes his present state.
        Seated with some gray beadsman, he regrets
His former feasting, though it swell'd his debts;
Topers once famed, his friends in earlier days,
Well he describes, and thinks description praise:
Each hero's worth with much delight he paints;
Martyrs they were, and he would make them saints.
"Alas! alas!" Old England now may say,
"My glory withers; it has had its day:
We're fallen on evil times; men read and think;
Our bold forefathers loved to fight and drink.
"Then lived the good 'Squire Asgill—what a change
Has death and fashion shown us at the Grange!
He bravely thought it best became his rank
That all his tenants and his tradesmen drank;
He was delighted from his favourite room
To see them 'cross the park go daily home
Praising aloud the liquor and the host,
And striving who should venerate him most.
        "No pride had he, and there was difference small

Between the master's and the servant's hall:
And here or there the guests were welcome all.
Of Heaven's free gifts he took no special care,
He never quarrell'd for a simple hare;
But sought, by giving sport, a sportman's name,
Himself a poacher, though at other game:
He never planted nor inclosed—his trees
Grew, like himself, untroubled and at ease:
Bounds of all kinds he hated, and had felt
Chok'd and imprison'd in a modern belt,
Which some rare genius now has twined about
The good old house, to keep old neighbours out.
Along his valleys, in the evening-hours,
The borough-damsels stray'd to gather flowers,
Or by the brakes and brushwood of the park,
To take their pleasant rambles in the dark.

    "Some prudes, of rigid kind, forbore to call
On the kind females—favourites at the hall;
But better nature saw, with much delight,
The different orders of mankind unite:
'Twas schooling pride to see the footman wait,
Smile on his sister and receive her plate.

    "His worship ever was a churchman true,
He held in scorn the Methodistic crew;
'May God defend the Church, and save the King,'
He'd pray devoutly and divinely sing.
Admit that he the holy day would spend
As priests approved not, still he was a friend:
Much then I blame the preacher, as too nice,
To call such trifles by the name of vice;
Hinting, though gently and with cautious speech,
Of good example—'tis their trade to preach.
But still 'twas pity, when the worthy 'squire
Stuck to the church, what more could they require?
'Twas almost joining that fanatic crew,
To throw such morals at his honour's pew;
A weaker man, had he been so reviled,
Had left the place—he only swore and smiled.

    "But think, ye rectors and ye curates, think,
Who are your friends, and at their frailties wink;
Conceive not—mounted on your Sunday-throne,
Your firebrands fall upon your foes alone;
They strike your patrons—and should all withdraw,
In whom your wisdoms may discern a flaw,
You would the flower of all your audience lose,

And spend your crackers on their empty pews.
　　"The father dead, the son has found a wife,
And lives a formal, proud, unsocial life;—
The lands are now inclosed; the tenants all,
Save at a rent-day, never see the hall;
No lass is suffer'd o'er the walks to come,
And if there's love, they have it all at home.
　　"Oh! could the ghost of our good 'squire arise,
And see such change; would it believe its eyes?
Would it not glide about from place to place,
And mourn the manners of a feebler race?
At that long table, where the servants found
Mirth and abundance while the year went round;
Where a huge pollard on the winter-fire,
At a huge distance made them all retire;
Where not a measure in the room was kept,
And but one rule—they tippled till they slept—
There would it see a pale old hag preside,
A thing made up of stinginess and pride;
Who carves the meat, as if the flesh could feel;
Careless whose flesh must miss the plenteous meal;
Here would the ghost a small coal-fire behold,
Not fit to keep one body from the cold;
Then would it flit to higher rooms, and stay
To view a dull, dress'd company at play;
All the old comfort, all the genial fare
For ever gone! how sternly would it stare:
And though it might not to their view appear,
'Twould cause among them lassitude and fear
Then wait to see—where he delight has seen—
The dire effect of fretfulness and spleen.
　　"Such were the worthies of these better days;
We had their blessings—they shall have our praise.
　　"Of Captain Dowling would you hear me speak?
I'd sit and sing his praises for a week:
He was a man, and man-like all his joy,—
I'm led to question was he ever boy?
Beef was his breakfast;—if from sea and salt,
It relish'd better with his wine of malt;
Then, till he dined, if walking in or out,
Whether the gravel teased him or the gout,
Though short in wind and flannell'd every limb,
He drank with all who had concerns with him:
Whatever trader, agent, merchant, came,
They found him ready, every hour the same;

Whatever liquors might between them pass,
He took them all, and never balk'd his glass:
Nay, with the seamen working in the ship,
At their request, he'd share the grog and flip.
But in the club-room was his chief delight,
And punch the favourite liquor of the night;
Man after man they from the trial shrank,
And Dowling ever was the last who drank:
Arrived at home, he, ere he sought his bed,
With pipe and brandy would compose his head,
Then half an hour was o'er the news beguiled,
When he retired as harmless as a child.
Set but aside the gravel and the gout.
And breathing short—his sand ran fairly out.

    "At fifty-five we lost him—after that
Life grows insipid and its pleasures flat;
He had indulged in all that man can have,
He did not drop a dotard to his grave;
Still to the last, his feet upon the chair,
With rattling lungs now gone beyond repair;
When on each feature death had fix'd his stamp,
And not a doctor could the body vamp;
Still at the last, to his beloved bowl
He clung, and cheer'd the sadness of his soul;
For though a man may not have much to fear,
Yet death looks ugly when the view is near:
—'I go,' he said, 'but still my friends shall say,
'Twas as a man—I did not sneak away;
An honest life with worthy souls I've spent,—
Come, fill my glass;' he took it and he went.

    "Poor Dolly Murray!—I might live to see
My hundredth year, but no such lass as she.
Easy by nature, in her humour gay,
She chose her comforts, ratafia and play:
She loved the social game, the decent glass,
And was a jovial, friendly, laughing lass;
We sat not then at Whist demure and still,
But pass'd the pleasant hours at gay Quadrille:
Lame in her side, we plac'd her in her seat,
Her hands were free, she cared not for her feet;
As the game ended, came the glass around
(So was the loser cheer'd, the winner crown'd).
Mistress of secrets, both the young and old
In her confided—not a tale she told;
Love never made impression on her mind,

She held him weak, and all his captives blind;
She suffer'd no man her free soul to vex,
Free from the weakness of her gentle sex;
One with whom ours unmoved conversing sate,
In cool discussion or in free debate.
    "Once in her chair we'd placed the good old lass,
Where first she took her preparation-glass;
By lucky thought she'd been that day at prayers,
And long before had fix'd her small affairs,
So all was easy—on her cards she cast
A smiling look; I saw the thought that pass'd:
'A king,' she call'd—though conscious of her skill.
'Do more,' I answer'd—'More,' she said, 'I will;'
And more she did—cards answer'd to her call,
She saw the mighty to her mightier fall:
'A vole! a vole!' she cried, "tis fairly won,
My game is ended and my work is done;'—
This said, she gently, with a single sigh,
Died as one taught and practised how to die.
    "Such were the dead-departed; I survive,
To breathe in pain among the dead-alive."
The bell then call'd these ancient men to pray,
"Again!" said Benbow,—"tolls it every day?
Where is the life I led?"—He sigh'd and walk'd his way. [7]

LETTER XVII.

Blessed is he that considereth the poor: the Lord will deliver him in time of trouble.

PSALM xli, 1.

Quas dederis, solas semper habebis opes.

MARTIAL.

Nil negat, et sese vel non poscentibus offert.

CLAUDIAN.

Decipias alios verbis voltuque benigno;
Nam mihi jam notus dissimulator eris.

MARTIAL.

THE HOSPITAL AND GOVERNORS.

Christian Charity anxious to provide for future as well as present Miseries—Hence the Hospital for the Diseased—Description of a recovered Patient—The Building: how erected—The Patrons and Governors—Eusebius—The more active Manager of Business, a moral and correct Contributor—One of different Description—Good, the Result, however intermixed with Imperfection.

AN ardent spirit dwells with Christian love,
The eagle's vigour in the pitying dove;
'Tis not enough that we with sorrow sigh,
That we the wants of pleading man supply,
That we in sympathy with sufferers feel,
Nor hear a grief without a wish to heal;
Not these suffice—to sickness, pain, and woe,
The Christian spirit loves with aid to go;
Will not be sought, waits not for want to plead,
But seeks the duty—nay, prevents the need;
Her utmost aid to every ill applies,
And plans relief for coining miseries.
　　Hence yonder Building rose: on either side
Far stretch'd the wards, all airy, warm, and wide;
And every ward has beds by comfort spread,
And smooth'd for him who suffers on the bed:
There all have kindness, most relief,—for some
Is cure complete,—it is the sufferer's home:
Fevers and chronic ills, corroding pains,

Each accidental mischief man sustains;
Fractures and wounds, and wither'd limbs and lame,
With all that, slow or sudden, vex our frame,
Have here attendance—here the sufferers lie,
(Where love and science every aid apply,)
And heal'd with rapture live, or soothed by comfort die.

See! one relieved from anguish, and to-day
Allow'd to walk and look an hour away;
Two months confined by fever, frenzy, pain,
He comes abroad and is himself again:
'Twas in the spring, when carried to the place,
The snow fell down and melted in his face.

'Tis summer now; all objects gay and new,
Smiling alike the viewer and the view:
He stops as one unwilling to advance,
Without another and another glance;
With what a pure and simple joy he sees
Those sheep and cattle browsing at their ease;
Easy himself, there's nothing breathes or moves,
But he would cherish—all that lives he loves:
Observing every ward as round he goes,
He thinks what pain, what danger they inclose;
Warm in his wish for all who suffer there,
At every view he meditates a prayer:
No evil counsels in his breast abide,
There joy, and love, and gratitude reside.

The wish that Roman necks in one were found,
That he who form'd the wish might deal the wound,
This man had never heard; but of the kind,
Is that desire which rises in his mind;
He'd have all English hands (for further he
Cannot conceive extends our charity),
All but his own, in one right-hand to grow,
And then what hearty shake would he bestow.

"How rose the Building?"—Piety first laid
A strong foundation, but she wanted aid;
To Wealth unwieldy was her prayer address'd,
Who largely gave, and she the donor bless'd:
Unwieldy Wealth then to his couch withdrew,
And took the sweetest sleep he ever knew.

Then busy Vanity sustained her part,
"And much," she said, "it moved her tender heart;
To her all kinds of man's distress were known,
And all her heart adopted as its own."
Then Science came—his talents he display'd,

And Charity with joy the dome survey'd;
Skill, Wealth, and Vanity, obtain the fame,
And Piety, the joy that makes no claim.

    Patrons there are, and Governors, from, whom
The greater aid and guiding orders come;
Who voluntary cares and labours take,
The sufferers' servants for the service' sake;
Of these a, part I give you—but a part,—
Some hearts are hidden, some have not a heart.

    First let me praise—for so I best shall paint
That pious moralist, that reasoning saint!
Can I of worth like thine, Eusebius, speak?
The man is willing, but the Muse is weak;—
'Tis thine to wait on woe! to soothe! to heal!
With learning social, and polite with zeal:
In thy pure breast although the passions dwell,
They're train'd by virtue, and no more rebel;
But have so long been active on her side,
That passion now might be itself the guide.

    Law, conscience, honour, all obey'd; all give
Th' approving voice, and make it bliss to live;
While faith, when life can nothing more supply,
Shall strengthen hope, and make it bliss to die.

    He preaches, speaks, and writes with manly sense,
No weak neglect, no labour'd eloquence;
Goodness and wisdom are in all his ways,
The rude revere him and the wicked praise.

    Upon humility his virtues grow,
And tower so high because so fix'd below;
As wider spreads the oak his boughs around,
When deeper with his roots he digs the solid ground.

    By him, from ward to ward, is every aid
The sufferer needs, with every care convey'd:
Like the good tree he brings his treasure forth,
And, like the tree, unconscious of his worth:
Meek as the poorest Publican is he,
And strict as lives the straitest Pharisee;
Of both, in him unite the better part,
The blameless conduct and the humble heart.

    Yet he escapes not; he, with some, is wise
In carnal things, and loves to moralize:
Others can doubt if all that Christian care
Has not its price—there's something he may share:
But this and ill severer he sustains,
As gold the fire, and as unhurt remains;

When most reviled, although he feels the smart,
It wakes to nobler deeds the wounded heart,
As the rich olive, beaten for its fruit,
Puts forth at every bruise a bearing shoot.

 A second friend we have, whose care and zeal
But few can equal—few indeed can feel;
He lived a life obscure, and profits made
In the coarse habits of a vulgar trade.
His brother, master of a hoy, he loved
So well, that he the calling disapproved:
"Alas! poor Tom!" the landman oft would sigh
When the gale freshen'd and the waves ran high;
And when they parted, with a tear he'd say,
"No more adventure!—here in safety stay."
Nor did he feign; with more than half he had
He would have kept the seaman, and been glad.
Alas! how few resist, when strongly tried—
A rich relation's nearer kinsman died;
He sicken'd, and to him the landman went,
And all his hours with cousin Ephraim spent.
This Thomas heard, and cared not: "I," quoth he,
"Have one in port upon the watch for me."
So Ephraim died, and when the will was shown,
Isaac, the landman, had the whole his own:
Who to his brother sent a moderate purse,
Which he return'd in anger, with his curse;
Then went to sea, and made his grog so strong,
He died before he could forgive the wrong.

 The rich man built a house, both large and high,
He enter'd in and set him down to sigh;
He planted ample woods and gardens fair,
And walk'd with anguish and compunction there:
The rich man's pines, to every friend a treat,
He saw with pain, and he refused to eat;
His daintiest food, his richest wines, were all
Turn'd by remorse to vinegar and gall:
The softest down by living body press'd,
The rich man bought, and tried to take his rest;
But care had thorns upon his pillow spread,
And scatter'd sand and nettles in his bed:
Nervous he grew,—would often sigh and groan,
He talk'd but little, and he walk'd alone;
Till by his priest convinced, that from one deed
Of genuine love would joy and health proceed,
He from that time with care and zeal began

To seek and soothe the grievous ills of man;
And as his hands their aid to grief apply,
He learns to smile and he forgets to sigh.

Now he can drink his wine and taste his food,
And feel the blessings Heav'n has dealt are good;
And, since the suffering seek the rich man's door,
He sleeps as soundly as when young and poor.

Here much he gives—is urgent more to gain;
He begs—rich beggars seldom sue in vain:
Preachers most famed he moves, the crowd to move,
And never wearies in the work of love:
He rules all business, settles all affairs;
He makes collections, he directs repairs;
And if he wrong'd one brother,—Heav'n forgive
The man by whom so many brethren live.

Then, 'mid our Signatures, a name appears,
Of one for wisdom famed above his years;
And these were forty: he was from his youth
A patient searcher after useful truth:
To language little of his time he gave,
To science less, nor was the Muse's slave;
Sober and grave, his college sent him down,
A fair example for his native town.
Slowly he speaks, and with such solemn air,
You'd thing a Socrates or Solon there;
For though a Christian, he's disposed to draw
His rules from reason's and from nature's law.
"Know," he exclaims, "my fellow mortals, know,
Virtue alone is happiness below;
And what is virtue? prudence first to choose
Life's real good,—the evil to refuse;
Add justice then, the eager hand to hold,
To curb the lust of power and thirst of gold;
Join temp'rance next, that cheerful health ensures.
And fortitude unmoved, that conquers or endures."

He speaks, and lo!—the very man you see,
Prudent and temperate, just and patient he,
By prudence taught his worldly wealth to keep,
No folly wastes, no avarice swells the heap:
He no man's debtor, no man's patron lives;
Save sound advice, he neither asks nor gives;
By no vain thoughts or erring fancy sway'd,

His words are weighty, or at least are weigh'd;
Temp'rate in every place—abroad, at home,
Thence will applause, and hence will profit come
And health from either—he in time prepares
For sickness, age, and their attendant cares,
But not for fancy's ills;—he never grieves
For love that wounds or friendship that deceives.
His patient soul endures what Heav'n ordains,
But neither feels nor fears ideal pains.

    "Is aught then wanted in a man so wise?"—
Alas!—I think he wants infirmities;
He wants the ties that knit us to our kind—
The cheerful, tender, soft, complacent mind.
That would the feelings, which he dreads, excite,
And make the virtues he approves delight;
What dying martyrs, saints, and patriots feel,
The strength of action and the warmth of zeal.

    Again attend!—and see a man whose cares
Are nicely placed on either world's affairs,—
Merchant and saint; 'tis doubtful if he knows
To which account he most regard bestows;
Of both he keeps his ledger:—there he reads
Of gainful ventures and of godly deeds;
There all he gets or loses find a place,
A lucky bargain and a lack of grace.

    The joys above this prudent man invite
To pay his tax—devotion!—day and night;
The pains of hell his timid bosom awe,
And force obedience to the church's law:
Hence that continual thought,—that solemn air,
Those sad good works, and that laborious prayer.

    All these (when conscience, waken'd and afraid,
To think how avarice calls and is obey'd)
He in his journal finds, and for his grief
Obtains the transient opium of relief.

    "Sink not, my soul!—my spirit, rise and look
O'er the fair entries of this precious book:
Here are the sins, our debts;—this fairer side
Has what to carnal wish our strenetb denied;
Has those religious duties every day
Paid,—which so few upon the Sabbath pay;
Here too are conquests over frail desires,
Attendance due on all the church requires;
Then alms I give—for I believe the word
Of holy writ, and lend unto the Lord,

And if not all th' importunate demand,
The fear of want restrains my ready hand:
—Behold! what sums I to the poor resign,
Sums placed in Heaven's own book, as well as mine:
Rest then, my spirit!—fastings, prayers, and alms,
Will soon suppress these idly-raised alarms,
And weigh'd against our frailties, set in view
A noble balance in our favour due:
Add that I yearly here affix my name,
Pledge for large payment—not from love of fame,
But to make peace within;—that peace to make,
"What sums I lavish! and what gains forsake!
Cheer up, my heart! let's cast off every doubt,
Pray without dread, and place our money out."
    Such the religion of a mind that steers
Its way to bliss, between its hopes and fears;
Whose passions in due bounds each other keep,
And thus subdued, they murmur till they sleep;
Whose virtues all their certain limits know,
Like well-dried herbs that neither fade nor grow;
Who for success and safety ever tries,
And with both worlds alternately complies.
    Such are the Guardians of this bless'd estate,
Whate'er without, they're praised within the gate;
That they are men, and have their faults, is true;
But here their worth alone appears in view:
The Muse indeed, who reads the very breast,
Has something of the secrets there express'd,
But yet in charity;—and when she sees
Such means for joy or comfort, health or ease,
And knows how much united minds effect,
She almost dreads their failings to detect;
But Truth commands:—in man's erroneous kind,
Virtues and frailties mingle in the mind,
Happy!—when fears to public spirit move,
And even vices do the work of love. [8]

LETTER XVIII.

Bene paupertas
Humili tecto contenta latet.
                    SENECA.

Omnes quibu' res sunt minu' secundae, magi' sunt, nescio quo modo,
Suspiciosi; ad contumeliam omnia accipiunt magis;
Propter suam impotentiam se semper credunt negligi.
                                        TEPENT.

Show not to the poor thy pride,
Let their home a cottage be;
Nor the feeble body hide
In a palace fit for thee;
Let him not about him see
Lofty ceilings, ample halls,
Or a gate his boundary be,
Where nor friend or kinsman calls.

Let him not one walk behold,
That only one which he must tread,
Nor a chamber large and cold,
Where the aged and sick are led;
Better far his humble shed,
Humble sheds of neighbours by,
And the old and tatter'd bed,
Where he sleeps and hopes to die.

To quit of torpid sluggishness the cave,
And from the pow'rful arms of sloth be free,
'Tis rising from the dead—Alas! it cannot be.
                                        THOMSON.

THE POOR AND THEIR DWELLINGS. {9}

The Method of treating the Borough Paupers—Many maintained at
their own Dwellings—Some Characters of the poor—The
Schoolmistress, when aged—The Idiot—The poor Sailor—The
declined Tradesman and his Companion—This contrasted with the
Maintenance of the Poor in a common Mansion erected by the
Hundred—The Objections to this Method: Not Want, nor Cruelty, but
the necessary evils of this Mode—What they are—Instances of the
Evil—A Return to the Borough Poor—The Dwellings of these—The

Lanes and Byways—No Attention here paid to Convenience—The Pools in the Pathways—Amusements of Sea-port Children—The Town Flora—Herbs on Walls and vacant Spaces—A female Inhabitant of an Alley—A large Building let to several poor Inhabitants—Their Manners and Habits.

YES! we've our Borough-vices, and I know
How far they spread, how rapidly they grow;
Yet think not virtue quits the busy place,
Nor charity, the virtues crown and grace.
    "Our Poor, how feed we?"—To the most we give
A weekly dole, and at their homes they live;—
Others together dwell,—but when they come
To the low roof, they see a kind of home,
A social people whom they've ever known,
With their own thoughts, and manners like their own.
    At her old house, her dress, her air the same,
I see mine ancient Letter-loving dame:
"Learning, my child," said she "shall fame command;
Learning is better worth than house or land—
For houses perish, lands are gone and spent;
In learning then excel, for that's most excellent."
    "And what her learning?" 'Tis with awe to look
In every verse throughout one sacred book;
From this her joy, her hope, her peace is sought;
This she has learned, and she is nobly taught.
    If aught of mine have gain'd the public ear;
If RUTLAND deigns these humble Tales to hear;
If critics pardon what my friends approved;
Can I mine ancient Widow pass unmoved?
Shall I not think what pains the matron took,
When first I trembled o'er the gilded book?
How she, all patient, both at eve and morn,
Her needle pointed at the guarding horn;
And how she soothed me, when, with study sad,
I labour'd on to reach the final zad?
Shall I not grateful still the dame survey,
And ask the Muse the poet's debt to pay?
    Nor I alone, who hold a trifler's pen,
But half our bench of wealthy, weighty men,
Who rule our Borough, who enforce our laws;
They own the matron as the leading cause,
And feel the pleasing debt, and pay the just applause:
To her own house is borne the week's supply;
There she in credit lives, there hopes in peace to die.

With her a harmless Idiot we behold,
Who hoards up silver shells for shining gold:
These he preserves, with unremitted care,
To buy a seat, and reign the Borough's mayor:
Alas!—who could th' ambitious changeling tell,
That what he sought our rulers dared to sell?

    Near these a Sailor, in that hut of thatch
(A fish-boat's cabin is its nearest match),
Dwells, and the dungeon is to him a seat,
Large as he wishes—in his view complete:
A lockless coffer and a lidless hutch
That hold his stores, have room for twice as much:
His one spare shirt, long glass, and iron box,
Lie all in view; no need has he for locks:
Here he abides, and, as our strangers pass,
He shows the shipping, he presents the glass;
He makes (unask'd) their ports and business known,
And (kindly heard) turns quickly to his own,
Of noble captains, heroes every one,—
You might as soon have made the steeple run;
And then his messmates, if you're pleased to stay,
He'll one by one the gallant souls display,
And as the story verges to an end,
He'll wind from deed to deed, from friend to friend;
He'll speak of those long lost, the brave of old,
As princes gen'rous and as heroes bold;
Then will his feelings rise, till you may trace
Gloom, like a cloud, frown o'er his manly face,—
And then a tear or two, which sting his pride;
These he will dash indignantly aside,
And splice his tale;—now take him from his cot,
And for some cleaner berth exchange his lot,
How will he all that cruel aid deplore?
His heart will break, and he will fight no more.

    Here is the poor old Merchant: he declined,
And, as they say, is not in perfect mind;
In his poor house, with one poor maiden friend,
Quiet he paces to his journey's end.

    Rich in his youth, he traded and he fail'd;
Again he tried, again his fate prevail'd;
His spirits low, and his exertions small,
He fell perforce, he seem'd decreed to fall:
Like the gay knight, unapt to rise was he,
But downward sank with sad alacrity.
A borough-place we gain'd him—in disgrace

For gross neglect, he quickly lost the place;
But still he kept a kind of sullen pride,
Striving his wants to hinder or to hide;
At length, compell'd by very need, in grief
He wrote a proud petition for relief.
     "He did suppose a fall, like his, would prove
Of force to wake their sympathy and love;
Would make them feel the changes all may know,
And stir them up a due regard to show."
     His suit was granted;—to an ancient maid,
Relieved herself, relief for him was paid:
Here they together (meet companions) dwell,
And dismal tales of man's misfortunes tell:
"'Twas not a world for them, God help them, they
Could not deceive, nor flatter, nor betray;
But there's a happy change, a scene to come,
And they, God help them! shall be soon at home."
     If these no pleasures nor enjoyments gain,
Still none their spirits nor their speech restrain;
They sigh at ease, 'mid comforts they complain,
The poor will grieve, the poor will weep and sigh,
Both when they know, and when they know not why;
But we our bounty with such care bestow,
That cause for grieving they shall seldom know.
     Your Plan I love not; with a number you
Have placed your poor, your pitiable few:
There, in one house, throughout their lives to be,
The pauper-palace which they hate to see:
That giant-building, that high-bounding wall,
Those bare-worn walks, that lofty thund'ring hall,
That large loud clock, which tolls each dreaded hour,
Those gates and locks, and all those signs of power;
It is a prison, with a milder name,
Which few inhabit without dread or shame.
Be it agreed—the Poor who hither come
Partake of plenty, seldom found at home;
That airy rooms and decent beds are meant
To give the poor by day, by night, content;
That none are frighten'd, once admitted here,
By the stern looks of lordly Overseer:
Grant that the Guardians of the place attend,
And ready ear to each petition lend;
That they desire the grieving poor to show
What ills they feel, what partial acts they know;
Not without promise, nay desire to heal

Each wrong they suffer, and each woe they feel.
    Alas! their sorrows in their bosoms dwell;
They've much to suffer, but have nought to tell;
They have no evil in the place to state,
And dare not say it is the house they hate:
They own there's granted all such place can give,
But live repining, for 'tis there they live.
    Grandsires are there, who now no more must see,
No more must nurse upon the trembling knee,
The lost loved daughter's infant progeny:
Like death's dread mansion, this allows not place
For joyful meetings of a kindred race.
    Is not the matron there, to whom the son
Was wont at each declining day to run?
He (when his toil was over) gave delight,
By lifting up the latch, and one "Good night."
Yes, she is here; but nightly to her door
The son, still lab'ring, can return no more.
Widows are here, who in their huts were left,
Of husbands, children, plenty, ease bereft;
Yet all that grief within the humble shed
Was soften'd, softened in the humble bed:
But here, in all its force, remains the grief,
And not one softening object for relief.
    Who can, when here, the social neighbour meet?
Who learn the story current in the street?
Who to the long-known intimate impart
Facts they have learn'd or feelings of the heart?
They talk indeed, but who can choose a friend,
Or seek companions at their journey's end?
    Here are not those whom they when infants knew;
Who, with like fortune, up to manhood grew;
Who, with like troubles, at old age arrived;
Who, like themselves, the joy of life survived;
Whom time and custom so familiar made,
That looks the meaning in the mind convey'd:
But here to strangers, words nor looks impart
The various movements of the suffering heart;
Nor will that heart with those alliance own,
To whom its views and hopes are all unknown.
    What, if no grievous fears their lives annoy,
Is it not worse no prospects to enjoy?
'Tis cheerless living in such bounded view,
With nothing dreadful, but with nothing new;
Nothing to bring them joy, to make them weep,—

The day itself is, like the night, asleep;
Or on the sameness if a break be made,
'Tis by some pauper to his grave convey'd;
By smuggled news from neighb'ring village told,
News never true, or truth a twelvemonth old;
By some new inmate doom'd with them to dwell,
Or justice come to see that all goes well;
Or change of room, or hour of leave to crawl
On the black footway winding with the wall,
Till the stern bell forbids, or master's sterner call.

    Here too the mother sees her children train'd,
Her voice excluded and her feelings pain'd:
Who govern here, by general rules must move,
Where ruthless custom rends the bond of love.
Nations we know have nature's law transgress'd,
And snatch'd the infant from the parent's breast;
But still for public good the boy was train'd,
The mother suffer'd, but the matron gain'd:
Here nature's outrage serves no cause to aid;
The ill is felt, but not the Spartan made.

    Then too I own, it grieves me to behold
Those ever virtuous, helpless now and old,
By all for care and industry approved,
For truth respected, and for temper loved;
And who, by sickness and misfortune tried,
Gave want its worth and poverty its pride:
I own it grieves me to behold them sent
From their old home; 'tis pain, 'tis punishment,
To leave each scene familiar, every face,
For a new people and a stranger race;
For those who, sunk in sloth and dead to shame,
From scenes of guilt with daring spirits came;
Men, just and guileless, at such manners start,
And bless their God that time has fenced their heart,
Confirm'd their virtue, and expell'd the fear
Of vice in minds so simple and sincere.

    Here the good pauper, losing all the praise
By worthy deeds acquired in better days,
Breathes a few months, then, to his chamber led,
Expires, while strangers prattle round his bed.

    The grateful hunter, when his horse is old,
Wills not the useless favourite to be sold;
He knows his former worth, and gives him place
In some fair pasture, till he runs his race:
But has the labourer, has the seaman done

Less worthy service, though not dealt to one?
Shall we not then contribute to their ease,
In their old haunts, where ancient objects please?
That, till their sight shall fail them, they may trace
The well-known prospect and the long-loved face.
    The noble oak, in distant ages seen,
With far-stretch'd boughs and foliage fresh and green,
Though now its bare and forky branches show
How much it lacks the vital warmth below,
The stately ruin yet our wonder gains,
Nay, moves our pity, without thought of pains:
Much more shall real wants and cares of age
Our gentler passions in their cause engage;—
Drooping and burthen'd with a weight of years,
What venerable ruin man appears!
How worthy pity, love, respect, and grief—
He claims protection—he compels relief;—
And shall we send him from our view, to brave
The storms abroad, whom we at home might save,
And let a stranger dig our ancient brother's grave?
No! we will shield him from the storm he fears,
And when he falls, embalm him with our tears.

    Farewell to these: but all our poor to know,
Let's seek the winding Lane, the narrow Row,
Suburban prospects, where the traveller stops
To see the sloping tenement on props,
With building-yards immix'd, and humble sheds and shops;
Where the Cross-Keys and Plumber's-Arms invite
Laborious men to taste their coarse delight;
Where the low porches, stretching from the door,
Gave some distinction in the days of yore,
Yet now neglected, more offend the eye,
By gloom and ruin, than the cottage by:
Places like these the noblest town endures,
The gayest palace has its sinks and sewers.
    Here is no pavement, no inviting shop,
To give us shelter when compell'd to stop;
But plashy puddles stand along the way,
Fill'd by the rain of one tempestuous day;
And these so closely to the buildings run,
That you must ford them, for you cannot shun;
Though here and there convenient bricks are laid—

And door-side heaps afford tweir dubious aid,
    Lo! yonder shed; observe its garden-ground,
With the low paling, form'd of wreck, around:
There dwells a Fisher: if you view his boat,
With bed and barrel—'tis his house afloat;
Look at his house, where ropes, nets, blocks, abound,
Tar, pitch, and oakum—'tis his boat aground:
That space inclosed, but little he regards,
Spread o'er with relics of masts, sails, and yards:
Fish by the wall, on spit of elder, rest,
Of all his food, the cheapest and the best,
By his own labour caught, for his own hunger dress'd.
    Here our reformers come not; none object
To paths polluted, or upbraid neglect;
None care that ashy heaps at doors are cast,
That coal-dust flies along the blinding blast:
None heed the stagnant pools on either side,
Where new-launch'd ships of infant-sailors ride:
Rodneys in rags here British valour boast,
And lisping Nelsons fright the Gallic coast.
They fix the rudder, set the swelling sail,
They point the bowsprit, and they blow the gale:
True to her port, the frigate scuds away,
And o'er that frowning ocean finds her bay:
Her owner rigg'd her, and he knows her worth,
And sees her, fearless, gunwale-deep go forth;
Dreadless he views his sea, by breezes curl'd,
When inch-high billows vex the watery world.
    There, fed by food they love, to rankest size,
Around the dwellings docks and wormwood rise;
Here the strong mallow strikes her slimy root,
Here the dull nightshade hangs her deadly fruit:
On hills of dust the henbane's faded green,
And pencil'd flower of sickly scent is seen;
At the wall's base the fiery nettle springs,
With fruit globose and fierce with poison'd stings;
Above (the growth of many a year) is spread
The yellow level of the stone-crop's bed:
In every chink delights the fern to grow,
With glossy leaf and tawny bloom below;
These, with our sea-weeds, rolling up and down,
Form the contracted Flora of the town.
    Say, wilt thou more of scenes so sordid know?
Then will I lead thee down the dusty Row;
By the warm alley and the long close lane,—

There mark the fractured door and paper'd pane,
Where flags the noon-tide air, and, as we pass,
We fear to breathe the putrefying mass:
But fearless yonder matron; she disdains
To sigh for zephyrs from ambrosial plains;
But mends her meshes torn, and pours her lay
All in the stifling fervour of the day.

    Her naked children round the alley run,
And roll'd in dust, are bronzed beneath the sun,
Or gambol round the dame, who, loosely dress'd,
Woos the coy breeze to fan the open breast:
She, once a handmaid, strove by decent art
To charm her sailor's eye and touch his heart;
Her bosom then was veil'd in kerchief clean,
And fancy left to form the charms unseen.

    But when a wife, she lost her former care,
Nor thought on charms, nor time for dress could spare;
Careless she found her friends who dwelt beside,
No rival beauty kept alive her pride:
Still in her bosom virtue keeps her place,
But decency is gone, the virtues' guard and grace.

    See that long boarded Building!—By these stairs
Each humble tenant to that home repairs—
By one large window lighted—it was made
For some bold project, some design in trade:
This fail'd,—and one, a humourist in his way,
(Ill was the humour), bought it in decay;
Nor will he sell, repair, or take it down;
'Tis his,—what cares he for the talk of town?
"No! he will let it to the poor;—a home
Where he delights to see the creatures come:"
"They may be thieves;"—"Well, so are richer men;"
"Or idlers, cheats, or prostitutes;"—"What then?"
"Outcasts pursued by justice, vile and base;"—
"They need the more his pity and the place:"
Convert to system his vain mind has built,
He gives asylum to deceit and guilt.

    In this vast room, each place by habit fix'd,
Are sexes, families, and ages mix'd—
To union forced by crime, by fear, by need,
And all in morals and in modes agreed;
Some ruin'd men, who from mankind remove;
Some ruin'd females, who yet talk of love;
And some grown old in idleness—the prey
To vicious spleen, still railing through the day;

And need and misery, vice and danger bind,
In sad alliance each degraded mind.

    That window view!—oil'd paper and old glass
Stain the strong rays, which, though impeded, pass,
And give a dusty warmth to that huge room,
The conquer'd sunshine's melancholy gloom;
When all those western rays, without so bright,
Within become a ghastly glimmering light,
As pale and faint upon the floor they fall,
Or feebly gleam on the opposing wall:
That floor, once oak, now pieced with fir unplaned,
Or, where not pieced, in places bored and stain'd;
That wall once whiten'd, now an odious sight,
Stain'd with all hues, except its ancient white;
The only door is fasten'd by a pin,
Or stubborn bar that none may hurry in:
For this poor room, like rooms of greater pride,
At times contains what prudent men would hide.

    Where'er the floor allows an even space,
Chalking and marks of various games have place;
Boys, without foresight, pleased in halters swing;
On a fix'd hook men cast a flying ring;
While gin and snuff their female neighbours share,
And the black beverage in the fractured ware.

    On swinging shelf are things incongruous stored,—
Scraps of their food,—the cards and cribbage-board,—
With pipes and pouches; while on peg below,
Hang a lost member's fiddle and its bow;
That still reminds them how he'd dance and play,
Ere sent untimely to the Convicts' Bay.

    Here by a curtain, by a blanket there,
Are various beds conceal'd, but none with care;
Where some by day and some by night, as best
Suit their employments, seek uncertain rest;
The drowsy children at their pleasure creep
To the known crib, and there securely sleep.

    Each end contains a grate, and these beside
Are hung utensils for their boil'd and fried—
All used at any hour, by night, by day,
As suit the purse, the person, or the prey.

    Above the fire, the mantel-shelf contains
Of china-ware some poor unmatched remains;
There many a tea-cup's gaudy fragment stands,
All placed by vanity's unwearied hands;
For here she lives, e'en here she looks about,

To find some small consoling objects out:
Nor heed these Spartan dames their house, not sit
'Mid cares domestic,—they nor sew nor knit;
But of their fate discourse, their ways, their wars,
With arm'd authorities, their 'scapes and scars:
These lead to present evils, and a cup,
If fortune grant it, winds description up.

  High hung at either end, and next the wall,
Two ancient mirrors show the forms of all,
In all their force;—these aid them in their dress,
But with the good, the evils too express,
Doubling each look of care, each token of distress.

LETTER XIX.

THE POOR OF THE BOROUGH.

Nam dives qui fieri vult,
Et cito vult fieri; sed quae reverentia legum,
Quis metus, aut pudor est unquam properantis avari?
JUVENAL, Satire xiv.

Nocte brevem si forte indulsit cura soporem,
Et toto versata thoro jam membra quiescunt,
Continuo templum et violati Numinis aras,
Et quod praecipuis mentem suboribus urget,
Te videt in somnis; tua sacra et major imago
Humana turbat pavidum, cogitque fateri.
JUVENAL, Satire xiii.

THE PARISH-CLERK.

The Parish-Clerk began his Duties with the late Vicar, a grave and austere Man; one fully orthodox; a Detecter and Opposer of the Wiles of Satan—His opinion of his own Fortitude—The more frail offended by these Professions—His good advice gives further Provocation— They invent stratagems to overcome his Virtue—His Triumph—He is yet not invulnerable: is assaulted by fear of Want, and Avarice—He gradually yields to the Seduction—He reasons with himself, and is persuaded—He offends, but with Terror; repeats his Offence; grows familiar with Crime: is detected—His Sufferings and Death.

WITH our late Vicar, and his age the same,
His clerk, hight Jachin, to his office came;
The like slow speech was his, the like tall slender frame:
But Jachin was the gravest man on ground,
And heard his master's jokes with look profound;
For worldly wealth this man of letters sigh'd,
And had a sprinkling of the spirit's pride:
But he was sober, chaste, devout and just,
One whom his neighbours could believe and trust:
Of none suspected, neither man nor maid
By him were wrong'd, or were of him afraid.
    There was indeed a frown, a trick of state
In Jachin;—formal was his air and gait:
But if he seem'd more solemn and less kind,
Than some light men to light affairs confined,

Still 'twas allow'd that he should so behave
As in high seat, and be severely grave.
    This book-taught man, to man's first foe profess'd
Defiance stern, and hate that knew not rest;
He held that Satan, since the world began,
In every act, had strife with every man;
That never evil deed on earth was done,
But of the acting parties he was one;
The flattering guide to make ill prospects clear;
To smooth rough ways the constant pioneer;
The ever-tempting, soothing, softening power,
Ready to cheat, seduce, deceive, devour.
"Me has the sly Seducer oft withstood,"
Said pious Jachin,—"but he gets no good;
I pass the house where swings the tempting sign,
And pointing, tell him, 'Satan, that is thine:'
I pass the damsels pacing down the street,
And look more grave and solemn when we meet;
Nor doth it irk me to rebuke their smiles,
Their wanton ambling and their watchful wiles:
Nay, like the good John Bunyan, when I view
Those forms, I'm angry at the ills they do;
That I could pinch and spoil, in sin's despite,
Beauties, which frail and evil thoughts excite.{10}
    "At feasts and banquets seldom am I found,
And (save at church) abhor a tuneful sound;
To plays and shows I run not to and fro,
And where my master goes, forbear to go."
    No wonder Satan took the thing amiss,
To be opposed by such a man as this—
A man so grave, important, cautious, wise,
Who dared not trust his feeling or his eyes;
No wonder he should lurk and lie in wait,
Should fit his hooks and ponder on his bait;
Should on his movements keep a watchful eye;
For he pursued a fish who led the fry.
    With his own peace our Clerk was not content;
He tried, good man! to make his friends repent.
    "Nay, nay, my friends, from inns and taverns fly;
You may suppress your thirst, but not supply:
A foolish proverb says, 'the devil's at home;'
But he is there, and tempts in every room:
Men feel, they know not why, such places please;
His are the spells—they're idleness and ease;
Magic of fatal kind he throws around,

Where care is banish'd, but the heart is bound.

    "Think not of beauty;—when a maid you meet,
Turn from her view and step across the street;
Dread all the sex: their looks create a charm,
A smile should fright you and a word alarm:
E'en I myself, with all my watchful care,
Have for an instant felt the insidious snare;
And caught my sinful eyes at the endang'ring stars;
Till I was forced to smite my bounding breast
With forceful blow, and bid the bold-one rest.

    "Go not with crowds when they to pleasure run,
But public joy in private safety shun:
When bells, diverted from their true intent,
Ring loud for some deluded mortal sent
To hear or make long speech in parliament;
What time the many, that unruly beast,
Roars its rough joy and shares the final feast?
Then heed my counsel, shut thine ears and eyes;
A few will hear me—for the few are wise."

    Not Satan's friends, nor Satan's self could bear,
The cautious man who took of souls such care;
An interloper,—one who, out of place,
Had volunteered upon the side of grace:
There was his master ready once a week
To give advice; what further need he seek?
"Amen, so be it:"—what had he to do
With more than this?—'twas insolent and new;
And some determined on a way to see
How frail he was, that so it might not be.

    First they essay'd to tempt our saint to sin,
By points of doctrine argued at an inn;
Where he might warmly reason, deeply drink,
Then lose all power to argue and to think.

    In vain they tried; he took the question up,
Clear'd every doubt, and barely touch'd the cup:
By many a text he proved his doctrine sound,
And look'd in triumph on the tempters round.

    Next 'twas their care an artful lass to find,
Who might consult him, as perplex'd in mind;
She they conceived might put her case with fears,
With tender tremblings and seducing tears;
She might such charms of various kind display,
That he would feel their force and melt away:
For why of nymphs such caution and such dread,
Unless he felt, and fear'd to be misled?

She came, she spake: he calmly heard her case,
And plainly told her 'twas a want of grace;
Bade her "such fancies and affections check,
And wear a thicker muslin on her neck."
Abased, his human foes the combat fled,
And the stern clerk yet higher held his head.
They were indeed a weak, impatient set,
But their shrewd prompter had his engines yet;
Had various means to make a mortal trip,
Who shunn'd a flowing bowl and rosy lip;
And knew a thousand ways his heart to move,
Who flies from banquets and who laughs at love.

    Thus far the playful Muse has lent her aid,
But now departs, of graver theme afraid;
Her may we seek in more appropriate time,—
There is no jesting with distress and crime.

    Our worthy Clerk had now arrived at fame,
Such as but few in his degree might claim;
But he was poor, and wanted not the sense
That lowly rates the praise without the pence:
He saw the common herd with reverence treat
The weakest burgess whom they chanced to meet;
While few respected his exalted views,
And all beheld his doublet and his shoes:
None, when they meet, would to his parts allow
(Save his poor boys) a hearing or a bow:
To this false judgment of the vulgar mind,
He was not fully, as a saint, resign'd;
He found it much his jealous soul affect,
To fear derision and to find neglect.

    The year was bad, the christening-fees were small,
The weddings few, the parties paupers all:
Desire of gain with fear of want combined,
Raised sad commotion in his wounded mind;
Wealth was in all his thoughts, his views, his dreams,
And prompted base desires and baseless schemes.

    Alas! how often erring mortals keep
The strongest watch against the foes who sleep;
While the more wakeful, bold, and artful foe
Is suffer'd guardless and unmark'd to go.

    Once in a month the sacramental bread
Our Clerk with wine upon the table spread:
The custom this, that as the vicar reads,
He for our off'rings round the church proceeds;
Tall spacious seats the wealthier people hid,

And none had view of what his neighbour did:
Laid on the box and mingled when they fell,
Who should the worth of each oblation tell?
Now as poor Jachin took the usual round,
And saw the alms and heard the metal sound,
He had a thought—at first it was no more
Than—"these have cash and give it to the poor."
A second thought from this to work began—
"And can they give it to a poorer man?"
Proceeding thus,—"My merit could they know;
And knew my need, how freely they'd bestow;
But though they know not, these remain the same,
And are a strong, although a secret claim:
To me, alas! the want and worth are known;
Why then, in fact, 'tis but to take my own."
      Thought after thought pour'd in, a tempting train:—
"Suppose it done,—who is it could complain?
How could the poor? for they such trifles share,
As add no comfort, as suppress no care;
But many a pittance makes a worthy heap,—
What says the law? that silence puts to sleep:—
Nought then forbids, the danger could we shun,
And sure the business may be safely done.
      "But am I earnest?—earnest? No.—I say,
If such my mind, that I could plan a way;
Let me reflect;—I've not allow'd me time
To purse the pieces, and if dropp'd they'd chime:"
Fertile is evil in the soul of man.—
He paused,—said Jachin, "They may drop on bran.
Why then 'tis safe and (all consider'd) just,
The poor receive it,—'tis no breach of trust:
The old and widows may their trifles miss,
There must be evil in a good like this:
But I'll be kind—the sick I'll visit twice,
When now but once, and freely give advice.
Yet let me think again:"—Again he tried,
For stronger reasons on his passion's side,
And quickly these were found, yet slowly he complied.
      The morning came: the common service done,
Shut every door,—the solemn rite begun,—
And, as the priest the sacred sayings read,
The clerk went forward, trembling as he tread:
O'er the tall pew he held the box, and heard
The offer'd piece, rejoicing as he fear'd:
Just by the pillar, as he cautious tripp'd,

And turn'd the aisle, he then a portion slipp'd
From the full store, and to the pocket sent,
But held a moment—and then down it went.

 The priest read on, on walk'd the man afraid,
Till a gold offering in the plate was laid:
Trembling he took it, for a moment stopp'd,
Then down it fell, and sounded as it dropp'd;
Amazed he started, for th' affrighted man,
Lost and bewilder'd, thought not of the bran.
But all were silent, all on things intent
Of high concern, none ear to money lent;
So on he walk'd, more cautious than before,
And gain'd the purposed sum and one piece more.

 "Practice makes perfect:" when the month came round,
He dropp'd the cash, nor listen'd for a sound:
But yet, when last of all th' assembled flock
He ate and drank,—it gave th' electric shock:
Oft was he forced his reasons to repeat,
Ere he could kneel in quiet at his seat;
But custom soothed him—ere a single year
All this was done without restraint or fear:
Cool and collected, easy and composed,
He was correct till all the service closed;
Then to his home, without a groan or sigh,
Gravely he went, and laid his treasure by.
Want will complain: some widows had express'd
A doubt if they were favour'd like the rest;
The rest described with like regret their dole,
And thus from parts they reason'd to the whole:
When all agreed some evil must be done,
Or rich men's hearts grew harder than a stone.

 Our easy vicar cut the matter short;
He would not listen to such vile report.

 All were not thus—there govern'd in that year
A stern stout churl, an angry overseer;
A tyrant fond of power, loud, lewd, and most severe:
Him the mild vicar, him the graver clerk,
Advised, reproved, but nothing would he mark.
Save the disgrace; "and that, my friends," said he,
"Will I avenge, whenever time may be."
And now, alas! 'twas time:—from man to man
Doubt and alarm and shrewd suspicions ran.

 With angry spirit and with sly intent,
This parish-ruler to the altar went:
A private mark he fix'd on shillings three,

And but one mark could in the money see:
Besides in peering round, he chanced to note
A sprinkling slight on Jachin's Sunday-coat:
All doubt was over:—when the flock were bless'd,
In wrath he rose, and thus his mind express'd:—
    "Foul deeds are here!" and saying this, he took
The Clerk, whose conscience, in her cold-fit, shook:
His pocket then was emptied on the place;
All saw his guilt; all witness'd his disgrace:
He fell, he fainted, not a groan, a look,
Escaped the culprit; 'twas a final stroke—
A death-wound never to be heal'd—a fall
That all had witness'd, and amazed were all.
    As he recover'd, to his mind it came,
"I owe to Satan this disgrace and shame:"
All the seduction now appear'd in view;
"Let me withdraw," he said, and he withdrew:
No one withheld him, all in union cried,
E'en the avenger,—"We are satisfied:"
For what has death in any form to give,
Equal to that man's terrors, if he live?
    He lived in freedom, but he hourly saw
How much more fatal justice is than law;
He saw another in his office reign,
And his mild master treat him with disdain:
He saw that all men shunn'd him, some reviled,
The harsh pass'd frowning, and the simple smiled;
The town maintain'd him, but with some reproof,
And clerks and scholars proudly kept aloof.
In each lone place, dejected and dismay'd,
Shrinking from view, his wasting form he laid;
Or to the restless sea and roaring wind
Gave the strong yearnings of a ruin'd mind:
On the broad beach, the silent summer-day,
Stretch'd on some wreck, he wore his life away;
Or where the river mingles with the sea,
Or on the mud-bank by the elder tree,
Or by the bounding marsh-dike, there was he:
And when unable to forsake the town,
In the blind courts he sat desponding down—
Always alone: then feebly would he crawl
The church-way walk, and lean upon the wall:
Too ill for this, he lay beside the door,
Compell'd to hear the reasoning of the poor:
He look'd so pale, so weak, the pitying crowd

Their firm belief of his repentance vow'd;
They saw him then so ghastly and so thin,
That they exclaim'd, "Is this the work of sin?"
    "Yes," in his better moments, he replied,
"Of sinful avarice and the spirit's pride;—
While yet untempted, I was safe and well;
Temptation came; I reason'd, and I fell:
To be man's guide and glory I design'd,
A rare example for our sinful kind;
But now my weakness and my guilt I see,
And am a warning—man, be warn'd by me!"
    He said, and saw no more the human face;
To a lone loft he went, his dying place,
And, as the vicar of his state inquired,
Turn'd to the wall and silently expired!

LETTER XX.

THE POOR OF THE BOROUGH.

Patience and sorrow strove
Who should express her goodliest.
                    SHAKESPEARE.

"No charms she now can boast,"—'tis true,
But other charmers wither too:
"And she is old,"—the fact I know,
And old will other heroines grow;
But not like them has she been laid,
In ruin'd castle sore dismay'd;
Where naughty man and ghostly spright
Fill'd her pure mind with awe and dread,
Stalk'd round the room, put out the light,
And shook the curtains round her bed.
No cruel uncle kept her land,
No tyrant father forced her hand;
She had no vixen virgin-aunt,
Without whose aid she could not eat,
And yet who poison'd all her meat,
With gibe and sneer and taunt.
Yet of the heroine she'd a share,—
She saved a lover from despair,
And granted all his wish in spite
Of what she knew and felt was right:
But, heroine then no more,
She own'd the fault, and wept and pray'd
And humbly took the parish aid,
And dwelt among the poor.

ELLEN ORFORD.{11}

The Widow's Cottage—Blind Ellen one—Hers not the Sorrows or
Adventures of Heroines—What these are, first described—Deserted
Wives; rash Lovers; courageous Damsels: in desolated Mansions; in
grievous Perplexity—These Evils, however severe, of short Duration—
Ellen's Story—Her Employment in Childhood—First Love; first
Adventure; its miserable Termination—An Idiot Daughter—A
Husband—Care in Business without Success—The Man's Despondency
and its Effect—Their Children: how disposed of—One particularly

unfortunate—Fate of the Daughter—Ellen keeps a School and is happy—becomes Blind; loses her School—Her Consolations.

OBSERVE yon tenement, apart and small,
Where the wet pebbles shine upon the wall;
Where the low benches lean beside the door,
And the red paling bounds the space before;
Where thrift and lavender, and lad's-love bloom,—
That humble dwelling is the widow's home;
There live a pair, for various fortunes known,
But the blind EUen will relate her own;—
Yet ere we hear the story she can tell,
On prouder sorrows let us briefly dwell.
  I've often marvell'd, when, by night, by day,
I've mark'd the manners moving in my way,
And heard the language and beheld the lives
Of lass and lover, goddesses and wives,
That books, which promise much of life to give,
Should show so little how we truly live.
  To me, it seems, their females and their men
Are but the creatures of the author's pen;
Nay, creatures borrow'd and again convey'd
From book to book—the shadows of a shade:
Life, if they'd search, would show them many a change;
The ruin sudden, and the misery strange!
With more of grievous, base, and dreadful things,
Than novelists relate or poet sings:
But they, who ought to look the world around,
Spy out a single spot in fairy-ground;
Where all, in turn, ideal forms behold,
And plots are laid and histories are told.
  Time have I lent—I would their debt were less—
To flow'ry pages of sublime distress;
And to the heroine's soul-distracting fears
I early gave my sixpences and tears:
Oft have I travell'd in these tender tales,
To Darnley-Cottages and Maple-Vales,
And watch'd the fair-one from the first-born sigh,
When Henry pass'd and gazed in passing by;
Till I beheld them pacing in the park
Close by a coppice where 'twas cold and dark;
When such affection with such fate appear'd,
Want and a father to be shunn'd and fear'd,
Without employment, prospect, cot, or cash;
That I have judged th' heroic souls were rash.

Now shifts the scene,—the fair in tower confined,
In all things suffers but in change of mind;
Now woo'd by greatness to a bed of state,
Now deeply threaten'd with a dungeon's grate;
Till, suffering much, and being tried enough,
She shines, triumphant maid!—temptation-proof.

    Then was I led to vengeful monks, who mix
With nymphs and swains, and play unpriestly tricks;
Then view'd banditti who in forest wide,
And cavern vast, indignant virgins hide;
Who, hemm'd with bands of sturdiest rogues about,
Find some strange succour, and come virgins out.

    I've watch'd a wint'ry night on castle-walls,
I've stalk'd by moonlight through deserted halls,
And when the weary world was sunk to rest,
I've had such sights as may not be express'd.

    Lo! that chateau, the western tower decay'd,
The peasants shun it,—they are all afraid;
For there was done a deed!—could walls reveal,
Or timbers tell it, how the heart would feel!
Most horrid was it:—for, behold, the floor
Has stain of blood, and will be clean no more:
Hark to the winds! which through the wide saloon
And the long passage send a dismal tune,—
Music that ghosts delight in; and now heed
Yon beauteous nymph, who must unmask the deed;
See! with majestic sweep she swims alone,
Through rooms, all dreary, guided by a groan:
Though windows rattle, and though tap'stries shake,
And the feet falter every step they take,
'Mid moans and gibing sprights she silent goes,
To find a something, which will soon expose
The villanies and wiles of her determined foes:
And, having thus adventured, thus endured,
Fame, wealth, and lover, are for life secured.

    Much have I fear'd, but am no more afraid,
When some chaste beauty, by some wretch betray'd,
Is drawn away with such distracted speed,
That she anticipates a dreadful deed:
Not so do I—Let solid walls impound
The captive fair, and dig a moat around;
Let there be brazen locks and bars of steel,
And keepers cruel, such as never feel;
With not a single note the purse supply,
And when she begs, let men and maids deny;

Be windows those from which she dares not fall,
And help so distant, 'tis in vain to call;
Still means of freedom will some power devise,
And from the baffled ruffian snatch his prize.

To Northern Wales, in some sequester'd spot,
I've follow'd fair Louisa to her cot:
Where, then a wretched and deserted bride,
The injur'd fair-one wished from man to hide;
Till by her fond repenting Belville found,
By some kind chance—the straying of a hound,
He at her feet craved mercy, nor in vain,
For the relenting dove flew back again.

There's something rapturous in distress, or oh!
Could Clementina bear her lot of woe?
Or what she underwent could maiden undergoe?
The day was fix'd; for so the lover sigh'd,
So knelt and craved, he couldn't be denied;
When, tale most dreadful! every hope adieu,—
For the fond lover is the brother too:
All other griefs abate; this monstrous grief
Has no remission, comfort, or relief;
Four ample volumes, through each page disclose,—
Good Heaven protect us! only woes on woes;
Till some strange means afford a sudden view
Of some vile plot, and every woe adieu!

Now, should we grant these beauties all endure
Severest pangs, they've still the speediest cure;
Before one charm be withered from the face,
Except the bloom, which shall again have place,
In wedlock ends each wish, in triumph all disgrace;
And life to come, we fairly may suppose,
One light, bright contrast to these wild dark woes.

These let us leave, and at her sorrows look,
Too often seen, but seldom in a book;
Let her who felt, relate them;—on her chair
The heroine sits—in former years, the fair,
Now aged and poor; but Ellen Orford knows
That we should humbly take what Heaven bestows.

"My father died—again my mother wed,
And found the comforts of her life were fled;
Her angry husband, vex'd through half his years
By loss and troubles, filled her soul with fears:
Their children many, and 'twas my poor place
To nurse and wait on all the infant-race;
Labour and hunger were indeed my part,

And should have strengthen'd an erroneous heart.
    "Sore was the grief to see him angry come,
And teased with business, make distress at home;
The father's fury and the children's cries
I soon could bear, but not my mother's sighs;
For she look'd back on comforts, and would say,
'I wrong'd thee, Ellen,' and then turn away:
Thus, for my age's good, my youth was tried,
And this my fortune till my mother died.
    "So, amid sorrow much and little cheer—
A common case—I pass'd my twentieth year;
For these are frequent evils; thousands share
An equal grief—the like domestic care.
    "Then in my days of bloom, of health, and youth,
One, much above me, vow'd his love and truth:
We often met, he dreading to be seen,
And much I question'd what such dread might mean;
Yet I believed him true; my simple heart
And undirected reason took his part.
    "Can he who loves me, whom I love, deceive?
Can I such wrong of one so kind believe,
Who lives but in my smile, who trembles when I grieve?
    "He dared not marry, but we met to prove
What sad encroachments and deceits has love:
Weak that I was, when he, rebuked, withdrew,
I let him see that I was wretched too;
When less my caution, I had still the pain
Of his or mine own weakness to complain.
    "Happy the lovers class'd alike in life,
Or happier yet the rich endowing wife;
But most aggrieved the fond believing maid.
Of her rich lover tenderly afraid:
You judge th' event; for grievous was my fate,
Painful to feel, and shameful to relate:
Ah! sad it was my burthen to sustain,
When the least misery was the dread of pain;
When I have grieving told him my disgrace,
And plainly mark'd indifference in his face.
    "Hard! with these fears and terrors to behold
The cause of all, the faithless lover, cold;
Impatient grown at every wish denied,
And barely civil, soothed and gratified;
Peevish when urged to think of vows so strong,
And angry when I spake of crime and wrong.
All this I felt, and still the sorrow grew,

Because I felt that I deserved it too,
And begg'd my infant stranger to forgive
The mother's shame, which in herself must live.
When known that shame, I, soon expell'd from home,
With a frail sister shared a hovel's gloom;
There barely fed—(what could I more request?)
My infant slumberer sleeping at my breast,
I from my window saw his blooming bride,
And my seducer smiling at her side;
Hope lived till then; I sank upon the floor,
And grief and thought and feeling were no more:
Although revived, I judged that life would close,
And went to rest, to wonder that I rose:
My dreams were dismal,—wheresoe'er I stray'd,
I seem'd ashamed, alarm'd, despised, betray'd;
Always in grief, in guilt, disgraced, forlorn,
Mourning that one so weak, so vile, was born;
The earth a desert, tumult in the sea,
The birds affrighten'd fled from tree to tree,
Obscured the setting sun, and every thing like me.
But Heav'n had mercy, and my need at length
Urged me to labour, and renew'd my strength.
I strove for patience as a sinner must,
Yet felt th' opinion of the world unjust:
There was my lover, in his joy esteem'd,
And I, in my distress, as guilty deemed;
Yet sure, not all the guilt and shame belong
To her who feels and suffers for the wrong:
The cheat at play may use the wealth he's won,
But is not honour'd for the mischief done;
The cheat in love may use each villain art,
And boast the deed that breaks the victim's heart.
    "Four years were past; I might again have found
Some erring wish, but for another wound:
Lovely my daughter grew, her face was fair,
But no expression ever brighten'd there;
I doubted long, and vainly strove to make
Some certain meaning of the words she spake;
But meaning there was none, and I survey'd
With dread the beauties of my idiot-maid.
Still I submitted;—Oh! 'tis meet and fit
In all we feel to make the heart submit;
Gloomy and calm my days, but I had then,
It seem'd, attractions for the eyes of men:
The sober master of a decent trade

O'erlook'd my errors, and his offer made;
Reason assented:—true, my heart denied,
'But thou,' I said,'shalt be no more my guide.'
    "When wed, our toil and trouble, pains and care,
Of means to live procured us humble share;
Five were our sons,—and we, though careful, found
Our hopes declining as the year came round:
For I perceived, yet would not soon perceive,
My husband stealing from my view to grieve:
Silent he grew, and when he spoke he sigh'd,
And surly look'd, and peevishly replied:
Pensive by nature, he had gone of late
To those who preach'd of destiny and fate,
Of things foredoom'd, and of election-grace,
And how in vain we strive to run our race;
That all by works and moral worth we gain
Is to perceive our care and labour vain;
That still the more we pay, our debts the more remain;
That he who feels not the mysterious call,
Lies bound in sin, still grov'ling from the fall.
My husband felt not:—our persuasion, prayer,
And our best reason, darken'd his despair;
His very nature changed; he now reviled
My former conduct,—he reproach'd my child:
He talked of bastard slips, and cursed his bed,
And from our kindness to concealment fled;
For ever to some evil change inclined,
To every gloomy thought he lent his mind,
Nor rest would give to us, nor rest himself could find;
His son suspended saw him, long bereft
Of life, nor prospect of revival left.
    "With him died all our prospects, and once more
I shared th' allotments of the parish poor;
They took my children too, and this I know
Was just and lawful, but I felt the blow:
My idiot-maid and one unhealthy boy
Were left, a mother's misery and her joy.
    "Three sons I follow'd to the grave, and one—
Oh! can I speak of that unhappy son?
Would all the memory of that time were fled,
And all those horrors, with my child, were dead!
Before the world seduced him, what a grace
And smile of gladness shone upon his face!
Then, he had knowledge; finely would he write;
Study to him was pleasure and delight;

Great was his courage, and but few could stand
Against the sleight and vigour of his hand;
The maidens loved him;—when he came to die,
No, not the coldest could suppress a sigh:
Here I must cease—how can I say, my child
Was by the bad of either sex beguiled?
Worst of the bad—they taught him that the laws
Made wrong and right; there was no other cause,
That all religion was the trade of priests,
And men, when dead, must perish like the beasts:—
And he, so lively and so gay, before—
Ah; spare a mother—I can tell no more.
    "Int'rest was made that they should not destroy
The comely form of my deluded boy—
But pardon came not; damp the place and deep
Where he was kept, as they'd a tiger keep;
For he, unhappy! had before them all
Vow'd he'd escape, whatever might befall.
He'd means of dress, and dress'd beyond his means,
And so to see him in such dismal scenes,
I cannot speak it—cannot bear to tell
Of that sad hour—I heard the passing bell!
    "Slowly they went; he smiled, and look'd so smart,
Yet sure he shudder'd when he saw the cart,
And gave a look—until my dying day,
That look will never from my mind away:
Oft as I sit, and ever in my dreams,
I see that look, and they have heard my screams.
    "Now let me speak no more—yet all declared
That one so young, in pity, should be spared.
And one so manly;—on his graceful neck,
That chains of jewels may be proud to deck,
To a small mole a mother's lips have press'd—
And there the cord—my breath is sore oppress'd.
    "I now can speak again:—my elder boy
Was that year drown'd,—a seaman in a hoy:
He left a numerous race; of these would some
In their young troubles to my cottage come,
And these I taught—an humble teacher I—
Upon their heavenly Parent to rely.
    "Alas! I needed such reliance more:
My idiot-girl, so simply gay before,
Now wept in pain: some wretch had found a time,
Depraved and wicked, for that coward crime;
I had indeed my doubt, but I suppress'd

The thought that day and night disturb'd my rest;
She and that sick-pale brother—but why strive
To keep the terrors of that time alive?
    "The hour arrived, the new, th' undreaded pain,
That came with violence, and yet came in vain.
I saw her die: her brother too is dead;
Nor own'd such crime—what is it that I dread?
    "The parish aid withdrawn, I look'd around,
And in my school a bless'd subsistence found—
My winter-calm of life: to be of use
Would pleasant thoughts and heavenly hopes produce;
I loved them all; it soothed me to presage
The various trials of their riper age,
Then dwell on mine, and bless the Power who gave
Pains to correct us, and remorse to save.
    "Yes! these were days of peace, but they are past,—
A trial came, I will believe, a last;
I lost my sight, and my employment gone,
Useless I live, but to the day live on;
Those eyes which long the light of heaven enjoy'd,
Were not by pain, by agony destroy'd:
My senses fail not all; I speak, I pray;
By night my rest, my food I take by day;
And, as my mind looks cheerful to my end,
I love mankind, and call my GOD my friend."

LETTER XXI.

THE POOR OF THE BOROUGH.

Now the Spirit speaketh expressly, that, in the latter times, some shall depart from the faith, giving heed to seducing spirits and doctrines of devils.

Epistle to Timothy.

ABEL KEENE.

Abel, a poor man, Teacher of a School of the lower Order; is placed in the Office of a Merchant; is alarmed by Discourses of the Clerks; unable to reply; becomes a Convert; dresses, drinks, and ridicules his former conduct—The Remonstrance of his Sister, a devout Maiden—Its Effect—The Merchant dies—Abel returns to Poverty unpitied; but relieved—His abject Condition—His Melancholy—He wanders about; is found—His own Account of himself and the Revolutions in his Mind.

A QUIET, simple man was Abel Keene,
He meant no harm, nor did he often mean;
He kept a school of loud rebellious boys,
And growing old, grew nervous with the noise;
When a kind merchant hired his useful pen,
And made him happiest of accompting men;
With glee he rose to every easy day,
When half the labour brought him twice the pay.
　　There were young clerks, and there the merchant's son,
Choice spirits all, who wish'd him to be one;
It must, no question, give them lively joy,
Hopes long indulged to combat and destroy;
At these they levelled all their skill and strength,—
He fell not quickly, but he fell at length:
They quoted books, to him both bold and new,
And scorn'd as fables all he held as true;
"Such monkish stories, and such nursery lies,"
That he was struck with terror and surprise.
　　"What! all his life had he the laws obey'd,
Which they broke through and were not once afraid?
Had he so long his evil passions check'd,
And yet at last had nothing to expect?
While they their lives in joy and pleasure led,
And then had nothing at the end to dread?

Was all his priest with so much zeal convey'd
A part! a speech! for which the man was paid!
And were his pious books, his solemn prayers,
Not worth one tale of the admir'd Voltaire's?
Then was it time, while yet some years remain'd,
To drink untroubled and to think unchain'd,
And on all pleasues, which his purse could give,
Freely to seize, and while he lived, to live."

    Much time he pass'd in this important strife,
The bliss or bane of his remaining life;
For converts all are made with care and grief,
And pangs attend the birth of unbelief;
Nor pass they soon;—with awe and fear he took
The flowery way, and cast back many a look.

    The youths applauded much his wise design,
With weighty reasoning o'er their evening wine;
And much in private 'twould their mirth improve,
To hear how Abel spake of life and love;
To hear him own what grievous pains it cost,
Ere the old saint was in the sinner lost,
Ere his poor mind, with every deed alarm'd,
By wit was settled, and by vice was charm'd.

    For Abel enter'd in his bold career,
Like boys on ice, with pleasure and with fear;
Lingering, yet longing for the joy, he went,
Repenting now, now dreading to repent:
With awkward pace, and with himself at war,
Far gone, yet frighten'd that he went so far;
Oft for his efforts he'd solicit praise,
And then proceed with blunders and delays:
The young more aptly passions' calls pursue,
But age and weakness start at scenes so new,
And tremble, when they've done, for all they dared to do.

    At length example Abel's dread removed,
With small concern he sought the joys he loved;
Not resting here, he claim'd his share of fame,
And first their votary, then their wit became;
His jest was bitter and his satire bold,
When he his tales of formal brethren told;
What time with pious neighbours he discuss'd,
Their boasted treasure and their boundless trust:
"Such were our dreams," the jovial elder cried;
"Awake and live," his youthful friends replied.

    Now the gay clerk a modest drab despised,
And clad him smartly, as his friends advised;

So fine a coat upon his back he threw,
That not an alley-boy old Abel knew;
Broad polish'd buttons blazed that coat upon,
And just beneath the watch's trinkets shone,—
A splendid watch, that pointed out the time,
To fly from business and make free with crime:
The crimson waistcoat and the silken hose
Rank'd the lean man among the Borough beaux:
His raven hair he cropp'd with fierce disdain,
And light elastic locks encased his brain:
More pliant pupil who could hope to find,
Se deck'd in person and so changed in mind?
    When Abel walked the streets, with pleasent mien
He met his friends, delighted to be seen;
And when he rode along the public way,
No beau so gaudy, and no youth so gay.
    His pious sister, now an ancient maid,
For Abel fearing, first in secret pray'd;
Then thus in love and scorn her notions she convey'd.
    "Alas! my brother! can I see thee pace
Hoodwink'd to hell, and not lament thy case,
Nor stretch my feeble hand to stop thy headlong race?
Lo! thou art bound; a slave in Satan's chain;
The righteous Abel turn'd the wretched Cain;
His brother's blood against the murderer cried,
Against thee thine, unhappy suicide!
Are all our pious nights and peaceful days,
Our evening readings and our morning praise,
Our spirits' comfort in the trials sent,
Our hearts' rejoicings in the blessings lent,
All that o'er grief a cheering influence shed,
Are these for ever and for ever fled?
    "When in the years gone by, the trying years,
When faith and hope had strife with wants and fears,
Thy nerves have trembled till thou couldst not eat
(Dress'd by this hand) thy mess of simple meat;
When, grieved by fastings, gall'd by fates severe,
Slow pass'd the days of the successless year;
Still in these gloomy hours, my brother then
Had glorious views, unseen by prosperous men:
And when thy heart has felt its wish denied,
What gracious texts hast thou to grief applied;
Till thou hast enter'd in thine humble bed,
By lofty hopes and heavenly musings fed;
Then I have seen thy lively looks express

The spirit's comforts in the man's distress.
　　"Then didst thou cry, exulting, 'Yes, 'tis fit,
'Tis meet and right, my heart! that we submit:'
And wilt thou, Abel, thy new pleasures weigh
Against such triumphs?—Oh? repent and pray.
　　"What are thy pleasures?—with the gay to sit,
And thy poor brain torment for awkward wit;
All thy good thoughts (thou hat'st them) to restrain,
And give a wicked pleasure to the vain;
Thy long, lean frame by fashion to attire,
That lads may laugh and wantons may admire;
To raise the mirth of boys, and not to see,
Unhappy maniac! that they laugh at thee
　　"These boyish follies, which alone the boy
Can idly act, or gracefully enjoy,
Add new reproaches to thy fallen state,
And make men scorn what they would only hate.
　　"What pains, my brother, dost thou take to prove
A taste for follies which thou canst not love!
Why do thy stiffening limbs the steed bestride—
That lads may laugh to see thou canst not ride?
And why (I feel the crimson tinge my cheek)
Dost thou by night in Diamond-Alley sneak?
　　"Farewell! the parish will thy sister keep,
Where she in peace shall pray and sing and sleep,
Save when for thee she mourns, thou wicked, wandering sheep.
When youth is fallen, there's hope the young may rise,
But fallen age for ever hopeless lies;
Torn up by storms, and placed in earth once more,
The younger tree may sun and soil restore;
But when the old and sapless trunk lies low,
No care or soil can former life bestow;
Reserved for burning is the worthless tree—
And what, O Abel! is reserved for thee?"
　　These angry words our hero deeply felt,
Though hard his heart, and indisposed to melt!
To gain relief he took a glass the more,
And then went on as careless as before;
Thenceforth, uncheck'd, amusements he partook,
And (save his ledger) saw no decent book;
Him found the merchant punctual at his task,
And that performed, he'd nothing more to ask;
He cared not how old Abel play'd the fool,
No master he, beyond the hours of school:
Thus they proceeding, had their wine and joke,

Till merchant Dixon felt a warning stroke,
And, after struggling half a gloomy week,
Left his poor clerk another friend to seek.

    Alas! the son, who led the saint astray,
Forgot the man whose follies made him gay;
He cared no more for Abel in his need,
Than Abel cared about his hackney steed:
He now, alas! had all his earnings spent,
And thus was left to languish and repent;
No school nor clerkship found he in the place,
Now lost to fortune, as before to grace.

    For town-relief the grieving man applied,
And begg'd with tears what some with scorn denied;
Others look'd down upon the glowing vest,
And frowning, ask'd him at what price he dress'd?
Happy for him his country's laws are mild,
They must support him, though they still reviled;
Grieved, abject, scorn'd, insulted, and betray'd,
Of God unmindful, and of man afraid,—
No more he talk'd; 'twas pain, 'twas shame to speak,
His heart was sinking, and his frame was weak.
His sister died with such serene delight,
He once again began to think her right;
Poor like himself, the happy spinster lay,
And sweet assurance bless'd her dying-day:
Poor like the spinster, he, when death was nigh,
Assured of nothing, felt afraid to die.
The cheerful clerks who sometimes pass'd the door,
Just mention'd "Abel!" and then thought no more.
So Abel, pondering on his state forlorn,
Look'd round for comfort, and was chased by scorn.
And now we saw him on the beach reclined,
Or causeless walking in the wintry wind;
And when it raised a loud and angry sea,
He stood and gazed, in wretched reverie:
He heeded not the frost, the rain, the snow,
Close by the sea he walk'd alone and slow:
Sometimes his frame through many an hour he spread
Upon a tombstone, moveless as the dead;
And was there found a sad and silent place,
There would he creep with slow and measured pace;
Then would he wander by the river's side,
And fix his eyes upon the falling tide;
The deep dry ditch, the rushes in the fen,
And mossy crag-pits were his lodgings then:

There, to his discontented thought a prey,
The melancholy mortal pined away.

    The neighb'ring poor at length began to speak
Of Abel's ramblings—he'd been gone a week;
They knew not where, and little care they took
For one so friendless and so poor to look.
At last a stranger, in a pedlar's shed,
Beheld him hanging—he had long been dead.
He left a paper, penn'd at sundry times,
Entitled thus—"My Groanings and my Crimes!"

    "I was a Christian man, and none could lay
Aught to my charge; I walk'd the narrow way:
All then was simple faith, serene and pure,
My hope was stedfast and my prospects sure;
Then was I tried by want and sickness sore,
But these I clapp'd my shield of faith before,
And cares and wants and man's rebukes I bore:
Alas! new foes assail'd me; I was vain,
They stung my pride and they confused my brain:
Oh! these deluders! with what glee they saw
Their simple dupe transgress the righteous law;
'Twas joy to them to view that dreadful strife,
When faith and frailty warr'd for more than life;
So with their pleasures they beguiled the heart,
Then with their logic they allay'd the smart;
They proved (so thought I then) with reasons strong,
That no man's feelings ever lead him wrong:
And thus I went, as on the varnish'd ice,
The smooth career of unbelief and vice.
Oft would the youths, with sprightly speech and bold,
Their witty tales of naughty priests unfold;
'Twas all a craft,' they said, 'a cunning trade;
Not she the priests, but priests Religion made.'
So I believed:"—No, Abel! to thy grief:
So thou relinquish'dst all that was belief:—
"I grew as very flint, and when the rest
Laugh'd at devotion, I enjoy'd the jest;
But this all vanish'd like the morning-dew,
When unemploy'd, and poor again I grew;
Yea! I was doubly poor, for I was wicked too.

    "The mouse that trespass'd and the treasure stole,
Found his lean body fitted to the hole;
Till, having fatted, he was forced to stay,
And, fasting, starve his stolen bulk away:
Ah! worse for me—grown poor, I yet remain

In sinful bonds, and pray and fast in vain.

"At length I thought, although these friends of sin
Have spread their net, and caught their prey therein;
Though my hard heart could not for mercy call,
Because though great my grief, my faith was small;
Yet, as the sick on skilful men rely,
The soul diseased may to a doctor fly.

"A famous one there was, whose skill had wrought
Cures past belief, and him the sinners sought;
Numbers there were defiled by mire and filth,
Whom he recovered by his goodly tilth:
'Come then,' I said, 'let me the man behold,
And tell my case:'—I saw him and I told.

"With trembling voice, 'Oh! reverend sir,' I said,
'I once believed, and I was then misled;
And now such doubts my sinful soul beset,
I dare not say that I'm a Christian yet;
Canst thou, good sir, by thy superior skill,
Inform my judgment and direct my will?
Ah! give thy cordial; let my soul have rest,
And be the outward man alone distress'd;
For at my state I tremble.'—'Tremble more,'
Said the good man, 'and then rejoice therefore!
'Tis good to tremble; prospects then are fair,
When the lost soul is plunged in deep despair:
Once thou wert simply honest, just, and pure,
Whole, as thou thought'st, and never wish'd a cure:
Now thou hast plunged in folly, shame, disgrace,
Now thou'rt an object meet for healing grace;
No merit thine, no virtue, hope, belief,
Nothing hast thou, but misery, sin, and grief;
The best, the only titles to relief.'
'What must I do,' I said, 'my soul to free?'—
'Do nothing, man; it will be done for thee.'
'But must I not, my reverend guide, believe?'—
'If thou art call'd, thou wilt the faith receive.'
'But I repent not.'—Angry he replied,
'If thou art call'd, though needest nought beside:
Attend on us, and if 'tis Heaven's decree,
The call will come,—if not, ah! woe for thee.'

"There then I waited, ever on the watch,
A spark of hope, a ray of light to catch;
His words fell softly like the flakes of snow,
But I could never find my heart o'erflow:
He cried aloud, till in the flock began

The sigh, the tear, as caught from man to man;
They wept and they rejoiced, and there was I
Hard as a flint, and as the desert dry:
To me no tokens of the call would come,
I felt my sentence, and received my doom;
But I complain'd—'Let thy repinings cease,
Oh! man of sin, for they thy guilt increase;
It bloweth where it listeth;—die in peace.'
—In peace, and perish?' I replied; 'impart
Some better comfort to a burthen'd heart.'
'Alas!' the priest return'd, 'can I direct
The heavenly call?—Do I proclaim th' elect?
Raise not thy voice against th' Eternal will,
But take thy part with sinners, and be still.'
    "Alas, for me! no more the times of peace
Are mine on earth—in death my pains may cease.
    "Foes to my soul! ye young seducers, know
What serious ills from your amusements flow;
Opinions you with so much ease profess,
Overwhelm the simple and their minds oppress:
Let such be happy, nor with reasons strong,
That make them wretched, prove their notions wrong;
Let them proceed in that they deem the way,
Fast when they will, and at their pleasure pray:
Yes, I have pity for my brethren's lot,
And so had Dives, but it help'd him not:
And is it thus?—I'm full of doubts:—Adieu!
Perhaps his reverence is mistaken too."{12}

LETTER XXII.

THE POOR OF THE BOROUGH.

> Methought the souls of all that I had murder'd
> Came to my tent, and every one did threat...
> > SHAKESPEARE, Richard III.

> The time hath been,
> That, when the brains were out, the man would die,
> And there an end: but now they rise again,
> With twenty mortal murders on their crowns,
> And push us from our stools.
> > SHAKESPEARE, Macbeth.

PETER GRIMES.

The Father of Peter a Fisherman—Peter's early Conduct—His Grief for the old Man—He takes an Apprentice—The Boy's Suffering and Fate—A second Boy; how he died—Peter acquitted—A third Apprentice—A Voyage by Sea: the Boy does not return—Evil Report on Peter: he is tried and threatened—Lives alone—His melancholy and incipient Madness—Is observed and visited—He escapes and is taken: is lodged in a parish-house: Women attend and watch him—He speaks in a Delirium; grows more collected—His Account of his Feelings and visionary Terrors previous to his Death.

OLD Peter Grimes made fishing his employ,
His wife he cabin'd with him and his boy,
And seem'd that life laborious to enjoy:
To town came quiet Peter with his fish,
And had of all a civil word and wish.
He left his trade upon the Sabbath-day,
And took young Peter in his hand to pray:
But soon the stubborn boy from care broke loose,
At first refused, then added his abuse:
His father's love he scorn'd, his power defied,
But being drunk, wept sorely when he died.
    Yes! then he wept, and to his mind there came
Much of his conduct, and he felt the shame,—
How he had oft the good old man reviled,
And never paid the duty of a child;
How, when the father in his Bible read,
He in contempt and anger left the shed:

"It is the word of life," the parent cried;
—"This is the life itself," the boy replied.
And while old Peter in amazement stood,
Gave the hot spirits to his boiling blood:—
How he, with oath and furious speech, began
To prove his freedom and assert the man;
And when the parent check'd his impious rage,
How he had cursed the tyranny of age,—
Nay, once had dealt the sacrilegious blow
On his bare head, and laid his parent low;
The father groan'd—"If thou art old," said he,
"And hast a son—thou wilt remember me:
Thy mother left me in a happy time,
Thou kill'dst not her—heav'n spares the double crime."
    On an inn-settle, in his maudlin grief,
This he resolved, and drank for his relief.
    Now lived the youth in freedom, but debarr'd
From constant pleasures, and he thought it hard;
Hard that he could not every wish obey,
But must awhile relinquish ale and play;
Hard! that he could not to his cards attend,
But must acquire the money he would spend.
    With greedy eye he look'd on all he saw,
He knew not justice, and he laugh'd at law;
On all he mark'd, he stretch'd his ready hand;
He fish'd by water and he filch'd by land:
Oft in the night has Peter dropp'd his oar,
Fled from his boat, and sought for prey on shore;
Oft up the hedge-row glided, on his back
Bearing the orchard's produce in a sack,
Or farm-yard load, tugg'd fiercely from the stack;
And as these wrongs to greater numbers rose,
The more he look'd on all men as his foes.
    He built a mud-wall'd hovel, where he kept
His various wealth, and there he oft-times slept;
But no success could please his cruel soul,
He wish'd for one to trouble and control;
He wanted some obedient boy to stand
And bear the blow of his outrageous hand;
And hoped to find in some propitious hour
A feeling creature subject to his power.
Peter had heard there were in London then,—
Still have they being!—workhouse-clearing men,
Who, undisturb'd by feelings just or kind,
Would parish-boys to needy tradesmen bind:

They in their want a trifling sum would take,
And toiling slaves of piteous orphans make.
　　Such Peter sought, and when a lad was found,
The sum was dealt him, and the slave was bound.
Some few in town observed in Peter's trap
A boy, with jacket blue and woollen cap;
But none inquired how Peter used the rope,
Or what the bruise that made the stripling stoop;
None could the ridges on his back behold,
None sought him shiv'ring in the winter's cold;
None put the question,—"Peter, dost thou give
The boy his food?—What, man! the lad must live:
Consider, Peter, let the child have bread,
He'll serve the better if he's stroked and fed."
None reason'd thus—and some, on hearing cries,
Said calmly, "Grimes is at his exercise."
　　Pinn'd, beaten, cold, pinch'd, threaten'd, and abused—
His efforts punish'd and his food refused,—
Awake tormented,—soon aroused from sleep,—
Struck if he wept, and yet compell'd to weep,
The trembling boy dropp'd down and strove to pray,
Received a blow, and trembling turn'd away,
Or sobb'd and hid his piteous face;—while he,
The savage master, grinn'd in horrid glee:
He'd now the power he ever loved to show,
A feeling being subject to his blow.
　　Thus lived the lad, in hunger, peril, pain,
His tears despised, his supplications vain:
Compe'lld by fear to lie, by need to steal,
His bed uneasy and unbless'd his meal,
For three sad years the boy his tortures bore,
And then his pains and trials were no more.
　　"How died he, Peter?" when the people said,
He growl'd—"I found him lifeless in his bed;"
Then tried for softer tone, and sigh'd, "Poor Sam is dead."
Yet murmurs were there, and some questions ask'd—
How he was fed, how punish'd, and how task'd?
Much they suspected, but they little proved,
And Peter pass'd untroubled and unmoved.
　　Another boy with equal ease was found,
The money granted, and the victim bound;
And what his fate?—One night it chanced he fell
From the boat's mast and perish'd in her well,
Where fish were living kept, and where the boy
(So reason'd men) could not himself destroy:—

"Yes! so it was" said Peter, "in his play,
(For he was idle both by night and day,)
He climb'd the main-mast and then fell below;"—
Then show'd his corpse, and pointed to the blow.
"What said the jury?"—they were long in doubt,
But sturdy Peter faced the matter out:
So they dismissed him, saying at the time,
"Keep fast your hatchway when you've boys who climb."
This hit the conscience, and he colour'd more
Than for the closest questions put before.

Thus all his fears the verdict set aside,
And at the slave-shop Peter still applied.

Then came a boy, of manners soft and mild,—
Our seamen's wives with grief beheld the child;
All thought (the poor themselves) that he was one
Of gentle blood, some noble sinner's son,
Who had, belike, deceived some humble maid,
Whom he had first seduced and then betray'd:—
However this, he seem'd a gracious lad,
In grief submissive, and with patience sad.

Passive he labour'd, till his slender frame
Bent with his loads, and he at length was lame:
Strange that a frame so weak could bear so long
The grossest insult and the foulest wrong;
But there were causes—in the town they gave
Fire, food, and comfort, to the gentle slave;
And though stern Peter, with a cruel hand,
And knotted rope, enforced the rude command,
Yet he consider'd what he'd lately felt,
And his vile blows with selfish pity dealt.

One day such draughts the cruel fisher made,
He could not vend them in his borough-trade,
But sail'd for London-mart: the boy was ill,
But ever humbled to his master's will;
And on the river, where they smoothly sail'd,
He strove with terror and awhile prevail'd;
But new to danger on the angry sea,
He clung affrighten'd to his master's knee:
The boat grew leaky and the wind was strong,
Rough was the passage and the time was long;
His liquor fail'd, and Peter's wrath arose,—
No more is known—the rest we must suppose,
Or learn of Peter:—Peter says, he "spied
The stripling's danger and for harbour tried;
Meantime the fish, and then th' apprentice died."

The pitying women raised a clamour round,
And weeping said, "Thou hast thy 'prentice drown'd."
　　Now the stern man was summon'd to the hall,
To tell his tale before the burghers all:
He gave th' account; profess'd the lad he loved,
And kept his brazen features all unmoved.
　　The mayor himself with tone severe replied,—
"Henceforth with thee shall never boy abide;
Hire thee a freeman, whom thou durst not beat,
But who, in thy despite, will sleep and eat:
Free thou art now!—again shouldst thou appear,
Thou'lt find thy sentence, like thy soul, severe."
　　Alas! for Peter not a helping hand,
So was he hated, could he now command;
Alone he row'd his boat, alone he cast
His nets beside, or made his anchor fast:
To hold a rope or hear a curse was none,—
He toil'd and rail'd; he groan'd and swore alone.
　　Thus by himself compell'd to live each day,
To wait for certain hours the tide's delay;
At the same time the same dull views to see,
The bounding marsh-bank and the blighted tree;
The water only, when the tides were high,
When low, the mud half cover'd and half-dry;
The sun-burnt tar that blisters on the planks,
And bank-side stakes in their uneven ranks;
Heaps of entangled weeds that slowly float,
As the tide rolls by the impeded boat.
　　When tides were neap, and, in the sultry day,
Through the tall bounding mud-banks made their way,
Which on each side rose swelling, and below
The dark warm flood ran silently and slow;
There anchoring, Peter chose from man to hide,
There hang his head, and view the lazy tide
In its hot slimy channel slowly glide;
Where the small eels that left the deeper way
For the warm shore, within the shallows play;
Where gaping mussels, left upon the mud,
Slope their slow passage to the fallen flood;—
Here dull and hopeless he'd lie down and trace
How sidelong crabs had scrawl'd their crooked race,
Or sadly listen to the tuneless cry
Of fishing gull or clanging golden-eye;
What time the sea-birds to the marsh would come.
And the loud bittern, from the bull-rush home,

Gave from the salt ditch side the bellowing boom:
He nursed the feelings these dull scenes produce,
And loved to stop beside the opening sluice;
Where the small stream, confined in narrow bound,
Ran with a dull, unvaried, sadd'ning sound;
Where all, presented to the eye or ear,
Oppress'd the soul with misery, grief, and fear.

    Besides these objects, there were places three,
Which Peter seem'd with certain dread to see;
When he drew near them he would turn from each,
And loudly whistle till he pass'd the reach.

    A change of scene to him brought no relief,
In town, 'twas plain, men took him for a thief:
The sailor's wives would stop him in the street,
And say, "Now, Peter, thou'st no boy to beat;"
Infants at play when they perceived him, ran,
Warning each other—"That's the wicked man;"
He growl'd an oath, and in an angry tone
Cursed the whole place and wish'd to be alone.

    Alone he was, the same dull scenes in view,
And still more gloomy in his sight they grew:
Though man he hated, yet employ'd alone
At bootless labour, he would swear and groan,
Cursing the shoals that glided by the spot,
And gulls that caught them when his arts could not.

    Cold nervous tremblings shook his sturdy frame,
And strange disease—he couldn't say the name;
Wild were his dreams, and oft he rose in fright,
Waked by his view of horrors in the night,—
Horrors that would the sternest minds amaze,
Horrors that demons might be proud to raise:
And though he felt forsaken, grieved at heart,
To think he lived from all mankind apart;
Yet, if a man approach'd, in terrors he would start.

    A winter pass'd since Peter saw the town,
And summer lodgers were again come down;
These, idly curious, with their glasses spied
The ships in bay as anchor'd for the tide,—
The river's craft,—the bustle of the quay,—
And sea-port views, which landmen love to see.

    One, up the river, had a man and boat
Seen day by day, now anchor'd, now afloat;
Fisher he seem'd, yet used no net nor hook;
Of sea-fowl swimming by no heed he took,
But on the gliding waves still fix'd his lazy look:

At certain stations he would view the stream,
As if he stood bewilder'd in a dream,
Or that some power had chain'd him for a time,
To feel a curse or meditate on crime.

    This known, some curious, some in pity went,
And others question'd—"Wretch, dost thou repent?"
He heard, he trembled, and in fear resign'd
His boat: new terror fill'd his restless mind;
Furious he grew, and up the country ran,
And there they seized him—a distemper'd man:—
Him we received, and to a parish-bed,
Follow'd and cursed, the groaning man was led.

    Here when they saw him, whom they used to shun,
A lost, lone man, so harass'd and undone;
Our gentle females, ever prompt to feel,
Perceived compassion on their anger steal;
His crimes they could not from their memories blot,
But they were grieved, and trembled at his lot.

    A priest too came, to whom his words are told;
And all the signs they shudder'd to behold.

    "Look! look!" they cried; "His limbs with horror shake
And as he grinds his teeth, what noise they make!
How glare his angry eyes, and yet he's not awake:
See! what cold drops upon his forehead stand,
And how he clenches that broad bony hand."

    The Priest attending, found he spoke at times
As one alluding to his fears and crimes;
"It was the fall," he mutter'd, "I can show
The manner how,—I never struck a blow:"—
And then aloud,—"Unhand me, free my chain;
On oath he fell—it struck him to the brain:—
Why ask my father?—that old man will swear
Against my life; besides, he wasn't there:
What, all agreed?—Am I to die to-day?—
My Lord, in mercy give me time to pray."

    Then as they watch'd him, calmer he became,
And grew so weak he couldn't move his frame,
But murmuring spake—while they could see and hear
The start of terror and the groan of fear;
See the large dew-beads on his forehead rise,
And the cold death-drop glaze his sunken eyes:
Nor yet he died, but with unwonted force
Seem'd with some fancied being to discourse:
He knew not us, or with accustom'd art
He hid the knowledge, yet exposed his heart;

'Twas part confession and the rest defence,
A madman's tale, with gleams of waking sense.
    "I'll tell you all," he said, "The very day
When the old man first placed them in my way:
My father's spirit—he who always tried
To give me trouble, when he lived and died—
When he was gone he could not be content
To see my days in painful labour spent,
But would appoint his meetings, and he made
Me watch at these, and so neglect my trade.
    "'Twas one hot noon, all silent, still, serene,
No living being had I lately seen;
I paddled up and down and dipp'd my net,
But (such his pleasure) I could nothing get,—
A father's pleasure, when his toil was done,
To plague and torture thus an only son!
And so I sat and look'd upon the stream,
How it ran on and felt as in a dream:
But dream it was not: No!—I fix'd my eyes
On the mid stream and saw the spirits rise:
I saw my father on the water stand,
And hold a thin pale boy in either hand;
And there they glided ghastly on the top
Of the salt flood, and never touch'd a drop:
I would have struck them, but they knew th' intent,
And smiled upon the oar, and down they went.
    "Now, from that day, whenever I began
To dip my net, there stood the hard old man—
He and those boys: I humbled me and pray'd
They would be gone; they heeded not, but stay'd:
Nor could I turn, nor would the boat go by,
But, gazing on the spirits, there was I:
They bade me leap to death, but I was loth to die:
And every day, as sure as day arose,
Would these three spirits meet me ere the close;
To hear and mark them daily was my doom,
And 'Come,' they said, with weak, sad voices, 'Come.'
To row away, with all my strength I tried,
But there were they hard by me in the tide,
The three unbodied forms—and 'Come, still come,' they cried.
    "Fathers should pity—but this old man shook
His hoary locks, and froze me by a look:
Thrice when I struck them, through the water came
A hollow groan, that weaken'd all my frame:
'Father!' said I, 'Have mercy:' he replied,

I know not what—the angry spirit lied,—
'Didst thou not draw thy knife?' said he:—'Twas true,
But I had pity and my arm withdrew:
He cried for mercy, which I kindly gave,
But he has no compassion in his grave.

    "There were three places, where they ever rose,—
The whole long river has not such as those—
Places accursed, where, if a man remain,
He'll see the things which strike him to the brain;
And there they made me on my paddle lean,
And look at them for hours;—accursed scene!
When they would glide to that smooth eddy-space,
Then bid me leap and join them in the place;
And at my groans each little villain sprite
Enjoy'd my pains and vanish'd in delight.

    "In one fierce summer-day, when my poor brain
Was burning hot, and cruel was my pain,
Then came this father-foe, and there he stood
With his two boys again upon the flood:
There was more mischief in their eyes, more glee
In their pale faces, when they glared at me:
Still they did force me on the oar to rest,
And when they saw me fainting and oppress'd,
He with his hand, the old man, scoop'd the flood,
And there came flame about him mix'd with blood;
He bade me stoop and look upon the place,
Then flung the hot-red liquor in my face;
Burning it blazed, and then I roar'd for pain,
I thought the demons would have turn'd my brain.

    "Still there they stood, and forced me to behold
A place of horrors—they can not be told—
Where the flood open'd, there I heard the shriek
Of tortured guilt—no earthly tongue can speak:
'All days alike! for ever!' did they say,
'And unremitted torments every day'—
Yes, so they said"—But here he ceased and gazed
On all around, affrighten'd and amazed;
And still he tried to speak, and look'd in dread
Of frighten'd females gathering round his bed;
Then dropp'd exhausted, and appear'd at rest,
Till the strong foe the vital powers possess'd;
Then with an inward, broken voice he cried,
"Again they come!" and mutter'd as he died.{13}

LETTER XXIII.

Poena autem vehemens ac multo saevior illis,
Quas et Caeditius gravis invenit aut Rhadamanthus,
Nocte dieque suum gestare in pectore testem.
                    JUVENAL, Satire xiii.

.... Think my former state a happy dream,
From which awaked, the truth of what we are
Shows us but this,—I am sworn brother now
To grim Necessity, and he and I
Will keep a league till death.
                    SHAKESPEARE, Richard II.

PRISONS. {14}

The Mind of Man accommodates itself to all Situations; Prisons otherwise would be intolerable—Debtors: their different kinds: three particularly described; others more briefly—An arrested Prisoner: his Account of his Feelings and his Situation—The Alleviations of a Prison—Prisoners for Crimes—Two Condemned: a vindictive Female: a Highwayman—The Interval between Condemnation and Execution—His Feelings as the Time approaches—His Dream.

'TIS well—that Man to all the varying states
Of good and ill his mind accommodates;
He not alone progressive grief sustains,
But soon submits to unexperienced pains:
Change after change, all climes his body bears;
His mind repeated shocks of changing cares:
Faith and fair Virtue arm the nobler breast;
Hope and mere want of feeling aid the rest.
    Or who could bear to lose the balmy air
Of summer's breath, from all things fresh and fair,
With all that man admires or loves below;
All earth and water, wood and vale bestow,
Where rosy pleasures smile, whence real blessings flow;
With sight and sound of every kind that lives,
And crowning all with joy that freedom gives?
    Who could from these, in some unhappy day,
Bear to be drawn by ruthless arms away,
To the vile nuisance of a noisome room,
Where only insolence and misery come?
(Save that the curious will by chance appear,

Or some in pity drop a fruitless tear);
To a damp Prison, where the very sight
Of the warm sun is favour and not right;
Where all we hear or see the feelings shock,
The oath and groan, the fetter and the lock?

Who could bear this and live?—Oh! many a year
All this is borne, and miseries more severe;
And some there are, familiar with the scene,
Who live in mirth, though few become serene.

Far as I might the inward man perceive,
There was a constant effort—not to grieve:
Not to despair, for better days would come,
And the freed debtor smile again at home:
Subdued his habits, he may peace regain,
And bless the woes that were not sent in vain.

Thus might we class the Debtors here confined,
The more deceived, the more deceitful kind;
Here are the guilty race, who mean to live
On credit, that credulity will give;
Who purchase, conscious they can never pay;
Who know their fate, and traffic to betray;
On whom no pity, fear, remorse, prevail.
Their aim a statute, their resource a jail;—
These are the public spoilers we regard,
No dun so harsh, no creditor so hard.

A second kind are they, who truly strive
To keep their sinking credit long alive;
Success, nay prudence, they may want, but yet
They would be solvent, and deplore a debt;
All means they use, to all expedients run,
And are by slow, sad steps, at last undone:
Justly, perhaps, you blame their want of skill,
But mourn their feelings and absolve their will.

There is a Debtor, who his trifling all
Spreads in a shop; it would not fill a stall:
There at one window his temptation lays,
And in new modes disposes and displays:
Above the door you shall his name behold,
And what he vends in ample letters told,
The words 'Repository,' 'Warehouse,' all
He uses to enlarge concerns so small:
He to his goods assigns some beauty's name,
Then in her reign, and hopes they'll share her fame,
And talks of credit, commerce, traffic, trade,
As one important by their profit made;

But who can paint the vacancy, the gloom,
And spare dimensions of one backward room?
Wherein he dines, if so 'tis fit to speak
Of one day's herring and the morrow's steak:
An anchorite in diet, all his care
Is to display his stock and vend his ware.
    Long waiting hopeless, then he tries to meet
A kinder fortune in a distant street;
There he again displays, increasing yet
Corroding sorrow and consuming debt:
Alas! he wants the requisites to rise—
The true connections, the availing ties:
They who proceed on certainties advance,
These are not times when men prevail by chance;
But still he tries, till, after years of pain,
He finds, with anguish, he has tried in vain.
Debtors are these on whom 'tis hard to press,
'Tis base, impolitic, and merciless.
    To these we add a miscellaneous kind,
By pleasure, pride, and indolence confined;
Those whom no calls, no warnings could divert,
The unexperienced, and the inexpert;
The builder, idler, schemer, gamester, sot,—
The follies different, but the same their lot;
Victims of horses, lasses, drinking, dice,
Of every passion, humour, whim, and vice.
See! that sad Merchant, who but yesterday
Had a vast household in command and pay;
He now entreats permission to employ
A boy he needs, and then entreats the boy.
    And there sits one improvident but kind,
Bound for a friend, whom honour could not bind;
Sighing, he speaks to any who appear,
"A treach'rous friend—'twas that which sent me here:
I was too kind,—I thought I could depend
On his bare word—he was a treach'rous friend."
    A Female too!—it is to her a home,
She came before—and she again will come:
Her friends have pity; when their anger drops,
They take her home;—she's tried her schools and shops—
Plan after plan;—but fortune would not mend,
She to herself was still the treach'rous friend;
And wheresoe'er began, all here was sure to end:
And there she sits, as thoughtless and as gay
As if she'd means, or not a debt to pay—

Or knew to-morrow she'd be call'd away—
Or felt a shilling and could dine to-day.

  While thus observing, I began to trace
The sober'd features of a well-known face—
Looks once familiar, manners form'd to please,
And all illumined by a heart at ease:
But fraud and flattery ever claim'd a part
(Still unresisted) of that easy heart;
But he at length beholds me—"Ah! my friend!
"And have thy pleasures this unlucky end?"
"Too sure," he said, and smiling as he sigh'd;
"I went astray, though Prudence seem'd my guide;
All she proposed I in my heart approved,
And she was honour'd, but my pleasure loved—
Pleasure, the mistress to whose arms I fled,
From wife-like lectures angry Prudence read.

  "Why speak the madness of a life like mine,
The powers of beauty, novelty, and wine?
Why paint the wanton smile, the venal vow,
Or friends whose worth I can appreciate now;
Oft I perceived my fate, and then could say,
I'll think to-morrow, I must live to-day:
So am I here—I own the laws are just—
And here, where thought is painful, think I must:
But speech is pleasant; this discourse with thee
Brings to my mind the sweets of liberty,
Breaks on the sameness of the place, and gives
The doubtful heart conviction that it lives.

  "Let me describe my anguish in the hour
When law detain'd me and I felt its power.

  "When, in that shipwreck, this I found my shore,
And join'd the wretched, who were wreck'd before;
When I perceived each feature in the face,
Pinch'd through neglect or turbid by disgrace;
When in these wasting forms affliction stood
In my afiiicted view, it chill'd my blood;—
And forth I rush'd, a quick retreat to make,
Till a loud laugh proclaim'd the dire mistake:
But when the groan had settled to a sigh,
When gloom became familiar to the eye,
When I perceive how others seem to rest,
With every evil rankling in my breast,—
Led by example, I put on the man,
Sing off my sighs, and trifle as I can.

  "Homer! nay Pope! (for never will I seek

Applause for learning—nought have I with Greek)
Gives us the secrets of his pagan hell,
Where ghost with ghost in sad communion dwell;
Where shade meets shade, and round the gloomy meads
They glide, and speak of old heroic deeds,—
What fields they conquer'd, and what foes they slew,
And sent to join the melancholy crew.
When a new spirit in that world was found,
A thousand shadowy forms came flitting round:
Those who had known him, fond inquiries made,—
'Of all we left, inform us, gentle shade,
Now as we lead thee in our realms to dwell,
Our twilight groves, and meads of asphodel.'
      "What paints the poet, is our station here,
Where we like ghosts and flitting shades appear:
This is the hell he sings, and here we meet,
And former deeds to new-made friends repeat;
Heroic deeds, which here obtain us fame,
And are in fact the causes why we came:
Yes! this dim region is old Homer's hell,
Abate but groves and meads of asphodel.
Here, when a stranger from your world we spy,
We gather round him and for news apply;
He hears unheeding, nor can speech endure,
But shivering gazes on the vast obscure:
We smiling pity, and by kindness show
We felt his feelings and his terrors know;
Then speak of comfort—time will give him sight,
Where now 'tis dark; where now 'tis woe—delight.
'Have hope,' we say, 'and soon the place to thee
Shall not a prison but a castle be:
When to the wretch whom care and guilt confound,
The world's a prison, with a wider bound;
Go where he may, he feels himself confined,
And wears the fetters of an abject mind.'
      "But now adieu! those giant-keys appear,
Thou art not worthy to be inmate here:
Go to thy world, and to the young declare
What we, our spirits and employments, are;
Tell them how we the ills of life endure,
Our empire stable, and our state secure;
Our dress, our diet, for their use describe,
And bid them haste to join the gen'rous tribe:
Go to thy world, and leave us here to dwell,
Who to its joys and comforts bid farewell."

Farewell to these; but other scenes I view,
And other griefs, and guilt of deeper hue;
Where Conscience gives to outward ills her pain,
Gloom to the night, and pressure to the chain:
Here separate cells awhile in misery keep
Two doom'd to suffer: there they strive for sleep;
By day indulged, in larger space they range,
Their bondage certain, but their bounds have change.

    One was a female, who had grievous ill
Wrought in revenge, and she enjoy'd it still:
With death before her, and her fate in view,
Unsated vengeance in her bosom grew:
Sullen she was and threat'ning; in her eye
Glared the stern triumph that she dared to die:
But first a being in the world must leave—
'Twas once reproach; 'twas now a short reprieve.

    She was a pauper bound, who early gave
Her mind to vice and doubly was a slave:
Upbraided, beaten, held by rough control,
Revenge sustain'd, inspired, and fill'd her soul:
She fired a full-stored barn, confess'd the fact,
And laugh'd at law and justified the act:
Our gentle Vicar tried his powers in vain,
She answer'd not, or answer'd with disdain;
Th' approaching fate she heard without a sigh,
And neither cared to live nor fear'd to die.

    Not so he felt, who with her was to pay
The forfeit, life—with dread he view'd the day,
And that short space which yet for him remain'd,
Till with his limbs his faculties were chain'd:
He paced his narrow bounds some ease to find,
But found it not,—no comfort reach'd his mind:
Each sense was palsied; when he tasted food,
He sigh'd and said, "Enough—'tis very good."
Since his dread sentence, nothing seem'd to be
As once it was—he seeing could not see,
Nor hearing, hear aright;—when first I came
Within his view, I fancied there was shame,
I judged resentment; I mistook the air,—
These fainter passions live not with despair;
Or but exist and die:—Hope, fear, and love,
Joy, doubt, and hate, may other spirits move,
But touch not his, who every waking hour
Has one fix'd dread, and always feels its power.

    "But will not mercy?"—No! she cannot plead

For such an outrage;—'twas a cruel deed:
He stopp'd a timid traveller;—to his breast,
With oaths and curses, was the danger press'd:—
No! he must suffer: pity we may find
For one man's pangs, but must not wrong mankind.

   Still I behold him, every thought employ'd
On one dire view!—all others are destroy'd;
This makes his features ghastly, gives the tone
Of his few words resemblance to a groan;
He takes his tasteless food, and when 'tis done,
Counts up his meals, now lessen'd by that one;
For expectation is on time intent,
Whether he brings us joy or punishment.

   Yes! e'en in sleep the impressions all remain,
He hears the sentence and he feels the chain;
He sees the judge and jury, when he shakes,
And loudly cries, "Not guilty," and awakes:
Then chilling tremblings o'er his body creep,
Till worn-out nature is compell'd to sleep.
Now comes the dream again: it shows each scene,
With each small circumstance that comes between—
The call to suffering and the very deed—
There crowds go with him, follow, and precede;
Some heartless shout, some pity, all condemn,
While he in fancied envy looks at them:
He seems the place for that sad act to see,
And dreams the very thirst which then will be:
A priest attends—it seems, the one he knew
In his best days, beneath whose care he grew.

   At this his terrors take a sudden flight,
He sees his native village with delight;
The house, the chamber, where he once array'd
His youthful person; where he knelt and pray'd:
Then too the comforts he enjoy'd at home,
The days of joy; the joys themselves are come;—
The hours of innocence;—the timid look
Of his loved maid, when first her hand he took,
And told his hope; her trembling joy appears,
Her forced reserve and his retreating fears.

   All now is present;—'tis a moment's gleam
Of former sunshine—stay, delightful dream!
Let him within his pleasant garden walk,
Give him her arm, of blessings let them talk.

   Yes! all are with him now, and all the while
Life's early prospects and his Fanny's smile:

Then come his sister and his village-friend,
And he will now the sweetest moments spend
Life has to yield;—No! never will he find
Again on earth such pleasure in his mind:
He goes through shrubby walks these friends among,
Love in their looks and honour on the tongue:
Nay, there's a charm beyond what nature shows,
The bloom is softer and more sweetly glows;—
Pierced by no crime, and urged by no desire
For more than true and honest hearts require,
They feel the calm delight, and thus proceed
Through the green lane,—then linger in the mead,—
Stray o'er the heath in all its purple bloom,—
And pluck the blossom where the wild bees hum;
Then through the broomy bound with ease they pass,
And press the sandy sheep-walk's slender grass,
Where dwarfish flowers among the gorse are spread,
And the lamb browses by the linnet's bed;
Then 'cross the bounding brook they make their way
O'er its rough bridge—and there behold the bay!—
The ocean smiling to the fervid sun—
The waves that faintly fall and slowly run—
The ships at distance and the boats at hand;
And now they walk upon the sea-side sand,
Counting the number and what kind they be,
Ships softly sinking in the sleepy sea:
Now arm in arm, now parted, they behold
The glitt'ring waters on the shingles roll'd:
The timid girls, half dreading their design,
Dip the small foot in the retarded brine,
And search for crimson weeds, which spreading flow,
Or lie like pictures on the sand below;
With all those bright red pebbles, that the sun
Through the small waves so softly shines upon;
And those live lucid jellies which the eye
Delights to trace as they swim glittering by:
Pearl-shells and rubied star-fish they admire,
And will arrange above the parlour fire,—
Tokens of bliss!—"Oh! horrible! a wave
Roars as it rises—save me, Edward! save!"
She cries:—Alas! the watchman on his way
Calls, and lets in—truth, terror, and the day!

LETTER XXIV.

Be it a weakness, it deserves some praise,—
We love the play-place of our early days;
The scene is touching, and the heart is stone
That feels not at that sight—and feels at none.
The wall on which we tried our graving skill;
The very name we carved subsisting still;
The bench on which we sat while deep employ'd,
Though mangled, hack'd, and hew'd, yet not destroy'd.
The little ones unbutton'd, glowing hot,
Playing our games, and on the very spot;
As happy as we once to kneel and draw
The chalky ring and knuckle down at taw.
This fond detachment to the well known place,
When first we started into life's long race,
Maintains its hold with such unfailing sway,
We feel it e'en in age and at our latest day.

COWPER.

Tu quoque ne metuas, quamvis schola verbere multo
Increpet et truculenta senex geret ora magister;
Degeneres animos timor arguit; at tibi consta
Intrepidus, nec te clamor plagaeque sonantes,
Nec matutinis agitet formido sub horis,
Quod sceptrum vibrat ferulae, quod multa supellex
Virgea, quod molis scuticam praetexit aluta,
Quod fervent trepido subsellia vestra tumultu,
Pompa loci, et vani fugiatur scena timoris.

AUSONIUS.

SCHOOLS. {15}

Schools of every Kind to be found in the Borough—The School for Infants—The School Preparatory: the Sagacity of the Mistress in foreseeing Character—Day Schools of the lower Kind—A Master with Talents adapted to such Pupils: one of superior Qualifications—Boarding Schools; that for young Ladies; one going first to the Governess, one finally returning Home—School for Youth: Master and Teacher; various Dispositions and Capacities—The Miser-Boy—The Bully-Boy—Sons of Farmers: how amused—What Study will effect, examined—A College Life: one sent from his College to a Benefice; one retained there in Dignity—The Advantage in either Case not

considerable—Where, then, the Good of a Literary Life?—Answered—
Conclusion.

To every class we have a School assign'd,
Rules for all ranks and food for every mind:
Yet one there is, that small regard to rule
Or study pays, and still is deem'd a School:
That, where a deaf, poor, patient widow sits,
And awes some thirty infants as she knits;
Infants of humble, busy wives, who pay
Some trifling price for freedom through the day:
At this good matron's hut the children meet,
Who thus becomes the mother of the street:
Her room is small they cannot widely stray,—
Her threshold high they cannot run away:
Though deaf, she sees the rebel-heroes shout,—
Though lame, her white rod nimbly walks about;
With band of yarn she keeps offenders in,
And to her gown the sturdiest rogue can pin:
Aided by these, and spells, and tell-tale birds,
Her power they dread and reverence her words.
    To Learning's second seats we now proceed,
Where humming students gilded primers read;
Or books with letters large and pictures gay,
To make their reading but a kind of play—
"Reading made easy," so the titles tell;
But they who read must first begin to spell:
There may be profit in these arts, but still
Learning is labour, call it what you will;
Upon the youthful mind a heavy load,
Nor must we hope to find the royal road.
Some will their easy steps to science show,
And some to heav'n itself their by-way know;
Ah! trust them not,—who fame or bliss would share,
Must learn by labour, and must live by care.
    Another matron, of superior kind,
For higher schools prepares the rising mind;
Preparatory she her Learning calls,
The step first made to colleges and halls.
    She early sees to what the mind will grow,
Nor abler judge of infant-powers I know:
She sees what soon the lively will impede,
And how the steadier will in turn succeed;
Observes the dawn of wisdom, fancy, taste,
And knows what parts will wear, and what will waste:

She marks the mind too lively, and at once
Sees the gay coxcomb and the rattling dunce.

    Long has she lived, and much she loves to trace
Her former pupils, now a lordly race;
Whom when she sees rich robes and furs bedeck,
She marks the pride which once she strove to check.
A Burgess comes, and she remembers well
How hard her task to make his worship spell;
Cold, selfish, dull, inanimate, unkind,
'Twas but by anger he display'd a mind:
Now civil, smiling, complaisant, and gay,
The world has worn th' unsocial crust away:
That sullen spirit now a softness wears,
And, save by fits, e'en dulness disappears:
But still the matron can the man behold,
Dull, selfish, hard, inanimate, and cold.
A Merchant passes,—"Probity and truth,
Prudence and patience, mark'd thee from thy youth."
Thus she observes, but oft retains her fears
For him, who now with name unstain'd appears:
Nor hope relinquishes, for one who yet
Is lost in error and involved in debt;
For latent evil in that heart she found,
More open here, but here the core was sound.

    Various our Day-Schools: here behold we one
Empty and still:—the morning duties done,
Soil'd, tatter'd, worn, and thrown in various heaps,
Appear their books, and there confusion sleeps;
The workmen all are from the Babel fled,
And lost their tools, till the return they dread:
Meantime the master, with his wig awry,
Prepares his books for business by-and-by:
Now all th' insignia of the monarch laid
Beside him rest, and none stand by afraid;
He, while his troop light-hearted leap and play,
Is all intent on duties of the day;
No more the tyrant stern or judge severe,
He feels the father's and the husband's fear.

    Ah! little think the timid trembling crowd,
That one so wise, so powerful, and so proud,
Should feel himself, and dread the humble ills
Of rent-day charges, and of coalman's bills;
That while they mercy from their judge implore,
He fears himself—a knocking at the door;
And feels the burthen as his neighbour states

His humble portion to the parish-rates.
They sit th' alloted hours, then eager run,
Rushing to pleasure when the duty's done;
His hour of leisure is of different kind,
Then cares domestic rush upon his mind,
And half the ease and comfort he enjoys,
Is when surrounded by slates, books, and boys.
Poor Reuben Dixon has the noisiest school
Of ragged lads, who ever bow'd to rule;
Low in his price—the men who heave our coals,
And clean our causeways, send him boys in shoals;
To see poor Reuben, with his fry beside,—
Their half-check'd rudeness and his half-scorn'd pride,—
Their room, the sty in which th' assembly meet,
In the close lane behind the Northgate-street;
T'observe his vain attempts to keep the peace,
Till tolls the bell, and strife and troubles cease,—
Calls for our praise; his labour praise deserves,
But not our pity; Reuben has no nerves:
'Mid noise and dirt, and stench, and play, and prate,
He calmly cuts the pen or views the slate.
But Leonard!—yes, for Leonard's fate I grieve,
Who loaths the station which he dares not leave:
He cannot dig, he will not beg his bread,
All his dependence rests upon his head;
And deeply skill'd in sciences and arts,
On vulgar lads he wastes superior parts.
Alas! what grief that feeling mind sustains,
In guiding hands and stirring torpid brains;
He whose proud mind from pole to pole will move,
And view the wonders of the worlds above;
Who thinks and reasons strongly:—hard his fate,
Confined for ever to the pen and slate:
True, he submits, and when the long dull day
Has slowly pass'd, in weary tasks, away,
To other worlds with cheerful view he looks,
And parts the night between repose and books.
Amid his labours, he has sometimes tried
To turn a little from his cares aside;
Pope, Milton, Dryden, with delight has seized,
His soul engaged and of his trouble eased:
When, with a heavy eye and ill-done sum,
No part conceived, a stupid boy will come;
Then Leonard first subdues the rising frown,
And bids the blockhead lay his blunders down;

O'er which disgusted he will turn his eye,
To his sad duty his sound mind apply,
And, vex'd in spirit, throw his pleasures by.
    Turn we to Schools which more than these afford—
The sound instruction and the wholesome board;
And first our School for Ladies;—pity calls
For one soft sigh, when we behold these walls,
Placed near the town, and where, from window high,
The fair, confined, may our free crowds espy,
With many a stranger gazing up and down,
And all the envied tumult of the town;
May, in the smiling summer-eve, when they
Are sent to sleep the pleasant hours away,
Behold the poor (whom they conceive the bless'd)
Employ'd for hours, and grieved they cannot rest.
    Here the fond girl, whose days are sad and few
Since dear mamma pronounced the last adieu,
Looks to the road, and fondly thinks she hears
The carriage-wheels, and struggles with her tears:
All yet is new, the misses great and small,
Madam herself, and teachers, odious all;
From laughter, pity, nay command, she turns,
But melts in softness, or with anger burns;
Nauseates her food, and wonders who can sleep
On such mean beds, where she can only weep:
She scorns condolence—but to all she hates
Slowly at length her mind accommodates;
Then looks on bondage with the same concern
As others felt, and finds that she must learn
As others learn'd—the common lot to share,
To search for comfort and submit to care.
    There are, 'tis said, who on these seats attend,
And to these ductile minds destruction vend;
Wretches—(to virtue, peace, and nature, foes)—
To these soft minds, their wicked trash expose;
Seize on the soul, ere passions take the sway,
And lead the heart, ere yet it feels, astray:
Smugglers obscene!—and can there be who take
Infernal pains the sleeping vice to wake?
Can there be those by whom the thought defiled
Enters the spotless bosom of a child?
By whom the ill is to the heart conveyed,
Who lend the foe, not yet in arms, their aid;
And sap the city-walls before the siege be laid?
    Oh! rather skulking in the by-ways steal,

And rob the poorest traveller of his meal;
Burst through the humblest trader's bolted door;
Bear from the widow's hut her winter-store;
With stolen steed, on highways take your stand,
Your lips with curses arm'd, with death your hand;—
Take all but life—the virtuous more would say,
Take life itself, dear as it is, away,
Rather than guilty thus the guileless soul betray.
  Years pass away—let us suppose them past,
Th' accomplish'd nymph for freedom looks at last;
All hardships over, which a school contains,
The spirit's bondage and the body's pains;
Where teachers make the heartless, trembling set
Of pupils suffer for their own regret;
Where winter's cold, attack'd by one poor fire,
Chills the fair child, commanded to retire;
She felt it keenly in the morning-air,
Keenly she felt it at the evening prayer.
More pleasant summer; but then walks were made,
Not a sweet ramble, but a slow parade;
They moved by pairs beside the hawthorn-hedge,
Only to set their feelings on an edge;
And now at eve, when all their spirits rise,
Are sent to rest, and all their pleasure dies;
Where yet they all the town-alert can see,
And distant plough-boys pacing o'er the lea.
  These and the tasks successive masters brought—
The French they conn'd, the curious works they wrought;
The hours they made their taper fingers strike
Note after note, all dull to them alike;
Their drawings, dancings on appointed days,
Playing with globes, and getting parts of plays:
The tender friendships made 'twixt heart and heart,
When the dear friends had nothing to impart:—
  All! all! are over;—now th' accomplish'd maid
Longs for the world, of nothing there afraid:
Dreams of delight invade her gentle breast,
And fancied lovers rob the heart of rest;
At the paternal door a carriage stands,
Love knits their hearts and Hymen joins their hands.
Ah! world unknown! how charming is thy view,
Thy pleasures many, and each pleasure new:
Ah! world experienced! what of thee is told?
How few thy pleasures, and those few how old!
  Within a silent street, and far apart

From noise of business, from a quay or mart,
Stands an old spacious building, and the din
You hear without, explains the work within;
Unlike the whispering of the nymphs, this noise
Loudly proclaims a "Boarding-School for Boys;"
The master heeds it not, for thirty years
Have render'd all familiar to his ears;
He sits in comfort, 'mid the various sound
Of mingled tones for ever flowing round:
Day after day he to his task attends,—
Unvaried toil, and care that never ends:
Boys in their works proceed; while his employ
Admits no change, or changes but the boy;
Yet time has made it easy;—he beside
Has power supreme, and power is sweet to pride:
But grant him pleasure; what can teachers feel,
Dependent helpers always at the wheel?
Their power despised, their compensation small,
Their labour dull, their life laborious all;
Set after set the lower lads to make
Fit for the class which their superiors take;
The road of learning for a time to track
In roughest state, and then again go back:
Just the same way, on other troops to wait,—
Attendants fix'd at learning's lower gate.

    The Day-tasks now are over—to their ground
Rush the gay crowd with joy-compelling sound;
Glad to elude the burthens of the day,
The eager parties hurry to their play:
Then in these hours of liberty we find
The native bias of the opening mind;
They yet possess not skill the mask to place,
And hide the passions glowing in the face;
Yet some are found—the close, the sly, the mean,
Who know already all must not be seen.

    Lo! one who walks apart, although so young,
He lays restraint upon his eye and tongue,
Nor will he into scrapes or dangers get,
And half the school are in the stripling's debt:
Suspicious, timid, he is much afraid
Of trick and plot:—he dreads to be betray'd:
He shuns all friendship, for he finds they lend
When lads begin to call each other friend:
Yet self with self has war; the tempting sight
Of fruit on sale provokes his appetite;—

See! how he walks the sweet seduction by;
That he is tempted, costs him first a sigh,—
'Tis dangerous to indulge, 'tis grievous to deny!
This he will choose, and whispering asks the price,
The purchase dreadful, but the portion nice:
Within the pocket he explores the pence;
Without, temptation strikes on either sense,
The sight, the smell;—but then he thinks again
Of money gone! while fruit nor taste remain.
Meantime there comes an eager thoughtless boy,
Who gives the price and only feels the joy:
Example dire: the youthful miser stops
And slowly back the treasured coinage drops:
Heroic deed! for should he now comply,
Can he tomorrow's appetite deny?
Beside, these spendthrifts who so freely live,
Cloy'd with their purchase, will a portion give:—
Here ends debate, he buttons up his store,
And feels the comfort that it burns no more.

    Unlike to him the Tyrant-boy, whose sway
All hearts acknowledge; him the crowds obey:
At his command they break through every rule;
Whoever governs, he controls the school:
'Tis not the distant emperor moves their fear,
But the proud viceroy who is ever near.

    Verres could do that mischief in a day,
For which not Rome, in all its power, could pay;
And these boy-tyrants will their slaves distress,
And do the wrongs no master can redress:
The mind they load with fear; it feels disdain
For its own baseness; yet it tries in vain
To shake th' admitted power:—the coward comes again:
'Tis more than present pain these tyrants give,
Long as we've life some strong impressions live;
And these young ruffians in the soul will sow
Seeds of all vices that on weakness grow.

    Hark! at his word the trembling younglings flee,
Where he is walking none must walk but he;
See! from the winter fire the weak retreat,
His the warm corner, his the favourite seat,
Save when he yields it to some slave to keep
Awhile, then back, at his return, to creep:
At his command his poor dependants fly,
And humbly bribe him as a proud ally;
Flatter'd by all, the notice he bestows,

Is gross abuse, and bantering and blows;
Yet he's a dunce, and, spite of all his fame
Without the desk, within he feels his shame:
For there the weaker boy, who felt his scorn,
For him corrects the blunders of the morn;
And he is taught, unpleasant truth! to find
The trembling body has the prouder mind.

Hark! to that shout, that burst of empty noise,
From a rude set of bluff, obstreperous boys;
They who, like colts let loose, with vigour bound,
And thoughtless spirit, o'er the beaten ground;
Fearless they leap, and every youngster feels
His Alma active in his hands and heels.

These are the sons of farmers, and they come
With partial fondness for the joys of home;
Their minds are coursing in their fathers' fields,
And e'en the dream a lively pleasure yields;
They, much enduring, sit th' allotted hours,
And o'er a grammar waste their sprightly powers;
They dance; but them can measured steps delight,
Whom horse and hounds to daring deeds excite?
Nor could they bear to wait from meal to meal,
Did they not slily to the chamber steal,
And there the produce of the basket seize,
The mother's gift! still studious of their ease.
Poor Alma, thus oppress'd forbears to rise,
But rests or revels in the arms and thighs.

"But is it sure that study will repay
The more attentive and forbearing?"—Nay!
The farm, the ship, the humble shop, have each
Gains which severest studies seldom reach.

At College place a youth, who means to raise
His state by merit and his name by praise;
Still much he hazards; there is serious strife
In the contentions of a scholar's life:
Not all the mind's attention, care, distress,
Nor diligence itself, ensure success:
His jealous heart a rival's powers may dread,
Till its strong feelings have confused his head,
And, after days and months, nay, years of pain,
He finds just lost the object he would gain.

But grant him this and all such life can give,
For other prospects he begins to live;
Begins to feel that man was form'd to look
And long for other objects than a book:

In his mind's eye his house and glebe he sees,
And farms and talks with farmers at his ease;
And time is lost, till fortune sends him forth
To a rude world unconscious of his worth;
There in some petty parish to reside,
The college boast, then turn'd the village guide:
And though awhile his flock and dairy please,
He soon reverts to former joys and ease,
Glad when a friend shall come to break his rest,
And speak of all the pleasures they possess'd,
Of masters, fellows, tutors, all with whom
They shared those pleasures, never more to come;
Till both conceive the times by bliss endear'd,
Which once so dismal and so dull appear'd.

But fix our Scholar, and suppose him crown'd
With all the glory gain'd on classic ground;
Suppose the world without a sigh resign'd,
And to his college all his care confined;
Give him all honours that such states allow,
The freshman's terror and the tradesman's bow;
Let his apartments with his taste agree,
And all his views be those he loves to see;
Let him each day behold the savoury treat,
For which he pays not, but is paid to eat;
These joys and glories soon delight no more,
Although, withheld, the mind is vex'd and sore;
The honour too is to the place confined,
Abroad they know not each superior mind:
Strangers no wranglers in these figures see,
Nor give they worship to a high degree;
Unlike the prophet's is the scholar's case,
His honour all is in his dwelling-place:
And there such honours are familiar things;
What is a monarch in a crowd of kings?
Like other sovereigns he's by forms address'd,
By statutes governed and with rules oppress'd.

When all these forms and duties die away,
And the day passes like the former day,
Then of exterior things at once bereft,
He's to himself and one attendant left;
Nay, John too goes; nor aught of service more
Remains for him; he gladly quits the door,
And, as he whistles to the college-gate,
He kindly pities his poor master's fate.

Books cannot always please, however good;

Minds are not ever craving for their food;
But sleep will soon the weary soul prepare
For cares to-morrow that were this day's care:
For forms, for feasts, that sundry times have past,
And formal feasts that will for ever last.
     "But then from Study will no comforts rise?"—
Yes! such as studious minds alone can prize;
Comforts, yea!—joys ineffable they find,
Who seek the prouder pleasures of the mind:
The soul, collected in those happy hours,
Then makes her efforts, then enjoys her powers;
And in those seasons feels herself repaid,
For labours past and honours long delay'd.
     No! 'tis not worldly gain, although by chance
The sons of learning may to wealth advance;
Nor station high, though in some favouring hour
The sons of learning may arrive at power;
Nor is it glory, though the public voice
Of honest praise will make the heart rejoice:
But 'tis the mind's own feelings give tho joy,
Pleasures she gathers in her own employ—
Pleasures that gain or praise cannot bestow,
Yet can dilate and raise them when they flow.
     For this the Poet looks thy world around,
Where form and life and reasoning man are found;
He loves the mind, in all its modes, to trace,
And all the manners of the changing race;
Silent he walks the road of life along,
And views the aims of its tumultuous throng:
He finds what shapes the Proteus-passions take,
And what strange waste of life and joy they make,
And loves to show them in their varied ways,
With honest blame or with unflattering praise:
'Tis good to know, 'tis pleasant to impart,
These turns and movements of the human heart:
The stronger features of the soul to paint,
And make distinct the latent and the faint;
MAN AS HE IS, to place in all men's view,
Yet none with rancour, none with scorn pursue:
Nor be it ever of my Portraits told—
"Here the strong lines of malice we behold."

     This let me hope, that when in public view

I bring my Pictures, men may feel them true:
"This is a likeness," may they all declare,
"And I have seen him, but I know not where:"
For I should mourn the mischief I had done,
If as the likeness all would fix on one.

    Man's Vice and Crime I combat as I can,
But to his GOD and conscience leave the Man;
I search (a Quixote!) all the land about,
To find its Giants and Enchanters out,—
(The Giant-Folly, the Enchanter-Vice,
Whom doubtless I shall vanquish in a trice;)—
But is there man whom I would injure?—No!
I am to him a fellow, not a foe,—
A fellow-sinner, who must rather dread
The bolt, than hurl it at another's head.
    No! let the guiltless, if there such be found,
Launch forth the spear, and deal the deadly wound.
How can I so the cause of Virtue aid,
Who am myself attainted and afraid?
Yet as I can, I point the powers of rhyme,
And, sparing criminals, attack the crime.

Footnotes:

{1} Note: Indentation and punctuation as original.

{2} The wants and mortifications of a poor clergyman are the subjects of one portion of this Letter; and he being represented as a stranger in the Borough, it may be necessary to make some apology for his appearance in the Poem. Previous to a late meeting of a literary society, whose benevolent purpose is well known to the public, I was induced by a friend to compose a few verses, in which, with the general commendation of the design, should be introduced a hint that the bounty might be farther extended; these verses, a gentleman did me the honour to recite at the meeting, and they were printed as an extract from the Poem, to which, in fact, they may be called an appendage.

{3} The account of Coddrington occurs in "The Mirrour for Magistrates." He suffered in the reign of Richard III.

{4} If I have in this letter praised the good-humour of a man confessedly too inattentive to business, and if, in another (AMUSEMENTS), I have written somewhat sarcastically of "the brick—floored parlour which the butcher lets," be credit given to me, that, in the one case, I had no intention to apologise for idleness, nor any design in the other to treat with contempt the resources of the poor. The good-humour is considered as the consolation of disappointment; and the room is so mentioned because the lodger is vain. Most of my readers will perceive this: but I shall be sorry if by any I am supposed to make pleas for the vices of men, or treat their wants or infirmities with derision or with disdain.

{5} The Letter on Itinerant Players will to some appear too harshly written, their profligacy exaggerated, and their distresses magnified; but though the respectability of a part of these people may give us a more favourable view of the whole body; though some actors be sober, and some managers prudent; still there is vice and misery left more than sufficient to justify my description. But, if I could find only one woman who (passing forty years on many stages and sustaining many principal characters) laments in her unrespected old age, that there was no workhouse to which she could legally sue for admission; if I could produce only one female, seduced upon the boards, and starved in her lodging, compelled by her poverty to sing, and by her sufferings to weep, without any prospect but misery, or any consolation but death; if I could exhibit only one youth who sought refuge from parental authority in the licentious freedom of a wandering company; yet, with three such examples, I should feel myself justified in the account I have given:—but such characters and sufferings are common, and there are few of these societies which could not show members of this description. To some, indeed, the life has its satisfactions: they never expected to be free from labour, and their present kind they think is light: they have no delicate ideas of shame, and therefore duns and hisses give them no other pain than what arises from the fear of not being trusted, joined with the apprehension that they may have nothing to subsist upon except their credit.

{6} For the Alms-house itself, its Governors, and Inhabitants, I have not much to offer in favour of the subject or of the character. One of these, Sir Denys Brand, may be considered as too highly placed for an author, who seldom ventures above middle life, to delineate; and, indeed, I had some idea of reserving him for another occasion, where he might have appeared with those in his own rank: but then it is most uncertain whether he would ever appear, and he has been so many years prepared for the public, whenever opportunity might offer that I have at length given him place, and though with his inferiors, yet as a ruler over them.

{7} Benbow may be thought too low and despicable to be admitted here; but he is a borough-character, and however disgusting in some respects a picture may be, it will please some, and be tolerated by many, if it can boast that one merit of being a faithful likeness.

{8} The characters of the Hospital Directors were written many years since and, so far as I was capable of judging, are drawn with fidelity. I mention this circumstance that, if any reader should find a difference in the versification or expression, he will be thus enabled to account for it.

{9} The Poor are here almost of necessity introduced, for they must be considered, in every place, as a large and interesting portion of its inhabitants. I am aware of the great difficulty of acquiring just notions on the maintenance and management of this class of our fellow subjects, and I forbear to express any opinion of the various modes which have been discussed or adopted: of one method only I venture to give my sentiments,— that of collecting the poor of a hundred into one building. This admission of a vast number of persons, of all ages and both sexes, of very different inclinations, habits, and capacities, into a society, must, at a first view I conceive, be looked upon as a cause of both vice and misery; nor does anything which I have heard or read invalidate the opinion: happily, the method is not a prevailing one, as these houses are, I believe, still confined to that part of the kingdom where they originated.

{10} John Bunyan, in one of the many productions of his zeal, has ventured to make public this extraordinary sentiment, which the frigid piety of our Clerk so readily adopted.

{11} The Life of Ellen Orford, though sufficiently burdened with error and misfortune, has in it little besides which resembles those of the unhappy men in the preceding Letters, and is still more unlike that of Grimes, in a subsequent one. There is in this character cheerfulness and resignation, a more uniform piety, and an immovable trust in the aid of religion. This, with the light texture of the introductory part, will, I hope, take off from that idea of sameness which the repetition of crimes and distresses is likely to create.

{12} It has been a subject of greater vexation to me than such trifle ought to be, that I could not, without destroying all appearance of arrangement, separate these melancholy narratives, and place the fallen Clerk in Office at a greater distance from the Clerk of the Parish, especially as they resembled each other in several particulars; both being tempted, seduced, and wretched. Yet there are, I conceive, considerable marks of distinction: their guilt is of different kind; nor would either have committed the offence of the other. The Clerk of the Parish could break the commandment, but he could not have been induced to have disowned an article of that creed for which he had so bravely contended, and on which he fully relied; and the upright mind of the Clerk in Office would have secured him from being guilty of wrong and robbery, though his weak and vacillating intellect could not preserve him from infidelity and profaneness. Their melancholy is nearly alike, but not its consequences. Jachin retained his belief, and though he hated life, he could never be induced to quit it voluntarily; but Abel was driven to terminate his misery in a way which the unfixedness of his religious opinions rather accelerated than retarded. I am, therefore, not without hope, that the more observant of my readers will perceive many marks of discrimination in these characters.

{13} The character of Grimes, his obduracy and apparent want of feeling, his gloomy kind of misanthropy, the progress of his madness, and the horrors of his imagination, I must leave to the judgment and observation of my readers. The mind here exhibited is one untouched by pity, unstung by remorse, and uncorrected by shame; yet is this hardihood of temper and spirit broken by want, disease, solitude, and disappointment: and he becomes the victim of a distempered and horror-stricken fancy. It is evident, therefore, that no feeble vision, no half-visible ghost, not the momentary glance of an unbodied being, nor the half-audible voice of an invisible one, would be created by the continual workings of distress on a mind so depraved and flinty. The ruffian of Mr Scott (Marmion) has a mind of this nature; he has no shame or remorse, but the corrosion of hopeless want, the wasting of unabating disease, and the gloom of unvaried solitude, will have their effect on every nature and the harder that nature is, and the longer time required to work upon it, so much the more strong and indelible is the impression. This is all the reason I am able to give, why a man of feeling so dull should yet become insane, and why the visions of his distempered brain should be of so horrible a nature.

{14} That a Letter on Prisons should follow the narratives of such characters as Keene and Grimes is unfortunate, but not to be easily avoided. I confess it is not pleasant to be detained so long by subjects so repulsive to the feelings of many as the sufferings of mankind; but, though I assuredly would have altered this arrangement, had I been able to have done it by substituting a better, yet am I not of opinion that my verses, or, indeed, the verses of any other person, can so represent the evils and distresses of life as to make any material impression on the mind, and much less any of injurious nature. Alas! sufferings real, evident, continually before us, have not effects very serious or lasting, even in the minds of the more reflecting and compassionate; nor, indeed, does it seem right that the pain caused by sympathy should serve for more than a stimulus to benevolence. If then the strength and solidity of truth placed before our eyes have effect so feeble and transitory, I need not be very apprehensive that my representations of Poor-houses and Prisons, of wants and sufferings, however faithfully taken, will excite any feelings which can be seriously lamented. It has always been held as a salutary exercise of the mind to contemplate the evils and miseries of our nature: I am not therefore without hope that even this gloomy subject of Imprisonment, and more especially the Dream of the Condemned Highwayman, will excite in some minds that mingled pity and abhorrence which, while it is not unpleasant to the feelings, is useful in its operation. It ties and binds us to all mankind by sensations common to us all, and in some degree connects us, without degradation, even to the most miserable and guilty of our fellow-men.

{15} Our concluding subject is Education; and some attempt is made to describe its various seminaries, from that of the poor widow who pronounces the alphabet for infants, to seats whence the light of learning is shed abroad on the world. If, in this Letter, I describe the lives of literary men as embittered by much evil; if they be often disappointed, and sometimes unfitted for the world they improve; let it be considered that they are described as men who possess that great pleasure, the exercise of their own talents, and the delight which flows from their own exertions: they have joy in their pursuits, and glory in their acquirements of knowledge. Their victory over difficulties affords the most rational cause of triumph, and the attainment of new ideas leads to incalculable riches, such as gratify the glorious avarice of aspiring and comprehensive minds. Here, then, I place the reward of Learning. Our Universities produce men of the first scholastic attainments, who are heirs to large possessions, or descendants from noble families. Now, to those so favoured, talents and acquirements are unquestionably means of arriving at the most elevated and important situations; but these must be the lot of a few: in general, the diligence, acuteness, and perseverance of a youth at the